I dedicate this book to my father James,
who has been with me every step of the way.....

Holywell Lane, Shoreditch   James Griffin Nov 2006

The Griffin Legacy

The extraordinary tale
of two ordinary
Victorian women as they fight
to save a publishing house

Alison Eddershaw

Griffin

Prologue

This is the story about two remarkable women. A story based entirely on fact that is not at all remarkable in today's world but was certainly extraordinary in Victorian Britain. Set against a backdrop of an age when feminism was yet to be born, this is a tale of determination in the face of adversity and hope at a time of despair. A look at how one family struggled to maintain their social position within fiercely divided class structures and how it was left to the women in the household to keep a flourishing business afloat. The plight of working widows was nothing unusual in working class society at this time when women and children worked to make ends meet and to prevent total destitution. In some industrial areas women provided a large proportion of the workforce, particularly in the textile towns, Midland Potteries and Scottish Jute industries. The same was not true for the middle and upper classes. In Lizzie and her mother's world women were not expected to even take an interest in what was emphatically considered 'men's work'. It was only a minority of single women, widows or married women who contributed to the family income. These were usually occupied in the arts (for example as musicians, artists or actresses), education (for example governesses) or writers. Very few entered the world of business and perhaps not surprisingly in her later years, Lizzie's focus shifted to her writing and to her church work (another socially accepted female profession coming to the fore).

Both women were unprecedented in their time and Lizzie paid a heavy price for her involvement in running the firm by sacrificing her femininity. She may have eventually gained the respect of her male colleagues but she was far less desirable as a possible wife and she forfeited her ability to become a mother. As we will discover, she did not set out to be a feminist. In many ways, she embodied the virtues displayed by Queen Victoria throughout her reign – reticence and propriety. Her upbringing was a classic example of middle class parenting. Lizzie's intelligence was apparent from a young age and she was encouraged by her parents to pursue her interest in music and language whilst being prepared for a life as a wife and mother. As with all her siblings, her upbringing was based on the solid foundations of Christianity and as the second eldest in the family, her childhood was spent basking in the love of both parents in relative luxury. Adolescence was taken up looking after her younger siblings and supporting her widowed mother before her world was turned upside-down.

Her destiny was thrust upon her and there is plenty of evidence to suggest she was a reluctant player in the drama. Many times she tried to withdraw from the Firm but she remained resolute, determined to fulfil her dying father's wish that the Griffin name would live on in the world of publishing.

Aside from the small matter of providing for his family, the Firm was Charles' life work, but in order to understand quite how important the business was to him, we have to go back to the beginning; to the very roots of the business, which were established back in 1820 by Charles' father Richard Thomas Griffin. In fact, the story does not even begin there, but goes back further still, to Charles' grandfather Joseph Griffin who, we believe, was instrumental in supporting his son and encouraging him to set up the business in the first place. These founding members of the Griffin Publishing business are detailed in the Appendix.

The Family Tree and Key Data that follows will help to identify some of the names that Lizzie mentions. We are fortunate in that many documents from the early history of the Firm survive and these letters and company ledgers, together with painstaking research into the family archives, has provided the skeleton of our story; the flesh is provided by family folklore and knowledge of the likely living conditions of the time.

Key Characters

Richard Thomas Griffin – founder of the Firm – named Richard Griffin & Co (RG & Co) – based in Glasgow. The first shop was opened in 1820 in Hutcheson Street, Glasgow.

"Quis Separabit nos?" - 'who shall separate us'- motto of the Firm under the symbol of an oak tree

Elizabeth Eaves – Richard's English wife

Sarah Bond – Richard Griffin's illegitimate daughter

Thomas Tegg - bookseller/ publisher in London. Richard Griffin undertook a five-year agreement to work for Thomas Tegg. A 50:50 partnership document was drawn up between Tegg and Richard to set up a new company, Richard Griffin & Company to be based in Glasgow with Tegg handling the London trade.

John Joseph Griffin – Richard's younger brother. Eminent chemist and author. Took over Richard Griffin and Co in 1832. Author of highly acclaimed Chemical Reactions, published by RG&Co, which ran to 10 editions.

John Bumpus – bookseller in Newgate Street, London. Partner of John Joseph Griffin. Richard Griffin invested in this firm: Bumpus & Griffin

J J Griffin & Co – set up in 1842 in Baker Street London by John Joseph, seller of scientific instruments, including the highly successful Griffin Beaker.

Encyclopaedia Metropolitana- purchased in 1848, split by the Firm into separate volumes. A financial risk for RG&Co but its strong focus on mechanics, engineering and the sciences made it a highly lucrative set of publications.

Charles Sharpe Griffin – wife of Jessie Jane Rae, father of Lizzie. Manager of RG&Co from 1845-1862. 1853 became Publisher to the University of Glasgow.

Lord Henry Brougham – Lord Chancellor in 1830, strong advocator of technical education. Friend of Charles and Godfather to Henry Brougham Griffin, born 1856.

10 Stationers' Hall Court – often referred to by Lizzie as the Warehouse. Traditional publishing centre in London and the Firm's London location from 1860-1881.

1861 Charles bought out his uncle John Joseph Griffin's interest in Richard Griffin & Co.

Henry Bohn- business partner taken on by Charles at the time of his final illness in 1861. Richard Griffin & Co became known as 'Griffin, Bohn and Company', with Bohn taking over the day to day running of the business as Charles' health deteriorated.

Dr Aitken – physician who attended Charles in London. He was also a friend and author. His late payment of royalties owed to him caused considerable strain and embarrassment to Jessie in 1865 and became known in the family as 'The Aitken Affair'.

William Collins – successful publisher based in Glasgow. Friend of Richard Griffin. Became Trustee of the Firm on Richard's death.

Mr William Ambrose – Lawyer and Advocate who ran the Griffin family affairs in Glasgow in the 1850s and 1860s, after the family moved back to London. Trustee of the Firm until his death in 1872.

Charles Griffin & Co – Firm's new name, following the Bohn buy out in 1862

Henry Knox – first Manager of Charles Griffin & Co, not popular with Jessie who felt his management was weak, leaving the Firm vulnerable to closure. Manager from 1862-1866.

Eliza Stewart – wife of James – sister of Jessie, approached for a £1000 loan for the business in 1862 (refused)

Mr Warner – traveller (or travelling salesman) for Charles Griffin & Co. Not trusted by Jessie, but close to Mr Knox.

Mr Meiklejohn - worked in the Accounts Department. Long standing employee who reported irregularities in the running of the business in 1864, fuelling Jessie's concerns over the management capabilities of Mr Knox.

Mr Crafter – Manager of Charles Griffin & Co from 1866-1871

Vallance and Vallance – English Lawyers acting on behalf of the Firm in London.

Family tree

Joseph GRIFFIN [1752-1838] = Mary KING [1757-1827]

- William Samuel GRIFFIN [1784-1870]
- Elisabeth GRIFFIN [1786-?]
- Richard Thomas GRIFFIN [1790-1832] = Elizabeth EAVES [1792-?]
- Sarah GRIFFIN [1796-?]
- James Joseph GRIFFIN [1802-1877]

[Issue]

Charles Sharpe GRIFFIN [1819-1862] = Jessie Jane RAE [1823-1909]

[Issue]

- Mary Anne Eliza GRIFFIN [1843-1902]
- **Elizabeth Eaves GRIFFIN** [1845-1899]
- Richard Thomas GRIFFIN [1847-1894]
- Alexander Jamieson GRIFFIN [1848-1877]
- Charles James GRIFFIN [1850-1907]
- Jessie Jane GRIFFIN [1852-1894]
- Helena GRIFFIN [1853-1853]
- John Joseph GRIFFIN [1854-1922]
- Henry Brougham GRIFFIN [1856-1894]
- Helen Florence GRIFFIN [1860-1927]
- Alice Edith GRIFFIN [1862-1913]

[Issue]

[See page 2]

[Issue]

Charles
James
GRIFFIN [from page 1

| Charles Rae GRIFFIN [1881-1962] | Leonard Stewart GRIFFIN [1883-1884] | Doris Mary GRIFFIN [1885-1979] | Helen Elnith Eaves GRIFFIN [1899-1984] |

[by 2nd marriage:]

| Charles Falkner Rae GRIFFIN [1908-1983] | Nancy Margaret GRIFFIN [1911-2002] | John Oswald GRIFFIN [1916-1995] | Rosamund Lydia GRIFFIN [1936-] | Thomas George Bowers GRIFFIN [1939-] |

[Issue]

| James Rae GRIFFIN [1938-2011] | Norah Patricia Lettice GRIFFIN [1942-] | Martin Brodie GRIFFIN [1947-] | Janet Louise GRIFFIN [1951-] |

[Issue]   [Issue]   [Issue]

[See page 3]

Chapter 1

I've spent much of the last few months trying not to look at my hands. Not an easy task I think you'll agree under the circumstances and I've even tried to wear tight fitting gloves on occasion to obscure my view, but my writing was almost illegible and I missed the feel of the smooth, solid pen beneath my fingers. I have learnt to quash the feeling of déjà vu I feel when I stare at the age spotted hinterland, veins running deep and strong, for it is not my own hand I see but my Mother's, the white delicate fingers firmly imprinted on my mind after years of studying her bent over her writing desk. We have always been a partnership Mother and I. We knew that we were doing something unusual. Two Victorian women 'meddling' in business affairs. Daring to enter a man's world. I want Mama to read and recall her part in the battle. Recently, when we have talked about it she has forgotten our conversation the following day but at least if she has my interpretation of key events on paper, it will continually spark some sort of memory for her. I would also love future generations of Griffins to understand the sacrifices she undertook. I find it tragic that only four children out of ten are still alive as I write. No wonder Mothers' mind is giving up. How can she bear to see the loss of her beloved offspring one-by-one as she herself continues to live? I have no time or space to document what happened to each of my siblings in detail, but I will be referring to all of them when I recount the struggle for the Family Firm. They are of course part of the story. Let me take you back now to the time of Papa's death. To focus on the years from 1862 to the time I am writing (1894). This is for you dearest Mama, my rock; my saviour; my life.

* * * * *

It was the silence that first alerted me that something had changed. The moment was suspended in time and the world seemed to slow down and pause for a second before resuming full speed as if the whole house had stopped breathing at the same moment my father took his final agonising breath, allowing time for the pain to be firmly lodged in our memories forever. Even the little ones sensed something was wrong and came out of the nursery in a subdued crocodile rather than their usual carefree bundle, little John trailing behind the others like an exhausted dog. Then, as if in slow motion, Mama descended the stairs in a trance like state, her pale face strained, dark bags under her eyes betraying the countless sleepless nights that had preceded this event. I distinctly remember what she was wearing at that moment. Funny the detail you recall and yet not that surprising given it was the last article of any colour she wore for a year following her bereavement. A deep ocean blue shift dress – no doubt chosen as it was a favourite of Papa's – that rustled at the hem, a green shawl clasped at her neck and only the absence of jewellery a sign that she had been up all night at her husband's bedside. Her words were surprisingly stark and I remember being a little surprised that she made no attempt to soften the blow: *"I'm afraid that Papa is dead."* She followed this with *"I'm so sorry"* as if she had in some way been responsible for his demise. In many ways she always felt that somehow she should have done more to help him. Even though Papa had been practically bedridden for months, we had all lived in hope that he would get better and no expense had been spared trying to make him well. Dr Aitken, a family friend as well as my father's practitioner, had practically lived in our house during the final few weeks. He may be a friend but he was still a practising Doctor and his bills mounted with every hour he spent at Coombe Lodge.

My older sister Mary Ann (or Polly as we called her) took charge when it became apparent that Mother was incapable of getting a grip on the situation. Ignoring the look of utter desolation in

Mother's eyes, she herded the subdued boys back into the nursery, closely followed by the nursemaid Bella, both clucking like old hens in their attempt to provide the maternal love that Mother was unable to dispense. Polly and I took refuge in the nursery, comforted by the furniture of our own childhood: the rocking chair, toy cupboard and high chair and by the distractions of Alice's gurgles and Helen and Harry's imaginary play.

We all saw Papa of course, as is the custom, but it was not our father who lay rigid on the bed, his body a thin bumpy line under the sheet, his face the colour of his white nightgown. I felt no connection. Mama had barely left his side in the hours following his death and sat on a little stool next to his pillow, proprietorially placing one hand on the bedspread above his head. *"Come nearer Lizzie. Say a prayer for Papa's soul"* she beseeched me, sensing my reluctance. *"He is with God and is no longer in any pain. We must be thankful for that, child, and be sure to follow his work"*. I took no notice of these words at the time, intent as I was to leave the room that smelt of beeswax, soot and another unidentifiable aromas that hung like a shroud around the bed. I tried to ignore the waves of nausea that threatened to overwhelm me and obeyed Mother, forcing myself to peck my father's hand, the feel of it like chilled baking parchment on my lips. I swallowed the lump that threatened to choke me as I took one final look at my dear father's face.

The older boys spent days in quiet retreat, exchanging the barest of grunts and only really appearing at mealtimes at Mama's insistence. Polly, Jessie and I sat on one side of the table and Richard, Alexander and Charles the other, with her at the head – the vacant chair opposite a mocking reminder of our loss. The younger ones were excused this ordeal and were allowed to eat in the kitchen or have high tea in the nursery with Bella. The day before Papa's funeral was particularly traumatic. We sat at the dinner table, poking at our food and Mother tried as usual to coax some kind of conversation with her sons. *"Richard I want you to speak to the rector tomorrow. It is important he knows he is welcome to come back to the house. Charles I've put a new coat on the chair in your room. John you can wear the black boots we bought for school. Your feet have clearly grown since your Uncle's funeral"*. And then she had done the unthinkable. It was as if uttering the word funeral had finally made her realise what was actually going to happen the following day. I clearly remember the unfamiliar sound as Mama's voice caught in a sob and she frantically reached inside her gown for her handkerchief. The boys' heads snapped up, their eyes betraying their shock and pain at their Mother's tears. In his defence, Richard did scrape back his chair and stretch a rangy arm awkwardly around his Mother. Charles and Alex didn't know where to look and I started to clear away our untouched plates in an attempt at distracting attention away from our weeping parent. It took several minutes for Mama to gain her composure before she rose from the chair dismissing us with a wave of her hand and a few comforting words: *"Dear children. Dear, dear children. How you are a comfort to me. I know you will make your father proud"*.

Papa. No longer would we hear the lilting timbre of his voice as he called out in greeting on his return home from the office. No longer would he tease Polly, Jessie and I about our hair, our dresses or our shoes, or listen to the boys as they struggled with their Latin, or take us out on trips up to town. Most of all I knew I'd miss Papa's kindness. His ability to sit quietly and listen to Polly as she gossiped about the handsome man and fine home that she would soon be acquiring (she lived in hope for a knight on a white horse to come and sweep her off her feet); his patience with Jessie as she struggled with her exercises; his chats with the older boys about their latest hobbies and his tolerance of the little ones as they chugged through the house in their world of make-believe. I will miss his interest in all of our lives and my heart ached as I considered how the little girls, Helen aged 2 and baby Alice would never at first hand experience their father's love.

The truth was that I was scared to enter my parents' bedroom after Papa had died. I had spent many hours in the weeks preceding his death in that room. Not only was it the warmest in the house – Mama was very particular about the fire being lit morning to night – it was also an opportunity for me to indulge in my favourite pastime without fear of reproach. Reading to Papa was my job and I relished it. After the daily update from the *Times* and the *London Chronicle*, which often prompted some discussion about the news of the day, Papa would lie back exhausted and listen as I read from his chosen book. During those long, long days when he could get no rest, the only thing that helped him to forget himself was first *The Old Curiosity Shop* then all the others, read aloud by me. I often used to think it a shame Dickens did not know how much pain and suffering he had eased. It saddens me still that Papa never got to read Dickens's later works, I just know he would have loved the gritty descriptions of dirty London in *Our Mutual Friend* and he missed out altogether on the delights of Henry James. On his brighter days Papa never asked for Dickens, it was always Browning or Carlyle or something equally highbrow. Of course Shakespeare was another favourite. The immortal bard; but Papa had to be in a certain mood to listen to a play reading and on several occasions towards the end of his life, we would start on his favoured choice and as the plights of Desdemona or Juliet grew ever graver he would give a pained sigh and point to the pile of literature beside his bed and I would resume my reading of *Rob Roy* and he would lie back, eyes closed as he let the descriptions of Sir Walter Scott's Mountain View wash over him. It was as if he could actually feel the soft breeze on his face, see the glittering lake before his eyes and smell the freshness of Scottish turf. Mind you, I did worry at times that the pace and excitement of the narrative may prove too much for him, but he never seemed to tire of this particular novel. I preferred Eliot, by far my favourite of her novels being *Daniel Deronda*, although I also enjoyed her other books like *The Mill on the Floss* and *Adam Bede* that were set at the turn of the century and Papa was equally fond of the former. Latterly it was the Good Book that Papa requested and we both drew comfort from the words of the Lord as his time drew to a close.

Papa was 41 years old when he died: the average life expectancy pretty much at that time, especially in the Home Counties where we lived. If we'd still been in Central London it would have been few year's younger and in Manchester it was as low as 24. I guess in that context he did rather well. He seemed quite old at the time but now I've reached well beyond that age myself I know it to be very young. We were never told exactly what he died of but it was definitely something to do with his digestive system. *"He's managed some of cook's special broth"* or *"Daddy said thank you for the scones"* Mama would proudly announce if Papa managed some morsel of food as if she were reporting some tremendous achievement. She'd emerge from his room with an empty tray and beaming smile, the frown that seemed to have become a permanent feature smoothing momentarily as she dared hope for recovery. And then there were the days when the food trays would return to the kitchen untouched, the days when Papa would sleep, surviving only on liquids accompanied by some kind of pungent remedy supplied by Dr Aitken.

As well as being our physician, Dr Aitken was a kind, loyal friend and he was also one of the Firm's authors, and I was to get to know him rather well in that capacity in the years that followed Papa's death. Neither of us would ever have imagined that, as I silently slipped into the room delivering refreshment, or helped prop father up on his pillows when he became weaker, we would one day have professional dealings. My role then was dutiful daughter and I was happy to oblige. I was, after all, still being educated. My sisters and I were lucky in that respect. We must take a moment to remember what it was like for middle class girls in the 1860's. Most girls – if given any education at all – were taught at home by a governess and Mothers gave small girls their first models of feminine behaviour. Hardly surprising therefore that Polly and I - with our Mother as Matriarch – were not typically educated in the traditional sexual division of labour given what was to happen after Papa's death. However conventions were followed up to a point. After a brief spell with a Governess, the boys were all sent away to boarding school whilst us older girls were educated at home, at least until we were old enough to be sent abroad to be 'finished'. We were lucky in that we were not expected to make much contribution to domestic work – that after all was the servant's job. However Polly and I (little Jessie was excused of course given her immobility) had to do more jobs around the house than the boys. When they were home for the long school holidays they had free time to do what they liked, but we had to help – especially on Bella's afternoon off in the week. Mother's view, like most of my friends' Mothers – was that there was no sense in coddling a girl. She may as well get accustomed to the kind of work she would eventually do – i.e. run a large household ready for such a time as we married.

Apart from this very boring domestic training, we girls were encouraged by both our parents to be educated in literature, music and art. Books were revered in our household, music practice encouraged and later we were given the opportunity to travel to broaden our minds. No wonder then that I thought nothing of stepping outside the stereotypical role of a young Victorian lady.

The boys were totally spoilt. Even from a very early age we girls were taught deference to our brothers. When they came home from boarding school in the holidays they were very often insufferable for the first week or so. They patronised us dreadfully, puffed up by a sense of their own self importance. Central to all our education was the moral and social teachings of the church. Both Papa and Mama were united on this and we were taught about sin and damnation and Papa used to read us long passages from the Bible. Just before father died Henry (aged about 7 and a half at the time) was given a stern talking to. His crime? He had taken one of cook's freshly baked buns and then denied it despite the presence of crumbs around his cheeky face and the evidence given by Charles who had witnessed the event (probably intending to follow suit had cook not returned that very moment from the depths of the larder). Mama was furious, her voice piercing through the closed kitchen door as she laid into her son. *"Henry you are to go without any supper and reflect on what you have done. 'Thou shall not steal' the eighth commandment and one you know very well at your age. I am disappointed in you."* Henry's sobs accompanied her speech and Mother's voice was noticeably softer in response *"Now don't ever do that again young man, if you were hungry as you say then you only had to have asked for a bun!"* I can remember smiling ironically at this as I slipped away from the door. Typical of my Mother to show sympathy to one of her precious boys the moment they turned on the tears. That would never have happened if one of her daughters had tried the same trick. Not that Mama didn't love us. She was an utterly devoted parent to all of her children. It was just that the boys were treated differently even then, and after Papa's death the boys became an even more 'precious commodity' to nurture and indulge. Sadly our parents' Scottish roots and this constant teaching of the benefits of self denial did not prevent the boys from going a little wayward in adult life. Although Mother and I have felt that their lack of paternal role model, just at the time they were preparing to be launched into the adult world, played a huge part in their troubles. The boys' love of drinking and gambling were lamentable but endured by Mother over the years for just that very reason. I have never been as forgiving but I can see her point.

My first indication that Mother was going to be strong and not collapse in a depressed heap (as my friend Eleanor's Mother had done when her husband was found dead in the garden) was about a week after the funeral. She seemed to pull herself together almost the moment the last of the Kentish soil was scattered over the coffin. So, unlike our dear Queen who had simply fallen apart when her beloved husband died at the same age as Papa, becoming a virtual recluse for nearly ten years. Mama was just as heartbroken, but at least Papa had had plenty of time to consider his funeral and to finalise his will. That certainly made it easier for her. He requested that he stay close to the family home so we buried him in the little churchyard of St Peter and St Paul's church in Swanscombe, just yards away from the house. After much agonising over what we should all wear (Mother at last settling on her best Parramatta silk trimmed with black crepe, a large jet brooch at her bosom, Polly and I in similar attire minus the jewellery, the boys with black gloves and handkerchiefs, the little ones in their Sunday best), Mama was determined to keep the funeral service simple and wanted the minimum of fuss. It was however, standing room only in the little church and mourners crammed into the porch and lined the path as we paraded after the pall bearers. I still get emotional when I think of all those sympathetic eyes staring at a time when we wished to be alone with our grief. Polly and I were upset that there was no headstone made to mark his grave. Even now Mother and I visit the little churchyard whenever time allows. But Mother's belief that Papa's spirit is with us always and his soul safe with God, meant she was scornful of our suggestion for a more elaborate memorial to him. Anyway, I never did tell her that I wrote to my Great Uncle in Scotland - Dr Low of Seafield House in Rothesay (husband of Mama's oldest sister) - about a month after we buried Papa. Polly and I discussed it and we felt he should have some kind of memorial in his beloved Scotland. We both wanted his name added to the family vault up in Glasgow where Grandfather and Grandmamma are buried and where little Helena was laid to rest. The trouble was it was complicated. After all, the vault was shared, as Grandfather had bought a half layer in 1827 after his Mother

Mary died. I wanted a proper monument to Papa and to my grandparents. Unfortunately my request to add the dates of death and names of my grandparents Richard and Elizabeth Eaves, their son Charles and little Helena fell on deaf ears. Uncle Low never objected but he was an old man by this point and he simply never got round to sorting it all out.

Mother's 'no nonsense' approach could have been misinterpreted as being cold but she is just a very private person. After her breakdown at the breakfast table there were no public tears. Just a strong acceptance that life must go on and we all took her lead, pulled together as a family, (at least in those early days) as if by an invisible thread. Unfortunately this feeling of togetherness did not last. Over the years the tides that separated us became stronger and we all drifted apart. For some it was inevitable due to the physical miles that distanced us, but even for those who stayed close by, as the months passed we had to fight to bridge the widening gap that started as a tiny crack when Papa was still newly in his grave.

My own involvement in the business side of Charles Griffin & Co did not start until some time after Papa's death, but at 17 years old, I was treated by Mama as an adult, and as such I was fully aware of my Mother's part in the drama. Polly and I were initially frightened when we discovered the precariousness of the situation for the first time. It was several days after the funeral and our new life was taking shape. We remained however, a skipper-less ship in those early dark days with Mother in deep mourning. I remember one particular Sunday when we had just finished our lunch having returned late from worship in our local church in Swanscombe after laying flowers at Papa's grave. I loved the peaceful, tranquil space of our church. The formality of the church rituals had become a great source of comfort to Polly, Mother and I. The solid feel of the cold pew beneath us, the creak of the bell rope, the patter of little feet as the school children marched in under the wing of their mistress.

Charlie and Henry who sat with the other boys on one side of the church were always under Mama's watchful gaze, their clean faces pink and shiny beneath broad shirt collars, hands firmly in pockets to fiddle with whatever they had managed to cram in there for distraction purposes. The girls sat on their own benches, in their time honoured costume of short white tippet (replaced by scarlet in winter) with a scratchy straw bonnet tied underneath each chin held by a band of broad ribbon, and it was Jessie's absence that always drew a melancholy sigh from Mother when she viewed these robust, if delicately dressed children. Jessie was quite happy to be left at home of course, in the company of one of the servants, to silently read her Bible and say her prayers but she did not appreciate all she missed, poor lamb. For it was the sound of the organ and the opportunity to sing that was the highlight for all of us Griffin attendees. We have since worshipped in a variety of churches and if truth be told, the presence of an organ was pretty much the prerequisite in our choice of worship when we came to a new location, but none have issued such a rich or sweet sound as the organ at Swanscombe. Not that it was always sympathetically played, as the regular organist was an elderly lady called Miss Spry, whose hands and feet worked extraordinarily hard each Sunday, pitching the Psalms in the very highest key that could be sustained without absolute breakdown.

St Peter and St Paul was an unremarkable building from the outside as it was made of brick and it has had its plasterwork repaired so many times it is hard to date, but parts of the nave I know go back to the Norman era and what the building lacked in beauty was more than made up by the churchyard. Hidden in a grove of elms and chestnuts, the area contained the usual variety of well kept, more recent graves, and those whose ancestors have long departed but it was the charming view that set this churchyard apart. Polly and I had been known to sit for an hour or more after laying our flowers at Papa's grave just staring out at England's green and pleasant land. This was the garden of England and the rich fruits of the soil were plain to see. Although only on a slight ridge, the air felt fresher and purer up at that spot and we used to envy the occupants of the nearby vicarage and also the handsome manor house with its tall gables and stacks of graceful chimneys, its square mullioned windows sharing 'our view'. Polly and I had lingered that day to reflect and to remember before heading home to our noisy household to prepare in haste for the midday meal.

By the time we had finished luncheon and checked on the little ones, Mother was in the drawing room – a quiet, if chilly haven in our noisy household, and she was reading a batch of letters. Polly and I slipped into the cool shadowy depths anxious not to disturb Mother as she sat staring at the letters in her hand. After exchanging a look, Polly and I took up our embroidery and sat in silence concentrating on our stitching, pointedly ignoring the thud of tiny feet above our head as Henry and Helen tore around the nursery. We assumed Mother was reading one of the many letters of condolence that continued to arrive at our house after she had put her simple message into the *Times* declaring Papa's demise. A pretty fair assumption given the amount of time she had sat staring hard at such letters, caressing the paper as she proudly read through the sugary accolades and gushing sympathy that filled each note, drawing comfort from their effusiveness. To me they were just words on a page but to Mother they meant the world. Anyway, that particular Sunday, it transpired that the serious expression and crisp notepaper on her lap were from a different source. This was business. Startled out of her reverie, Mama looked up and once again I was struck by how much older she looked. Her hair was in a bun at the base of her neck as was the fashion at the time and there were no grey strands (they were to appear much later in her life), neither was she lined or wrinkled, stiff limbed or creaky. She just looked old somehow. I think it was the dull expression, the worried frown that had ploughed a deep furrow across her forehead, shadowy against the pallor of her skin. The look she gave us that day was positively haunted as she informed us of the letter's contents:

"Girls, I have received some grave news. You remember I told you that one of the Executors Papa requested was to be Mr John Whitaker, a London publisher of some repute who had previously agreed to act when your father approached him last year?" We had both nodded, but I for one had no recollection of hearing of such a man and it was obvious from Polly's confused frown that she had no idea what an Executor even meant let alone what the consequences of this news might be. Anyway, back to Mama's conversation:

"Well I have received word from William that Mr Whitaker has now declined because" she had squinted at the paper in her hand at that point to ensure she got the words exactly right:

"Regrettably he has informed me by letter that he is too busy and he was anyway under the impression that there were to be only two Executors not six. Can you believe that, girls when Papa had always talked of the need for half a dozen? It was bad enough when Uncle John refused but I can now understand his reasons, but this is a double blow. I shall have to write at once to Mr Ambrose to implore him to try to persuade Mr Whitaker to reconsider."

Polly and I had simply nodded in agreement, anxious to please, but frankly we were both confused. What I did know at this point was that Mother was the only surviving family member who was an Executor of our Firm and I also knew that Papa's Uncle John Joseph – his former partner and the perfect choice for overseeing the business until the boys came of age – had refused this task. I remember Mama initially being distraught about that decision when the letter arrived from Mr Knox our family Solicitor in London who was dealing with Papa's will. It had taken many visits by my great uncle to convince her that he was not 'abandoning the family' as she had coldly accused him and he had repeatedly reassured her that he would continue to support us and the Firm while he still had breath in his body. But he was on old man (60 to be precise). Tired of running his own business let alone taking on another. He had been concentrating on passing the reins for his own highly successful company – John Joseph Griffin & Co makers of scientific equipment – to his own sons Charles and William – to free up more of his time for writing. A renowned author, he had just finished the tenth and last edition of his highly acclaimed book called *Chemical Reactions*. He managed to convince Mother that even if Henry Bohn's partnership did not flourish, other managers could be brought in to keep the Firm operating. Mama appeared to accept this position and an uneasy equilibrium returned. The weight of her new responsibility was a burden that Polly and I were fully aware of. Mother had changed. Not surprising given the loss of her devoted husband and a subtle yet distinctive shift in her character: the grit and determination that frankly had always been present in her were now focused not on her offspring but on the Firm. So it was that we sat in silence struggling to come up with something intelligent to say, whilst Mother poured out her woes. Luckily she appeared to solve her own quandary, with a nod in our direction as if we had somehow put the idea into her head, she told us: *"I shall write to Mr Collins forthwith. He will be able to convince Mr Whitaker that his knowledge and experience and his London location are essential if Griffins is to succeed"..*

I dared to speak at this point, concerned at the thought that the Firm may not succeed - a possibility that had not before entered my head.

"But Mama surely Mr Bohn will run the Firm satisfactorily until the boys take over?"

Polly had meanwhile resumed her embroidery, evidently bored with the conversation but something had kindled inside me. A small flame of interest that flickered and glowed at Mother's rather surprising reply:

"No, Elizabeth. We cannot sit back and rely solely on Mr Bohn. He is not, after all family and I am not convinced he will have the vision to keep Griffins on track".

Her insistence on ignoring the new name of the Firm only then seemed significant. Mama did not trust Papa's choice of business partner. I know it had been a very hard decision for Papa taking on a partner, and he did it with a heavy heart. But Papa was a realist. He understood his death was imminent and he realised the need to share the burden of running the company. Mama confessed to me that she urged him at the time to reconsider but deferred to his authority and Mr Bohn came with considerable business experience and an impressive lump sum to shore up the Firm's finances. After Papa's death Mother was determined to get rid of Bohn and return the company to family control. My sense of unease grew at this point but my interest was sparked. Long after Polly and I had been sent to check on Alice whose lusty wails echoed through the house, drowning out the noise of Henry's wooden truck that crashed and scraped along the wooden hallway, my mind was whirring. This was my first memory of the business and my interest was sufficiently aroused to follow up on this conversation over the course of the next few days.

Mama's letters to Mr Ambrose and to Mr Collins clearly came to nothing. The former came as no surprise. Mama had opened the letter from the Firm's Scottish attorney during breakfast time and her cluck of disapproval could be heard over the scraping and stirring around the table.

"It is with regret that I write to inform you that Mr Whitaker has reiterated his decision not to act as Executor to Griffin, Bohn and

Company", she read as if addressing a meeting. I seemed to be the only one listening and she turned her worried frown in my direction in acknowledgment of the fact. *"Why am I not surprised, Lizzie? I tell you why, it is because our Mr Ambrose is an incompetent fool. Sorry to be so blunt but that is my opinion and has been for some time. Papa had more faith in the man and for that reason alone he remains our family solicitor, but I have long suspected he puts his own interests before those of his clients and unless I see evidence to the contrary, I would even question whether his letter to Mr Whitaker was sufficiently imploring. I should have written directly myself. I have a good mind so to do"*.

During this little speech an eerie silence had descended on our table and all eyes were on our pink cheeked, wild eyed parent. She seemed to have momentarily taken leave of her senses. She was plainly livid, but to call Mr Ambrose a 'fool' in front of us was something none of us expected. We had of course met Mr Ambrose on several occasions, and we struggled to connect the respectable, grey haired gentleman, with his customary formal attire with a bumbling fool, despite a very strange habit of his that always came to mind whenever he was mentioned. This was his annoying way of tapping the cane that he always took with him, (despite appearing to have no walking impediment) on the floor to the rhythm of his speech. Anyway, the older boys were delighted by Mama's description and it was all they could do to stop themselves from sniggering out loud, but one glance at the Mother's face was enough to stifle any sound. As I have already mentioned, Mama had changed. A new outspoken creature had replaced our gentle, softly spoken Mother. Of course on reflection I expect that she was always outspoken; it was just that previously this was confined to private conversations she had had with Papa. I distinctly remember this outburst, because it was never repeated, at least not in such a public manner. As the years progressed it was I who bore the brunt of her frustrations and she used me as a sounding board - and I was perfectly happy with this role given my own growing interest in the business.

During that first year of widowhood Mama sought help wherever she could find it. Her one aim: to keep the Firm afloat until her sons came of age – a goal set out in Papa's will and one she was resolutely determined to achieve. Whatever it took. She even had a date to focus on – 23rd March 1868 – when Richard as the eldest son would be 21 years old. Unfortunately for all of us, this date – as set out in black and white in Papa's will – was not adhered to, as you are about to find out.

Luckily, although still in mourning, Mother's black mood lifted slightly over the months that followed as her attention was focused on sorting out her little family as well as finding out as much as she could about the business. She wasted no time on the latter, and spent many an evening (after she had overseen prayers) poring over some official document or other. Her main problem she confessed to me was getting her hands on such documents. For years she (and later I) struggled to get access to the company books. The company ledger was virtually kept under lock and key at the office in Stationer's Hall Court, and it was really only when Richard went into the Firm that she was able to see all the company records. Back in the early 1860's such records were considered no business of hers and it was a constant source of irritation for her that she was seen as a peripheral member of the team (and a woman to boot) with no need to get so heavily involved, despite her being the only Executor of the Firm in London and the only member of the Griffin family in such a position. And so it was that she spent those early weeks struggling to piece together information on how the business was structured, what books the Firm had in production and how their financial position stood from snippets provided by the office staff. We were desperate to establish how stable the Firm was and to identify its potential profitability.

Meanwhile I continued to take an interest from afar. I would be at the piano trying out a new piece, or sitting next to the fire unpicking a tangle of silk from my latest attempt at embroidery (Polly was infinitely better than I at sewing and would have got on better still had she not had to spend so much time rectifying my muddles), and I'd take note of Mama in the corner bent over her books. When Papa died she had insisted that his desk be moved from his study into the drawing room. It was ridiculous really as it was far too big for the room - the chunky mahogany legs had to press firmly against the dresser at one end and were dangerously close to the fireplace on the other, but Mama was not to be swayed. Its shiny surface gradually became covered with manuscripts, letters, ledgers and bound copies of Griffin publications as she delved deeper into the business world.

The issue over Executorships finally resolved itself after Mama had in the end succumbed and *"taken matters into my own hands"* when she had written directly to Mr Whitaker. She appeared to receive some comfort from his reply as I remember her telling me after another of my enquiries about the Firm's future that Mr Whitaker had sent a *"charming letter offering his support and advice whilst regretfully confirming his decision not to act"*. I was not so easily reassured and my sleepless nights continued. I had for some time taken to having nightmares about poverty and destitution, and poor Polly had to endure many an interrupted night as a consequence. Mama accepted Mr Whitaker's decision with good grace in much the same way she had with Uncle John. It would appear that although she had plenty of advisors, she was very much on her own when it came to sorting out the business. We can assume (I think) that both men did not expect Mama to take up the challenge, generously offering help and advice in the rather glib way that one does when one feels it unlikely to be called upon.

The older boys chose to spend as much time as possible away from the house. There was no village hall in Swanscombe at this time and instead, the main focal points were the triangular village green and fresh water well, the Church and the Public House, a thriving hostellery that contained a group of regulars who each had their own bar stool and tankard ready for the barmaid to serve them at the allotted time. The hard core of these regulars was the group of farm hands who formed the bedrock of our community but there were other local characters: the blacksmith, the joiner, the baker and butcher to name but a few, who if not at work, could always be found in the Dog and Duck. Papa never frequented this hostellery and it was painful for Mother and me therefore to have to turn a blind eye when the older boys returned home pink cheeked and silly, after 'taking the air'. Even at this stage they were not too young to be experimenting and I have often wondered if their lifelong struggle with the bottle was ignited at this time, shortly after Papa's death. Although not educated with the other local boys and girls at the little school in the next Parish, the boys inevitably mixed with these Kent youngsters during the holidays, albeit from afar. Mama and Papa did not encourage us to fraternise with the locals and we were initially treated with suspicion as incomers into the small close knit community. Gradually, through our Church attendances and invitations to a variety of 'at homes' we got to know other families of similar class, but from the time we first came to live in Swanscombe, Mother used Papa's illness as an excuse for turning down the majority of social engagements. It was only Polly's nagging that prevented us girls from becoming quite reclusive. Richard and Alec were allowed more freedom and as teenagers would boast to Polly and I of their adventures, especially after they had befriended Harry, one of the publican's sons, who had them up to all sorts of scrapes. Harry never once came into our house and remained a mystery to our parents, who used to encourage the boys to enjoy an 'outdoor life' after weeks spent in the class room at school.

Alec was especially thrilled to be released from the confines of his lessons and regularly bemoaned what he described as 'boring', 'tedious' and 'pointless' lessons in classical Latin, the weekly 'orations' and exercises in prose and verse which he personally detested. Poor Alex, he really was not an academic boy although his wit and sharp tongue belied this fact and, even as a youngster, he was quicker to grasp many instructions than either Richard or Charlie. Charles was really our shining intellect. He possessed a mathematical brain so sharp that he was correcting text books and helping his teachers in their calculations from a very young age. Not that they always appreciated his help, he often got into trouble for showing them up and was kept in late after lessons on numerous occasions just so the teachers could make him do extra sums. Richard was more artistic than Charlie and could have done so much better if he had applied himself, but his predisposition to minor childhood illnesses and an inherent laziness (that was sadly present in all the boys) meant he constantly underperformed. Henry was our technology expert and when he was old enough was a fantastic 'fixer' of things – invaluable in a household of women. All the boys had their talents but when it came to enjoying literature, it was really only Jessie and I who usually had our heads in a book. I'm smiling now as I write in remembrance of one novel that tempted my elder sister to spend her time reading: the scandalous *Madame Bovary*. This was a novel that was actually banned in our home until we were of age and of course this simply made it even more compelling. I sometimes blame young Emma for fuelling Polly's already romantic nature, by providing such a strong vision of passionate love, although naturally Polly was as shocked as I when she first read the novel and spent months gossiping with her friends over its contents.

At home we favoured the local circulating library and Papa had been a member of Mudie's Circulating Library in New Oxford Street and I am still a member now, visiting its new building on the same site or popping into the City branch. Papa and I consumed a whole variety of novels from Mudie's and as quickly as we read them more would appear on the shelves. It was a truly marvellous library and was one of my favourite places to visit in my youth. Of course in the last few years the railways have changed the book market beyond all recognition in a way that none of us anticipated. Travelling by horse drawn carriage is not conducive to reading but travelling by train is a much less bumpy ride and a market for train travellers and those waiting at stations has sprung up in recent years, fuelling demand for novels, serials, newspapers and of course of timetables and guidebooks. The latter was the only new genre to interest me and allowed me to become familiar with places previously unknown, fuelling my passion for foreign travel.

Polly had inherited the Scottish beauty gene, not I. It has been said that I have an 'interesting face' whatever that means, and I consider my best features to be my cornflower blue eyes, my slender frame and the straightness of my teeth. The rest of my appearance I would gladly change – especially my thick, unruly hair, neither properly curly like Polly's nor a glossy sheen like Jessie - my rather prominent straight nose and my height which has always been a source of amusement to my siblings but a great embarrassment to me, especially in my younger years when I towered over my sister and friends. Papa was ever thoughtful and refrained from teasing me about my long legs, especially after he had found me in tears one day following another session of teasing from the boys about my gangly limbs. On my more objective days, I think I have passable looks, certainly not repulsive, and I have seen many plainer girls go on to attract some handsome suitors. I think for me though it was also a feeling of not standing out from the crowd and not possessing the charm of my fellow sisterhood. Mama always used to say that to love me would be to love my brains and intelligence and looking back now, I think I simply missed the window of opportunity. For, when others were occupying that useless time when a girl finishes being educated until she assumes the place of a married woman, socialising in the right places, I was simply too busy to spend my time in this way, as you are about to find out.

Firstly, all society was tabooed for the six months following Papa's death, and then after that I was simply too busy with the family and the business. In truth I was also not particularly attracted by any potential suitors. There were, I confess, a couple of young men who caught my eye in the early days, but neither was remotely interested in me and I had none of the social tools needed to catch their eye and change their view. Then there was Thomas, the rector's son, a man some five years my senior with whom I felt some connection the moment I had been introduced. We were comfortable in each other's company and I sensed a kind, intuitive soul beneath his rather brusque manner. We had just reached the stage where we felt able to stay behind after evensong, with Polly of course, to help Thomas in his task of tidying up the church ready for the next service and I was secretly plucking up the courage to ask Mother to invite him over for tea, when Papa's illness prevented such a move. After we moved from Kent I wrote to Thomas for many months, but we soon lost touch when he left Swanscombe to take up a missionary post in Africa. Then as the years passed I think I was viewed by many men as harder and more masculine than is becoming in a woman and they were put off by my lack of 'softness'. I was anything but 'hard', decisive or forceful in the months succeeding my father's death. I felt like a newly sheared sheep, all pink and vulnerable and desperately sought comfort in the authority of others. Luckily Mama took charge, heading our household with admirable courage.

Money was Mother's immediate priority and, as well as researching her livelihood, she had to get to grips with the day to day essentials. As usual, she made decisions with confidence and clarity. She had written to Mr Ambrose about a month after Papa died to enquire whether to draw money from the family expenses from Griffin Bohn

& Co (as had previously been the case) or direct from him in Scotland. Poor Mama, she had spoken to me of her embarrassment at having to go up to town to Stationer's Hall Court *cap in hand* to ask for money from the accountant to keep our household solvent. The main issue though was the fact she struggled to plan her household budget. As is typical of the upper middle classes Mama was a stickler for keeping meticulous records of all household expenditure and living in this rather piecemeal fashion was far from ideal. However there was a more pressing problem. Mama was planning another major disruption to our lives and she needed to have full control of her budget if this was to come to fruition.

Chapter 2

At first Mother told none of us that she was planning to move house. Instead we all dealt with day to day tasks, appearing on the face of it to be bearing our loss well and even managing to laugh and joke at times, but all the while weighed down by grief, as if pulled by an invisible anchor. We older ones were the most visibly upset by our change of circumstances. I remember describing my misery to Polly one day as we sat moping in our bedroom. Polly, I now realise, was trying to put on a brave face, be the big supportive sister, but I mistook her apparently light hearted tale of our mutual friend Molly Jones' new hair style as a betrayal of our mourning, savagely berating her for her insensitivity and selfishness to dwell on such trivia. She let me rant and rave and then comforted me while I wept, finally stroking my hair as I hiccupped into my lace handkerchief, mumbling apologies at my loss of control. I explained to her then how I felt permanently sad and in discomfort, all the time something gnawing away inside spoiling my pleasure in life. She could sympathise as only someone in the same position could, describing her own grief as like having a sharp stone in her shoe. We all felt we were living under a scratchy grey blanket. Nothing was as much fun or as satisfying as before. Why read an interesting novel if you couldn't share a snippet? Why practise the piano when you had no desire to perform and the one who you most wanted to hear you was no longer there? Why dream of travel if you could barely summon the energy to go on a shopping trip?

The little ones appeared to carry on life as before and for that we were grateful, although their directness at times was painful. *"Why is Papa dead?"*, *"When is he coming back?"* was hard enough. *"I miss my Papa"* and *"Why did he have to die?"* were much harder to bear, particularly when they were accompanied by wracking sobs and eyes that begged for you to make it better and bring him back. The older boys were morose and moody. They didn't at first return to school (Richard had just finished his secondary education) and spent their days wandering the house arguing or pestering to be allowed to visit friends or go up to Town. Mama was typically indulgent, allowing Alexander to roam the countryside for hours at a time, giving money to 15 year old Richard to travel into London to do heaven knows what, and letting Charlie invite a school friend called George over to stay, who spent his time in our house teasing poor John mercilessly and worse still made fun of little Jessie when he thought none of us was looking. I grew to despise that boy and Polly and I had to be constantly on our guard when he was in our house. Mother seemed oblivious and spent an increasing amount of her time either at her writing table in her bedroom or at Papa's old desk in the drawing room.

Her moods were often dictated by the outcome of her correspondence. One example was on a particularly warm September morning when I'd woken feeling refreshed for the first time in weeks. I had often been woken by the cawing of crows as they flew from their rookery in the tallest tree in the garden (a tree I loved but which concerned Mother who felt it blocked out too much light), before sweeping past our lawn to alight in the meadow behind our house, and I had parted the curtain in our bedroom and stood for a while at the window observing the much loved view. That day, the clipped green grass was being gently whipped by the row of willow trees that protected the little stream at the bottom of the garden, as a light breeze brought the garden to life. Standing looking at that familiar scene I'd felt particularly close to Papa. Perhaps we could all survive after all? Just as the watery sun was struggling to burn through the autumn mist, for the first time I had the feeling he was still with me keeping a watch over us and I had a chance of shaking off my grey shroud. Just hours later I returned to that bedroom, shut out the cruel rays of the triumphant sun, flung myself onto my bed and cried my heart out. Even Polly did not try to comfort me; I was inconsolable for days and was furious with Mother for her insensitivity.

The reason for my dramatic change in mood was simple. A few words at the breakfast table. It had started when Mother had received bad news. Mary, the housekeeper, had come into the room with a couple of letters and had left them on the sideboard next to a plate of boiled eggs and a freshly baked loaf. No sooner had she popped the final piece of honeyed toast into her mouth, Mother gestured for Charles to pass her the letters and it took minutes of reading the first one for her mood to blacken. One look at her face and we knew we were in for a bad day. The boys crammed the last morsels of food into their mouths, mumbled their request to leave the table and barely waiting a moment for a reply they bolted. Polly and I were not so lucky. Polly was helping Jessie butter and cut up her bread whilst I was in charge of toddler Helen who seemed more interested in dropping her food onto the floor than actually getting it into her mouth. Just as I was trying to stop her from filling up her cup with soggy bread and totally oblivious to her children's table manners, Mother shared her news. She started by telling of her frustration with Mr Ambrose's reluctance to provide funds for her to buy dear Dr Aitken a ring or something similar in remembrance of Papa. Apparently he had still not sent the money she requested and this news appeared to trouble her greatly as there followed a ten minute diatribe on Mr Ambrose's incompetence during which she became redder in the face, spittle frothing at her lips, her hands shaking as she built up to a crescendo like a volcano about to explode. I even remember the precise time of this outburst as I glanced at the nearby carriage clock, which pointed to the hour of nine. We all avoided looking at the head of the table until she imparted her final blow. *"It is time to move from this house. We must plan for our future and must be practical in doing so. Swanscombe is too far from the Warehouse. We have no carriage to take us to the office and the journey is becoming very arduous. When Richard starts at the Firm we must be closer. You know how long it took me on the omnibus the other day. It would be impractical to suggest the boys tackle that journey twice a day. No, I have made my decision. It is time to relocate the family."*

I can still feel the searing hot tears that burned the back of my throat as I swallowed them down not daring to look at anyone as I felt physically winded from this latest body blow. We had not been in Kent long but it felt like home and Papa was sleeping in our churchyard. Papa had lived and died in this house. How could we move on?

I realise on reading this latest passage that I am in danger of portraying Mama as some kind of maudlin creature, a cold, hard woman with little regard for her family. Nothing could be further from the truth. We all felt loved, cherished and treasured by her and never once questioned her devotion to the family. We understood that in Papa's absence she was head of our household until the time that Richard came of age. In the meantime, we older ones appreciated Mother's mission. We had our nursemaid Bella and Mary to see to our physical needs and we had each other for emotional support. It was Mama's job to keep a roof over our head and to ensure that the boys were properly educated with a professional goal in mind. There was no question at this stage that all the boys would follow Papa's footsteps and enter the Firm. It was after all, Papa's wish and one even they at their tender ages would not question. And so it was that a move was planned. It was not the physical act of moving that distressed me so – we had after all moved a far greater distance from Scotland and had also moved from our house in Beckenham into Central London for a while when Papa had found the journey to work too much. It was just that I loved our house in Swanscombe. It felt safe and was Papa's final choice of home. When we were in London he had worried about the criminality that was never far from us in the Strand. The City was no longer the place where women could walk without fear. Anyway Papa and Mama chose to follow the latest fashion and move to the suburbs, away from the dirt and noise and industrial smoke, believing it was far better for Papa (and for us) to breathe cleaner air. There were other practical considerations. The house had a garden, its own privy (albeit not connected to any sewage system) and was close to the wide open spaces we all craved.

No, leaving Swanscombe was only difficult because at first I felt I was leaving Papa behind - a feeling that fortunately did not last after I realised Papa came with us in our hearts and minds, wherever we lived. In time I came to accept the practicality of Mother's decision. The distance from Stationer's Hall Court became an increasing problem and Mother was thinking ahead to Richard's daily journey to work and her own personal dislike of travelling. We were not rich enough to have our own means of transport and Richard would have had to take the horse omnibus which left Swanscombe at 7am and, although reasonable value, it still left a fair walk the other end as the nearest stop was over a mile from the office. Radical changes to London's transport links widened our choice of potential location. New railway lines were being developed all the time but this was the early 1860's when the railway companies were only just beginning to see the potential value of the working traveller. I think the most exciting thing that happened and the event that really caused a stir in our household was the first underground line. I clearly remember Charles, Alex and Richard being desperate to travel underground but Mama was adamant she would never descend into the bowels of the earth and it was many years before I was brave enough to try it out. Anyway, the trip from Paddington to Farringdon Street was a highlight for the boys who boasted about this outing for many years, but the underground did not help Mama's predicament. We lived too far away from the office and the family had to relocate.

Despite accepting this fact, I still felt devastated at having to move. I know I must not over glamorise our little Kentish village. We were after all one of the more affluent members of the community; the vast majority were not wealthy. An abiding memory for me was seeing on warmer days, the swarms of neglected children quarrelling and paddling in the ditches that ran alongside the main thoroughfare. Polly and I used to marvel at their numbers given the small cluster of houses in the locality, but in truth these children came from miles around to meet and play. Occasionally, unwashed and unkempt Mothers could also be seen as they pared potatoes and gossiped at their doors, but it was the children I remember most vividly. It wasn't the prettiest village around, and our house would not have particularly taken the eye of any passers-by, but it was home, and it was where my memories of Papa are strongest. The only other house I have ever felt attached to in the same way was the place where I was born in Scotland in Provan Side. My feelings for that house are tied up with my hankering for my homeland and my rose tinted memories of early family life. No, Coombe Lodge was by far the hardest for me to leave behind. It was only rented of course, but we loved it. A small village with around 400 houses, Swanscome itself lies four miles East of Dartford and our house was situated on a grassy ridge and commanded stunning views over the flat Kent countryside. The house had a large square garden, flanked on three sides by a beech hedge, the fourth by the row of willows already described. There were enough bedrooms to accommodate the servants who stayed in the two attic rooms. Papa was able to sit either on the couch or later propped up in his bed and looking out onto the patchwork of glistening green fields that spread out like a picture within the sash windows. He grew increasingly fond of this view as he became frailer and we'd sit together watching the clouds scud over paint box blue sky or listen to the rain battering the window and he'd feel part of the wider world even though his own environment was shrinking by the day. The maid at the time was particularly attentive to Papa, he being the master and a kind one at that. She kept the fireplace swept, the sheets cleaned every day and fresh water was kept beside his bed.

We were a progressive household in many ways. Papa had always been interested in new technology, keen to keep up to date with the latest gadgets of which there were many. The Great Exhibition which he had attended with great excitement fuelled by the fact that his uncle John Joseph was an exhibitor, had been talked about for months. Papa had told us about it in detail and I still feel disappointed that we were a little too young at the time to attend ourselves. Papa was all for taking Polly and I but Mama wouldn't hear of it *"The girls are far too young. It will be tedious for them. Besides I prefer to have them here with me,"* was her response to his pleas, and I recall the conversation precisely because it was such an untypical thing for Mother to say. We were still living in Scotland, and I recall quite vividly that we were all in the drawing room at the time after supper, Polly and I trying to play quietly so as not to be sent to bed and my ears pricked up at such an unlikely remark. Unfortunately my suggestion that it would be such fun to go to London with Papa was not well received and Polly was cross as we were both sent directly to bed and told off for listening into adult conversation. However, the next morning the matter was discussed again. I had been concentrating on spreading my oatcake with as thick a layer of creamy butter and golden honey as possible without it breaking (food being one of my great passions in life even at this young age) while Polly was still poking at her poached egg with a look of distaste as it slithered around her plate like a gruesome eyeball. I returned to the conversation when Mama reiterated to father that she did not want us to accompany him to England. It was strange as she was usually the one that encouraged us to try new things. She took us to the park to play, regularly planned outings by tram to go shopping or to visit relations and was the one to suggest that Papa took us out on foot to explore the city or the surrounding countryside. Of course at the time my six year old brain had no understanding of where the Great Exhibition was actually taking place. A 200 mile journey for him with two young girls in tow was a long way to travel especially given that only part of the railway network was efficiently running at this time and she was of course absolutely right that we would have found such a trip very long and very boring. Nevertheless it was uncharacteristic of Mama to be so adamant that we stayed behind. Perhaps she was struggling with her fifth child Charles, born the previous October (making five children under the age of 8), Papa working very long hours establishing the Firm; or possibly she was a little jealous at not being asked to go with him?

It was precisely the kind of event she would have loved to attend and Papa's descriptions of the show on his return was an equal fascination for her as for us. Prince Albert's vision was truly a fantastic spectacle and Uncle John and his scientific equipment business were lucky to have taken part. I know there were 100,000 exhibitors but even so, you had to prove you had something new or exciting to show and Great Uncle John's equipment was positioned alongside the very best of scientific instruments of the time. The publicity that he was given, not just for being there but for winning two medals – one for 'Graduated Class Instruments' - the inscription on the award being 'exceedingly accurate and good' – and the other for 'Economic and convenient chemical apparatus', was amazing and really boosted the company's sales. Mind you, I was less interested in the exhibitions Papa described than the wonder of the Exhibition Hall itself, fascinated by the scale of Joseph Paxton's design, the vast space incorporating thousands of panes of glass and over 300 iron columns. It was truly a spectacle to behold and Papa's excitement as he recalled what he'd seen from the shining alloy of steel and the 24 ton lump of coal at the entrance to the brightly coloured displays from the colonies was palpable, and I remember to this day the pang of regret I felt at not seeing these wonders first hand. Mother told me that Papa came back on such a high, more than ever convinced that Griffin's focus on technical publications was the right course to be taking. Britain after all, was the most advanced industrial and technological nation of the world and he was left with the strong feeling that London was the powerhouse; the place to be to capitalise on this new world.

I should quickly explain about Papa's Uncle John Joseph as he worked alongside Papa in Scotland and was his partner in the business for many years. Uncle John's primary interest was in scientific equipment and in particular the world of chemistry, and the Firm initially developed along two lines – the publishing side driven by Grandpapa and later Papa and the Scientific Equipment side which offered apparatus and instruments driven by John. Both businesses thrived and then in 1848 Uncle John moved to London as he wanted to develop his scientific apparatus specialities and was also keen to focus more of his time on his own writing. Mother has told me that the split came at a time when Papa was keen to have more autonomy over the Firm and whilst Uncle John continued to have close business links with Griffins (who continued to publish his writing), he was very busy building up his own company a business he called John Joseph Griffin & Co. This initially operated out of 53 Baker Street and it expanded rapidly over the years, especially when it took over a business from a Mr John Ward in March 1850 adding philosophical apparatus to his other categories. John Joseph remained a partner in Charles Griffin & Co however, and kept in close contact with Papa both before and after our move to London. Fortunately, God has given him good health unlike his brother and father who both died in their early forties, and he remained a major support to us throughout his life.

Of course, the wonders of the Great Exhibition and its Crystal Palace became quite well known to us when we moved to Lawrie Park. Although most of our visits were to concerts in the Great Hall, it was easy to see what an amazing effect the original edifice must have had in its Hyde Park setting.

Forgive the ramblings of an old woman. I am jumping between years in a very confusing way. If only I'd kept up the diary I started writing when we were first told we were moving from Scotland. We were all used to seeing Mama at her writing desk and her letters were legendary even when they were only of a personal nature. She was the one who kept in regular contact with her family and I recall as a little girl marvelling at the shape of the neat looped letters that packed each page, long before I could read their contents. Mother had given me a little notebook with a butterfly embroidered on the front that I have to this day. Intended to soften the blow, she had placed it in my eager hands whilst delivering the news that we would be leaving our birthplace. Not once did I consider how she must have felt. A true Scotswomen faced with leaving her family and friends behind. Instead all I could think about was my own sadness at leaving the home I loved. The boys were far too young to digest the monumental news of our move and after being called to order and stand quietly whilst Papa told us the plans, they embraced the idea of leaving Provan Side as a great adventure. Little Alex was the only one of the boys who demonstrated real sadness at our leaving and that was mainly because of his best friend Edward who lived a few doors away from us.

I was not a dedicated diarist and although I liked the look of the little book with its decorated cover and relished its leathery smell as it lay beside my bed, I did not keep much of a record of events – something I now regret. Even the diary I was given for 1860 is only half full with days of blank pages as if my life was conducted in little fits and starts. Looking back I didn't even mark the day of Papa's funeral, just his death and that was only 'Papa died today' – a banal statement with no reference to the ball of despair that lodged in my stomach for months afterwards. No my diary was not a place for me to spill out my heartaches, aspirations and emotions. That is not my way, although I can understand why Mother thought it may help. I was, after all, the one forever reading or scribbling in notebooks. It is just that I prefer fact to fiction; I like to further my education and share my new-found knowledge than idle away picking over my emotions. I don't want you to think I'm a cold person. Please do not misunderstand me. I am passionate in my own way and I hope I am sensitive to other people's feelings but I prefer to keep my inner thoughts locked away. I like to express myself through music, I am deeply spiritual and I like to use my language skills to further my education.

I suppose I am like Papa in that way. He truly loved books in any form, but he was also business-like in his approach to publishing. Some may say ruthless when it came to sorting out business affairs and selecting his authors, but in truth he was a realist. He recognised the need for Griffins to specialise and he was astute enough to embrace the burgeoning revolution in industry even back in the mid 19th Century when Glasgow was leading the way. How hard it must have been to move to another country, but of course we must remember that Papa was born in London. It was much worse for Mama. She had to leave her family, her friends and support network to set up a new life in an unknown city. Papa tried to make it better for her, but he had to work very long hours to set up the business and we had grown used to his absences in the lead up to our move because he had spent so much time down south. Now with the benefit of my advanced years, I understand how hard it must have been to leave his family and establish a business and start afresh somewhere new. Papa was forward thinking. He was a brave man especially as in truth he felt himself to be a Scot.

He had been less than a year old when he had moved away from London with his parents, Richard and Elizabeth. When they first came to Glasgow, it was light, clean and full of open spaces.

Between the 1760s and 1860's however, the population grew from 30,000 to over half a million people and with it came serious overcrowding and terrible inner city slums. By the time we left in 1859, the city had become known as the 'workshop of the Empire' and an industrial monster that had outgrown its own strength. The seriously cramped Wynds as they are known – narrow yards and closes – housed thousands of very poor folk with poor sanitation and high mortality and so in 1866 when the newspapers speak of The Glasgow City Improvement Act, we all rejoiced and were just sad that Papa had not lived to see the scale of the renovation. When we visited the city in the early 1870's we saw massive rebuilding. Slums were cleared, streets widened and whole districts rebuilt. Not that we ever ventured into the poorest closes before they were knocked down. But we had all read descriptions and heard father's account of the dark, little streets, with billowing washing, dirty cobbled yards with grey stone steps leading to the upstairs rooms filled with children in rags and weary women working desperately hard every day to eke out the pittance given to them to feed and clothe their families. Papa used to tell us how lucky we were to live in Provan Side with its double fronted bay windows overlooking the comforting expanse of St Martin's Green. Papa was proud of his Scottish upbringing although the influence of his English Mother meant that he was always made to remember his birthplace and Grandmamma by all accounts maintained "her little ways". I was only talking about her the other day to Mother. It's funny how much time she wants to spend speaking about the past and yet she is very forgetful about recent events. She can recall in detail what she ate the first time she dined with her future-in-laws. No Haggis in that household but a many course affair including Scotch broth and roast dinner with apple pie taken at 6.30 on the dot following Richard's return from the office. A protracted meal, which did not finish until gone 10 o'clock when supper was concluded with prayers with the servants and she remembers her relief when she was finally released from the table. Sadly, nowadays she cannot recollect what she requested cook to prepare for luncheon barely an hour after issuing her orders.

When we moved to England, it was left to Mother to keep up our Scottish traditions and remind us children of our roots. In truth, the younger children think of themselves as English and it is only Polly and I and the older boys who remember much of our birthplace. Mama has retained only a hint of a Scottish lilt but Polly and I relished the sound of our Mother tongue on our many trips north of the border. The maids at Aunt Eliza's house for example, where we were regular visitors, with their descriptions of our *"bonnie wee brothers and sisters"*. Their exclamations over little Henry, the *"laddie with the rid cheeks and spindly shanks"* and baby Alice, the *"bairn with the soft curly pow"*, bought nothing but delight to the Griffin clan, and we all secretly loved to be referred to as *"wee lambs"* even after we reached puberty! There was another reason why we particularly loved to visit Aunt Eliza and that was because of her beautiful home. To all accounts this was in fact a country house, with large sweeping main rooms running front to back and gardens so immense that they were referred by all as the grounds. Grand oaks and clumps of beeches separated a park of some acreage from the more formal gardens that immediately surrounded the house and the younger children loved to play hide and seek in the grounds when the weather allowed. I remember the smell of that garden best of all. The sweet, herby aroma that wafted through the family breakfast room on warmer days. It was years later that I'd discovered the source of such aromatic depths – banks of wild thyme and dells of honeysuckle grew close to the window and soft winds blew into that inviting room with the secrets of those hidden banks.

My own memories of Scotland have of course faded over time and probably because of our dramatic change in circumstances in 1862 when Papa died, it is Coombe Lodge and the early days of our bereavement that provide my sharpest recollections. Papa's will instructed his executors to pay an annuity of £300 to Mama (as well as give her the household furniture, silver plate, books etc to the value of £200) and £500 for refurbishing the house. He had left £15 a year to Sarah Bond, his illegitimate half sister (provided by Grandpapa!) as long as she had not married (which she never did) and another £15 to his Aunt Mrs Mary Eaves and £20 to GrandMother Mary Anne (Grandmamma Rae who we saw occasionally on visits back to Glasgow). As is customary, all of us children were listed in the will but Richard and Alexander came before Polly and me despite our being older in age.

So Mama had our existing furniture and a sizeable budget for refurbishment and she lost no time in those early weeks planning our move back into London. Looking back, her decision to relocate clearly gave her some focus during this bleak time. She talked to me about it years later and confessed to feeling totally numb and almost detached from daily life; so entrenched was she in her grief. As a self centred 17 year old it had not occurred to me to consider Mother's feelings in this decision. Whilst we drew comfort from routine, she craved new distractions and whilst we felt soothed by memories of our father in that house, she was tortured by them, wracked with misery at his absence. The area she chose to move us to was Islington in North London, not far from Uncle John who lived in Canonbury. We moved in mid October just weeks after Papa's death.

There was another reason why Mother was keen to leave Kent that we were not aware of at the time but came to light as soon as we moved. She clearly found Coombe Lodge substandard in terms of decor and had been disappointed by its state of repair. It provided the light and space Papa craved but mama was less impressed by the quality of its fixtures and fittings. I can remember her being irate when she received a letter from our old landlord Mr Goodeve. Her outrage disrupted another of our already noisy breakfast tables.

"Can you believe it girls? The nerve of Mr Goodeve to suggest that dilapidations in Swanscombe were caused by us during our short time there?" Even I felt riled by this accusation, thinking of our care of the house, our desire to get it comfortable for Papa and of course the servant's duty in keeping the place clean and tidy. We had often heard Mama bemoan the state of the place, particularly when we first moved in. I remember the very day we arrived, her instructing Mary to air the children's mattresses and cover them in calico before she would let the little ones sleep on them as they were very dirty. She had also had to replace broken tumblers in the bedroom and cover stained carpets and patch up broken oil lamps. Mother was used to more luxurious surroundings. Brought up in Linlothgowshire to the West of Edinburgh, the youngest of 15 children (and one of two sets of twins) with her father, James Rae a Sheriff Substitute (a man who helped the County Sheriff and his deputy with the daily running of the county court and therefore of some importance), the Rae clan were respected and wealthy members of society. They were a close family who kept in touch mostly via letter after we left Scotland. We didn't keep up with all of Mama's relations of course. I never met some of the older brothers and sisters who had died before I was born but Mother was closest to three of her sisters – the eldest Mary Ann (who married Uncle Low), Eliza (who married three times, the last husband being Uncle Stewart who we all knew well) and her unmarried sister Helen Rae who remained with their Mother (our GrandMother Rae) in Glasgow. Mama told us little about her childhood in fact but it was evidently a privileged one, despite the fact her own father died well before she married Papa in 1843, and this catastrophic event in her otherwise idyllic childhood had prompted their move from Edinburgh to Glasgow.

I digress, something you will be used to by now. I did want to point out the luxury Mother was used to as it makes it all the more remarkable that she coped so well with our change in circumstances. The letter from our old landlord did not put her in a good mood but in truth, her relationship with Mr Goodeve was a contributory factor in her decision to move from Coombe Lodge. Despite repeated requests to replace cracked china (or at least to lock it away) when we first moved in, the landlord refused and he ignored a similar request for bedroom tumblers (we used the dinner tumblers instead) and I lost count of the letters that past between them about the lack of garden tools and the soiled nature of the bed hangings. The fact that we never received a full inventory when we moved in was the main reason for the dispute and Mother was to learn from this experience. Never in all our subsequent moves did we have this problem.

Her primary concern in this case was choosing a good location. We had to be nearer to the Firm's offices at Stationers Hall Court and she chose an area that had recently been developed: Canonbury in North London. Canonbury Park Square to be precise. A very proud, formal little collection of newly built semi-detached houses, each facing a neatly clipped patch of grass enclosed on each side by a knee high box hedge. Each house had four storeys (to allow the servants to have the upper floor) with a three gabled roof, the central section containing the entrances and staircases and the other two gables (one each side) below which were the main rooms. Steps up from the street led to the reception rooms with the two floors of bedrooms above. A typical mid Victorian layout as you'll recognise but with one thing of note: no inside toilet or bathroom, as the houses were built before that sensible innovation became the norm. Houses I've since lived in that were built after the 1880's have all had an inside bathroom and our current flat has been adapted, although we may have the fanciest water closet you could wish for – all polished seat, painted cistern and china grip – but the sewage system is rendered useless most of the time, the drains still unable to cope with our household waste; but that is another story. Back in the 1860's we were used to using a commode and washstand and it was

Mary and her assistant at that time Clara, who really suffered. For it was they who lugged our water upstairs to the bedrooms and it was those poor dears who had to patiently fill the tin bath from water boiled on the kitchen range for our weekly bath. Poor Clara, she wasn't with us that long. I remember her as a neat, intelligent looking woman with a face as lined as a prune, but always spotless, in her freshly pressed uniform. Despite her outward appearance and in common with all our servants, she carried with her a faint pungent aroma; a blend of cooking smells, honest sweat and sooty fires. Anyway Canonbury Park Square may have been a step down in terms of size and status but it was only a small step. We had room to accommodate our servants, and they continued to help with the younger children; what is more, Polly took some comfort from the fact that, although she failed to persuade Mother to buy her preferred choice of carpet for the front room – a soft Axminster in gold and green - she won her battle over the curtains for the dining room: beautiful sheets of satin that shimmered against the early evening sunlight.

There was another matter that took up much of Mother's time as it was an issue that was much debated with Mr Collins, Uncle John and Mr Ambrose. I was only partially involved but I remember the angst that it caused and of course the implications were far reaching for the Firm. The problem was Papa's business partner Mr Bohn. Mother was determined that the business be returned to full Griffin ownership and she had never taken to Henry on the occasions they had met just before Papa died. The decision was taken, with the Executors approval, to borrow a considerable amount of money to pay back the half share that Mr Bohn had in the business. This debt was to hang over our heads until the latter part of the century, but it did at least make Mama very happy. So happy in fact that she could hardly wait to change the company name and was very proud when the legal documents were finalised in August 1862 and the business officially became Charles Griffin & Co.

After several months in the new house, it must have become apparent to Mother that our household outgoings were greater than our allowance and she started to look for different ways to balance the books. To make ends meet she was prepared to go to any lengths. She sold things: for example the oak cabinet, that had been given to her by an old relative and was once her pride and joy, was sold to a Mr Alexander, packed up before she could change her mind and sent to the station. I remember how pleased she seemed at the space it left behind. Not that she seemed worried by our smaller house and I'm ashamed to say it was Polly and I who were more likely to complain that our bedroom was too small, the parlour too cramped or the hall permanently cluttered. We soon had to make room for an even bigger household, as Mama's next money making venture was to take in lodgers. We also had to accommodate the boys in the school holidays, although not Richard who had by then started his apprenticeship in the book trade in Scotland. When Papa was alive Richard and Alexander spent their main Spring and Summer holidays boarded out closer to their school but after his death, when money was tighter they used to come home, their adolescent bulk adding to our congestion. I remember that Alex was particularly grumpy about this after we'd moved to Canonbury. A robust child, with a permanent restless air and ruddy complexion, he used to almost bounce off the walls in frustration at our cramped conditions, disappearing for hours to wander around the square and beyond, adding to Mother's general malaise by returning late for supper or making us the last family to file into our pew on Sunday mornings.

We were all affected by this move into the city but it was really Mother's distraction that was at the root of my problem. Polly and I had to take on a lot more of the childcare for the little ones. My favourite job was reading the bedtime story. This I remember as no chore. Little John would press his body as close to mine as possible, his hot chubby arm around my neck and Harry would back into my lap, thumb in mouth ready to hear the next instalment of *Tom Brown's*

School Days or *Uncle Tom's Cabin.* Polly preferred to spend her time making sure that little Alice and Helen were properly dressed (preferably like miniature ladies). They were both very tolerant of her attention. Helen in particular used to love to be dressed up and paraded around the house showing off her latest outfit – it's no wonder she has grown up to love fashionable clothes and shopping for accessories. Polly also put rags in their hair along with Jessie and took pride in their resulting head of shiny ringlets to match her own. I had no patience for such practice and favoured pulling my hair up into a bun although at night I secretly loved the feel of it as it swung like a glossy curtain down my back – far preferable to lying on a series of knots for the sake of fashion. I think Jessie felt the same but she was far more uncomplaining than I and was her usual placid amiable self whatever her fluctuating state of health. She was not however, a vacant child. Her restricted mobility allowed her many hours on the sofa to read or embroider and she was very patient and calm with the little boys even when she was going through the early stages of puberty. She was ten years old when we moved to Canonbury and required a lot of attention from Polly and I at this stage, particularly emotionally as she missed Papa so much. They had become especially close during his final illness and it was no secret that Papa had singled her out in his will, where he had stated that if she was ever bedridden or incapable of moving about she was to have a free life rent annuity in preference to the rest of us healthy children. This annuity was never needed as it happened, as Mother outlived Jessie but the fact that Papa stipulated such a clause was evidence of his devotion to his little invalid princess.

And so we all learnt to adapt to our new routine in London. The months slipped by and the family settled into an ordered life, structured by school terms, the days shaped by the Governess' lessons for the little ones. In due course Polly and I were sent to Germany to be 'finished' – a period of my life that started miserably for me due to extreme homesickness and ended very happily as I became accustomed to my new surroundings and indulged my passion for learning. I was inspired by my music teacher, an eccentric but gifted lady of indeterminate age who introduced me to the talent of the time in Europe. Work by Handel and Bach that influenced orchestral compositions the world over and stimulated my own creativity and up and coming young composers such as Debussy. Music has remained my passion throughout my life and I cannot imagine a world without symphonies, concertos, cantatas or chamber music. I'd love to say I supported British composers but if I'm honest, I favour non natives and I have always remained stubbornly loyal to my favourite composer, Beethoven throughout my life. A man so inspirational to me that my interest, I now see bordered on obsessional. I was, after all, an impressionable teenager. However my admiration and love of Beethoven has not dimmed over time and later culminated in my writing of his biography timed to mark the centenary of his birth. I am jumping ahead once again and anyway I did not seriously take up writing until the late 1860's/early 1870's although I was always a profuse letter writer, something I definitely inherited from Mama.

For our first year or so in Canonbury, Mother concentrated on sorting out the household accounts and spent time getting to know more about the business she had inherited. The two were of course intrinsically linked. Our future lay in the Firm's hands. Unfortunately for us, that meant relying on others. This became a matter of increasing frustration for Mother after it became apparent that not everyone involved felt as passionate or were as committed to the success of Griffins as we were. Mother found herself to be by far the most 'hands on' of the Trustees.

Her first task was to ensure that Mr Ambrose sorted out our finances. Not an easy one as it turned out as our Scottish advocate had a habit of disappearing for months when we needed him most, 'for the benefit of his health'. My memory of Mother's relationship with Mr Ambrose is tainted by the many arguments she had with him in later years but I assume at this stage they were actually on fairly civil terms. I did however find a copy of a letter Mother sent to him around this time and there is evidence of her exasperation with him even then. She clearly felt so strongly about the matters discussed that she kept two copies. Incidentally we always kept one copy of every business letter we ever sent, Mother and I, making the research for this book very easy. Remember, I was otherwise occupied myself during the first couple of years or so after we lost Papa, first helping to keep the house ticking over and then away to Germany; and so it was Mother who was left to get to grips with the Firm on her own. I have learnt a lot about her involvement through her letters and her own recollections of this period which are surprisingly clear.

The letter to Mr Ambrose I refer to was sent in December 1862, not long after our house move and it regarded our personal finances. We were all at home at the time but I have no recollection of this particular battle Mama was having. It was clear from the start that Mother took her role as Trustee very seriously, more so than the other members, who were to be fair, busy running their own lives. Mother had the most at stake in making Griffin's a success and that was evident from the outset. She felt concerned that Ambrose was disappearing for many months without clear reference to who would be authorising the Trust's bills in his absence. Also included in the letter were various monetary requests. I noticed these in particular because she was arguing the case for the £500 promised in the will for house refurbishment, which at this stage had not materialised. There were several issues: accounts for mourning and a claim for plate and linen were not in her view to come out of the £500 left by Papa but instead should come under either funeral costs or be covered by the £200 left specifically for household furniture. At this stage Mama had spent £250 of the £500 allocated for refurbishing our Canonbury home and as she writes ..."*as I have not yet obtained a Piano for the young ladies, I cannot possibly do with less than £300".* I'm so glad Mama stood out for the piano. I remember my absolute joy when the shiny beauty was delivered, as a rare moment of happiness at this bleak time. Of the £300 planned annual annuity for Mother there were also problems as she states in this same letter to Mr Ambrose, but she points out that she would happily defer £100 until the Trust could afford to pay it.

I find it interesting to note that her letter to Mr Ambrose also spells out how much she estimates each of us children cost. In many ways it's embarrassing given how little money poorer households have to manage with and yet for Mother it was a pitifully small amount after what she was used to. To think that she had to sit down and make this kind of calculation at all and then humble herself further by begging for funds shows her strength of character. This was a lady used to all the trappings of wealth and she was determined to ensure her children were given the best start in life. For each of us three girls – Polly, Jessie & I, she estimated that she needed £50 per annum; the three elder boys £80 each and the four little ones £20 each. The total: £470 per annum, a sum she asked to be paid quarterly from 11th November 1862. The cost of clothing, boarding and education for Richard and Alexander alone she felt would cost £100 – more than most employed working class families would be surviving on to feed, clothe and house their entire household. But the boys were our future. Alex remained at his Scottish school to finish his education, but the younger ones were sent to a more local school, so they were not so far from us in Canonbury. They were both weekly boarders and this meant a reduction in the cost of sending them to and fro in the holidays.

I have other letters written by Mama in these early months; many to Mr Ambrose, others to Mr Collins, her co-Trustee and a life saver for us in business terms even though he did not want to take on the running of Charles Griffin and Co. William Collins, although busy with his own thriving publishing business was a true friend of the family. He advanced £1000 in a short term loan, (a debt the Firm struggled to pay as it had initially been assumed it would be paid off by one of Mama's wealthier sisters – Eliza Stewart – but that was not to be the case), as the Firm was in financial difficulty. Cast afloat, a ship with no captain, the day to day management was taken on by a Manager - Henry Knox - an amiable, hard working man but 'not family' as Mother kept on reminding us. After several further attempts to glean more about the Firm's accounts via Mr Ambrose, Mama took a more direct approach and there are numerous letters in our files written directly to Mr Knox.

Still numb with grief and disorientated from our house move, we all tried to establish some kind of routine, mainly to keep our spirits up and to give the little ones a feeling of security. Christmas 1862 had all the hallmarks of being a sombre affair but we tried so hard to be jolly, and performed all our festive rituals whilst attempting to ignore the large Papa-shaped hole that filled our hearts. We stood around the piano and sang carols on Christmas Eve afternoon, the servants joining us for this annual treat, Polly and I stifling our yawns following several days of sleep deprivation. Not only had it fallen to us to send out the family Christmas cards (a tradition we had only recently adopted but one that had grown in line with the expansion of our extended family), we had also spent the previous two days at Church overseeing the donation of hundreds of gifts that we then sorted and sent out to be distributed to the poor of the parish. I had taken an hour or more packaging up a box of the most upmarket treats for the local poorhouse. We had left the boys in charge of purchasing and installing a tree to stand in the parlour. This was the first year we had bought a tree, a modern concession that Mother had agreed to on request from Richard and it became a favourite Christmas ritual ever since. Mama, Jessie and I particularly love the beautiful spicy aroma as you brush past the needles, the feeling of bringing nature indoors and for Mother it reminds her of her childhood home, which was nestled deep inside a valley overlooking a bank of majestic Scottish pines. There have been other new Christmas traditions included in the Griffin celebrations over the years and many have particularly appealed to the boys: the plum pudding for dessert, the Christmas cake inclusive of magic bean and the mountains of sugar topped mince pies baked by cook in the week running up to the big day. Our Christmas feast did not include such sweet treats in 1862, although there was plenty of other food on offer. We all felt saddened as we watched Richard taking the sharpened knife and attempting to carve the goose in the way his father had shown him, and when Henry knocked over one of the candles in the centre of our crowded table it took all of Mama's resolve not to chastise him too strongly, so taut were her nerves.

Luckily the present given session around the tree brought a smile to her face once more. I forget what gifts were exchanged other than Henry's toy soldier, a present received with such joy and excitement that his infectious grin more than compensated for his earlier clumsiness and we all rejoiced at the sound of his high pitched laughter as he sprang around the room clutching his prize. Our Christmas break was a time for us to close ranks and forget our worries, albeit temporarily. Boxing Day saw Mother back at her desk, her shoulders hunched over her paperwork once more as she took on the heavy mantle of head of household.

The Firm was at this time vulnerable to closure – indeed other Trustees clearly suggested this might be the best course of action (certainly it would have been easiest for them). But we had the most to lose from such an event and Mother begged for a longer trial, writing to her Co-Trustees: *"Eight months not being sufficient to warrant us in taking such a step"*. The struggle for financial backing continued, Mother had to re-pay William Collins £1000 or risk losing a vital ally and when it became apparent that Eliza was not able to settle the debt (her husband being seriously ill at the time), she suggested to Mr Ambrose that stocks be sold off to settle *"the liabilities which now oppress us"*. Her plan was a sensible and astute one. Although it would mean Papa's large scale plans for the business would have to be dropped, a clearing of debts was the most prudent option to carry on a smaller business advantageously.

Sadly, no-one was to act on her advice and Mama turned to Mr Collins stressing that selling off £4 or £5000 of stock and copyrights was their only hope. Poor Mother, she seemed to be getting nowhere. She once explained to me that it was hardly surprising that decision-making took so long: trying to run a London business partly in Glasgow, with the only London Trustee being a woman would have presented problems. With Mr Ambrose away so much it was left to William (himself a 'rival' publisher) to deal with day to day matters. Mama herself faced a steep learning curve. I remember the many hours she spent bent over the gas light at Papa's old desk and my feeling of frustration at times at her lack of interest in my piano playing, Polly's embroidery or the boys' model carriage. When I was about ten years old I had dreamt of becoming a famous pianist regularly performing my own compositions in front of packed crowds and I clung to that hope until it became apparent that my musical ability was good but not exceptional. I had a precocious talent that manifested itself very young due largely to my ability to read music at the same time that I learnt to read words on a page, and fuelled by the adoration of my Scottish piano teacher. Once I had reached the age of about twelve, it was my love of reading that overtook my obsession with the piano, and I then dreamt of becoming a famous writer. Even at this tender age, I viewed my future very differently to Polly, whose aim in life was to marry and bear children. I wanted to become a famous travel writer, a woman of independent means, supported by my loving parents. I nurtured this dream until my father's death and I think the realisation that my life was to take a different path was very hard for me to deal with, as I saw my world shrinking, confined to the four walls of my family home, and I often felt trapped. I now feel somewhat ashamed of my intolerance but I had felt resentful at being forced to take on more household responsibility and was often moody and unsupportive. Such is the selfishness of youth I suppose and Mother was forgiving and still keen for us girls to finish our education. My stay in Germany was a chance for me to escape the household stresses and in her defence, Mother sent a stream of letters that focused on the family rather than the business, and I found this a great comfort. *"Mama is busy"*, *"shush little one or Mother will be cross"* and *"show Mama later"* were common phrases in our house during the holiday time. It is only now at my advanced age that I can see that Mama had no choice. She missed out on the early childhood of the little ones simply because she had to fight for our livelihood.

By the end of 1863, early 1864, it became apparent that Mother's earlier suggestion to sell off stock was now vital. Early in the New Year, Uncle John took Mother to the Warehouse in Stationer's Hall Court to see what could be done. On 19th January they returned to see what had happened but Mr Knox had not even prepared the list John Joseph had asked for. It was apparent that Mother had concerns about the day to day running of the business. Not only had it been left to her to get to grips with the many bills the Firm owed and sort out how these should be paid (she learnt to her cost as Trustee when the 'bad debts' rolled in during the early months), there is also a copy of a letter written to Uncle John which expresses her *"fear that (Knox) is out of his depth in his present position"*. There were also reports of the attitude of another member of staff, Meiklejohn who had asked for a pay rise citing a discrepancy between his money and that of others in the Firm. It was left to Mother to explain to him that the travellers (salesmen) were paid extra because they received productivity bonuses and anyway unlike the others in the Firm he had received a pay rise at his last review. Mama was not afraid of confrontation and displayed keen management skills (presumably learnt whilst running a large and busy household) as well as a growing business aptitude.

Meanwhile she struggled with balancing our own books. Our household expenses were spiralling and she had particular problems funding Alexander's board. I knew nothing of this at the time but I came across a letter written to Mr Collins dated 22nd January 1864 telling him that she was under pressure to settle her account from Alex's headmaster - a Mr Wilson. At this time she had paid the first six months bill (£44) but could not find the balance of £34 and so took on two boarders to try to raise the extra cash. We were quite happy about having extra people in the house. I confess to dreading my return from Germany. I had fallen deeply in love with the country and was settled and happy there and felt uneasy about returning to my family responsibilities. However, one lodger who was taken in to help balance our books greatly brightened my young life and made my transition back home more bearable. James Rae, my cousin and of no romantic interest to me I hasten to add – was a fine young man. Small in stature, with sandy hair, a smattering of freckles across his nose and bright blue eyes, he was very charismatic, had a quick wit and keen sense of fun. He quickly became an adored extra playmate for the little ones and a great sparring partner for Polly and I. He had been sent from Scotland by my Aunt to find a job and, encouraged by Mama, he became interested in publishing and took time to study the various catalogues and paperwork about Charles Griffin and Co that were in danger of taking over our house. James used to accompany Polly and I to the theatre. Shakespeare was naturally a favourite and a trip to Covent Garden or Drury Lane was a regular treat at this time and one which Mama could occasionally be persuaded to join us. We never took her to contemporary productions mind. I remember one evening we had booked to attend a play at the Sadler's Well theatre. Richard was to accompany us that evening, as James had a prior engagement. However Polly and I ended up going alone, as Richard had a chill and was advised to stay indoors. It had taken us several hours to persuade Mother to allow us to go unchaperoned. Neither of us knew what to expect from Henry Irving's production and we never did enlighten Mama as to the play's contents, but it was rather an eye-opener to us both and a play I remember clearly to this day. The melodrama – called The Bells as I recall – thrived on cliché of course but was thrilling nevertheless and the description, conspiracy, revenge and violence not to mention romantic passion kept us spell bound throughout and provided us with much gossip for months afterwards.

Uncle John continued to support and was a regular visitor, as he lived only round the corner from us in Douglas Road – a newly developed and highly desirable location in Islington. He was by then an old man in his 60's and had plenty to occupy him – his own scientific business was thriving and his writing career continued to impress. The mid 1860's saw the production at John Joseph Griffin & Sons of the squat spouted beaker known as 'The Griffin Beaker' – a name that greatly impressed us in our Griffin household along with their other trademarked equipment such as the Griffin Furnace. Anyway, these Griffin beakers came in several sizes and nested together and were to bring much profit to this already successful business. Luckily his sons were able to help and this allowed Uncle John to support his brother's family through this difficult time. Although he was far too busy to take over completely, he remained a loyal friend and experienced advisor to Mother. In January 1864 he had been two or three times to the Warehouse to spend time looking over stock with Mr Knox and he shared many of Mother's growing concerns over the Manager's competence. It became apparent that Mr Knox had authorized the travellers to offer heavily reduced prices (which the Trustees had not agreed to) and this forced Mother to keep an even keener eye on day to day operations.

One of her ideas was to suggest putting her nephew James into the Firm as sub-manager and she wrote to Mr Collins with this suggestion on the 10th March 1864. She also suggested that James replace Mr Warner (another traveller for whom she had little respect and whose name you will see referred to later in this book). By this time, James had been living in our house for three months and had impressed Mother with his intelligence and enthusiasm. He had had the wit to keep his childish humour to the nursery and his faint lilting accent and Scottish ways had won her over in the first few days of his stay.

Sadly her suggestion fell on deaf ears and James was forced to accept a position in a rival firm – Cassells on Ludgate Hill in April 1864. Perhaps demoralised by this but also, she confessed to me later, a *"little upset"* at not being taken seriously, especially after it became apparent decisions were made between Collins and Knox that she was not party to, she again wrote to Uncle John begging him to become a Trustee. The reason given: *"I have no authority at Stationer's Hall Court".* Mr Collins also wrote to Uncle John as he had had enough and he hoped that the older man would take over his position as Trustee. Uncle John's letter declining this request written from his house in Douglas Road on 19th April 1864 is important enough to our story to be reproduced almost in full (I will omit a couple of paragraphs where he repeats himself).

My Dear Mrs Griffin

I have read Mr Collins's letter of 13th April, and now return it to you.

I am not surprised at his finding difficulties in the working of the Trusteeship. – When I urged him and Mr Ambrose to decline the Trusteeship and to leave the affairs in your hands, I did so in the conviction that their acceptance of the Trusteeship would prejudice the estate; for it appeared to me to be impossible that a complicated publishing business in London could be successfully directed by two men living in Glasgow, one of them totally ignorant of the trade, and the other entirely occupied by a complex business of his own. Events have justified my anticipations. You have been kept in constant trouble and anxiety, and Mr Collins now admits that the business is not successful, and hints that Mr Ambrose may resolve to wind it up.

These are his words: – 'If the next balance is not more favourable than the last, Mr Ambrose may insist on winding up the business', and then he proposes that, in the event of your wishing to continue the business, Mr JJG should undertake the office of Trustee, because he, (Mr Collins) would not himself take the responsibility of carrying on the business against Mr Ambrose's opinion.

Now if I were inclined to become a trustee I should ask for information's sake, what had been done during the twenty months that the Trustees have had the Estate in their hands? What is the state of that last balance-sheet which Mr Collins seems to deplore? When I put a question to you some months ago about that last balance-sheet, you said you did not know what was the balance; that you had asked for a copy of the balance-sheet, but that it had never been given to you. That neglect I consider very singular. <u>You</u>, one of the Trustees, a principal legatee, and the Mother of the family whose fate is bound up with this trust, seem to be kept in ignorance of the real state of your affairs, and not to know whether you are going forward or backwards. You have two Co-Trustees, a paid legal agent in Glasgow, an accountant, several clerks, and a manager of the business, but with this extensive and expensive staff of officers, you cannot have prepared a copy of that 'last balance' which you are told was so bad as to foreshadow a disastrous fate for your business and family.

Neither I, nor any man, without that balance sheet, and other information, could form a fair opinion of the propriety of becoming a Trustee, or the possibility of recovering lost ground and doing any good.

Let me recall the fact that last year I suggested, and you recommended to your Co-Trustees, a plan for realising part of your stock, and paying off some of the heavy debts that oppress the Estate.

That plan was ridiculed by Mr Ambrose and rejected, and it now appears that when he went abroad, he left behind him a threat that if the <u>next</u> balance was not more favourable that the <u>last</u>, he would insist on a winding up the business.

If I inquire what measures Mr Ambrose after scornfully rejecting your recommendation, took to render the next balance more favourable than the last? I fancy the answer must be that he did then, what he has done since, nothing at all........

.......How can Mr Collins recommend to me the occupation of a post which he finds to be so dangerous and so unpleasant? At any rate, I on my part, decline the offer. I could never think of joining Mr Ambrose either in his passive policy of doing nothing, or in his active policy of putting an end to a business, which, if I were a Trustee, I should consider it to be my sworn duty to preserve for the benefit of the family that was confined to my guardianship.

Even if I were not infirm, I should for these reasons feel it my duty to decline Mr Collins's proposal, and I will thank you to let him know that I do so; and you may add that I could never agree to appear before the public as the co-trustee with Mr Ambrose, and as giving countenance to the dilatory policy which I disapprove of.

I am, my dear Mrs Griffin, yours truly.

On 20th April 1864 Mother sent a copy of Uncle John's letter to Mr Collins. In it she notes Collin's wish to retire but put her own points in a typically forthright manner. *"There is one thing that I will not hear of and that is the selling of the business; it would ruin the family.....Mr Ambrose cannot know [how little such a sale would realise], or he would not have proposed such a thing. It is not fair to judge the business after so short a trial.... I am certain that if I could get Mr Griffin's plans carried out.... It would go satisfactorily and well. "*

When I started writing this book Mother spent some time (at my request) going over this period of her life as I was largely unaware until the summer of that year that such a struggle was ensuing. I have to confess to being too wrapped up in my own life and in particular was concentrating on furthering my education. I worried about Mother of course, but in the slightly distracted way of youth when no problem is insurmountable – no mountain too high to climb. I had not realised that the Firm was taken right to the brink. Mother said that she'd had to spend months following Mr Collins request to withdraw and Mr Ambrose's suggestion to wind up the Firm, reminding Mr Knox of the need to dispose of part of the premises – either by selling the lease or taking in tenants. He was typically slow in responding, and offered a lease that Mother thought was too low before finally sorting out a tenant that summer. By that time, Richard had started at the Firm. This event generated much excitement in the Griffin household.

Poor Richard. Our expectations were too high and I now suspect he was rather out of his depth the moment he stepped through the door. Not that he instantly became Manager. As expected, he was very much the office junior. He had to learn the trade from the bottom up - something he struggled with from the beginning. Part of the reason for his frustration was that he felt he had more experience than he was given credit for. He had not entered the Firm straight from school but, after he'd finished his education at Mr Walker's Academy in Scotland (where Papa himself had been educated), he had gone to the Bible Warehouse in Hutcheson Street in Glasgow not far from Papa's old offices . Papa had arranged this placement before his death as he was keen for Richard to learn the bookbinding side of the business as well as the publishing side, and the firm he chose: J & R Neil Bookbinders and Bible Warehouse to give its full title – is a company that Griffins has retained a bookbinding connection with up until this day. In the autumn of 1862, Richard left Neil's and came down to London and Mama could not wait for her son to enter the Firm, so anxious was she to have family involved as soon as possible. We all knew Richard wasn't that happy under Mr Knox and he certainly left us in no doubt that he thought his talents were wasted. Mother, to be fair, was more circumspect, treading a fine line in between promoting her son and acknowledging a certain arrogance fuelled by his age and his position as male head of our household. She did not however, stand in his way when he chose to push himself forward. Mother showed me (with some amusement it has to be said) a copy of a letter she received from Mr Knox that had been written by Richard to Mr Collins, not long after he had started at Charles Griffin and Co.

London, 2/4/63

Dear Sir,
I do not like being at the counter and feel that I ought by this time to be in some other department, it is now six months or more since I first came down from the Bible Warehouse.

If you could have time to write and ask Mr Knox (if you approve) to change my position it would oblige (sic)

Yours very truly
R. T. Griffin

I have the letter now in my hand, written in Richard's untidy scrawl and annotated in pencil with the words 'better consult Mrs G as to this, HK'. Mr Knox, rather prudently, decided to refer the matter to Mother after receiving it from Mr Collins in Glasgow. Mama said she was equally prudent in sending a reply to Mr Knox along the lines of 'I leave this decision to you' in acknowledgement of the fact that he was in full control of managing his staff.

Mother used Richard's journey from our home in Canonbury Park Square to the office each day as a channel for her correspondence with Mr Knox. Her regular letters - which were generally concerning Trust matters and requests for money against her annual income allowance, often asking him to 'cash the enclosed' and expecting him to send the appropriate notes or gold by return - were all carried by Richard. Unfortunatley for Richard, he was not a robust young man, often suffering ill health. Mama, so recently bereaved, was over-protective in my view and often imposed

Motherly sanctions on his movements. She would write to Mr Knox asking his permission to keep Richard at home when he had a cold as it usually went to his chest and laid him low for several days. Mother herself was in good health at this time, (considering the stress she was under), but the mental strain and physical demands of late nights poring over books and regular trips to Stationer's Hall Court to keep an eye on things eventually took their toll over the years, as you will find out later.

Meantime, Polly and I continued to help out at home. By now little Alice was two years old; Helen was three and a half, Henry seven and John Joseph nine years. Mother had arranged for the younger boys to attend a school not far from Islington and that left us girls at home with the nursemaid Lily (who had replaced a weeping Bella after an unplanned pregnancy put a premature end to her time with us) and cook Caroline who had moved with us from Kent as her family was in London. Polly was becoming frustrated at her circumstances and, at the tender age of twenty-one, was worried she may be left a spinster. The fact that Mama shunned the local 'at home' circuit was a source of irritation for Polly (but a relief to me) and she was also disappointed not to be able to attend the London Season.

Whilst my life was about to become very much consumed by business as I started to take over much of the letter writing duties in the summer of 1864, Polly concentrated on expanding her horizons and bettering her chances of finding a husband. Shopping was becoming a major leisure pursuit and Polly's favourite was a department store nearby that stocked finest firs, silk and jewellery as well as fashionable drapery. Polly preferred to shop with a friend and would never venture out alone, apart from one occasion which sticks in my mind. I remember it clearly as it came about by accident. She had been planning a trip into town to visit a newly opened department store with a friend called Margaret - a girl whose love of shopping even surpassed her own - and they were to be accompanied on this trip by Margaret's Mother Daphne. The day of the aforementioned trip dawned and Polly set off in a fervour of excitement, clutching her new parasol and cloaked in an air of anticipation. A new department store to explore was Polly's idea of heaven. Having waved her off as she departed to call for Margaret who lived in a nearby street, we thought nothing of Polly and her trip until her return much earlier than we expected, just as we had been called into luncheon. Polly arrived home with a bag in one hand, hat box in another and the younger girls clung to her skirts, clambering to see what she had bought. I knew at once that something was amiss but my question as to how she had enjoyed her day was answered in a perfunctory manner and it was only in the privacy of our bedroom that the tale unfolded. Polly, it transpired, had arrived at Margaret's house to the sound of her friend's sobbing and her Mother's soothing voice before Daphne had joined her in the hall to inform her that her friend had a slight chill and needed to stay indoors. Daphne was a kind lady, full of apologies for Polly's wasted trip, explaining that she had only put her foot down when she had seen her daughter's flushed cheeks and heard the muffled cough as she was finding her shoes. Polly was naturally devastated. So much so she had taken the most unlikely decision to instruct her driver to continue on their intended journey into the West End. I remember being shocked at the time by Polly's daring and in awe of her determination. It would be some years before I myself was to travel alone into the office. Although confessing to feeling a little anxious about shopping unaccompanied, Polly was secretly proud of her bravery and grew ever more independent from that day on.

Mother has only recently stopped worrying about me travelling alone around London (principally because she is now not aware of much of her surroundings). She need not have worried so much over the years, as I have been a particularly cautious traveller following an uncomfortable experience once when I was accosted by a middle aged man who thought I was a fallen woman (despite me being dressed in one of my best cape and bonnets). I naturally never told Mother of this unfortunate incident or she would have insisted I was always accompanied by one of the boys, but it did mean that I travelled in a Hansom whenever possible.

Sensing that her eldest daughter was feeling increasingly trapped at Canonbury Park Square, Mama arranged for her to go to Scotland to spend time with her relatives. She was to travel by train (a great excitement) and Mr Knox had kindly offered to take her to the station, but in fact she ended up going by sea and departed in August 1864, leaving me alone to juggle the dual demands of a large household and a business obsessed Mother.

I found an undated letter recently which must have been written around the autumn of that year due to its contents. It's a letter to Mr Collins from Mother that clearly demonstrates how closely involved she was in running the Firm. She reports on a visit to Stationer's Hall Court where she cross-questioned the long standing employee Mr Meiklejohn in front of the manager Mr Knox. Meiklejohn had reported irregularities in the business and, after asking for details, Mother agreed that *"Things are managed in a very unsatisfactory way"*. I should say by the way that Mr Meiklejohn was part of the Accountancy team and he was reporting on deficiencies in the record keeping of the production department – an issue I myself was to raise when I became more involved in the business. I have no recollection of this particular incident at the time but when I mentioned it to Mother recently she recalled this as being the occasion when Mr Knox asked for an assistant, claiming overwork. His suggested 'right hand man' was Mr Warner – a gentleman that Mother did not trust describing him as 'unsteady'. Instead she once again proposed that he took on my cousin James Rae but again it fell on deaf ears. Mother's frustration with Mr Knox was clear from her correspondence but he was not her only worry. As well as expressing grave concerns to Mr Collins (she once wrote *"it is dreadful to have our property at the mercy of so incompetent a man as Mr Knox"*), she also had problems, once again, with our own dear solicitor Mr Ambrose.

Neither man would have been used to having their professional competence questioned, let alone by a woman!

The months passed. Mr Collins oversaw the subletting of part of the Warehouse premises and by October 1864 the financial situation seemed to be more stable. However, whilst she was satisfied with the accounts given by Mr Smart (the Firm's Accountants) at the Autumn Trustee meeting, she realised there was still much to be done and urged Mr Knox to reconsider selling old stock and some copyrights to shore up the finances.

Although I took on some of the personal and business letter writing around this time (willingly I might add), Mother continued with her own correspondence. I suppose in many ways I became her personal assistant. Writing a letter is our main means of communication and with the rest of the Trustees hundreds of miles away north of the border, there were always issues that had to be dealt with. Often letters crossed in the post and the delay could be extremely frustrating, sometimes leading to misunderstanding. One example of this happening was in response to a personnel issue at the Firm. Mr Warner, presumably put out at not being made Mr Knox's assistant, was causing problems. He demanded a pay rise and when he was refused, he became vocal in his disapproval of the management team at Griffins. Publishing was (and still is for that matter) a small world and his claims were not helpful for the reputation of the Firm. I have several letters from Mother that hint at what happened. On 21st February 1865 she wrote to Mr Collins replying most firmly to a suggestion that the Firm gave Mr Warner a subscription (i.e. a monetary gift in lieu of a pension).

> *"I consider that we are not called upon to do anything for Mr Warner after the manner in which he has behaved. Even if the Estate were in a position to pension him off, his conduct has not been such to deserve it….Please let Mr Ambrose know my views on the subject."*

This letter was followed by another to Mr Collins after he advised her that withholding Griffin's name from the list would denote 'extreme shabbiness or poverty'. Mother backed down on the matter but not after putting her own view across: *"When I advised such a measure, I was ignorant of the purpose for which the money was wanted, as I had been confined to the house for more than a month"* (at the time she had thought Warner wished to set up a rival Firm of his own). *"It is my impression that our house has suffered greatly through having such a representative as Warner. For he has done all he could to bring it into bad repute by giving out everywhere that we were excessively mean…Now if he made £500 a year (as he stated in court not long ago) this cannot be true. You remember also his lifting our money and using it for his own purposes; and I consider that a man, who is capable of acting in such a way, is not eligible to our encouragement."*

She does however leave the final decision on Warner to Ambrose and Collins and the matter is dealt with.

My own letters to the Firm initially focused on more mundane matters. I remember my first correspondence clearly because I was so proud to take on the role from Mother (who was busy attending to Alice at the time after she had kept her awake for several nights laid low with a fever). It was a letter to Mr Knox about a parcel that was being sent to our old neighbour in Sydenham. It was too large to go by carrier and I wrote to ask if one of the lads could take it – a request that was granted of course. I remember that Alec had by now entered the Firm (somewhat grudgingly) and he had leapt at the chance to escape the office for the afternoon.

It was not all work and household chores for me. While my sister pursued her romantic quest I was happy to bury my nose in a book and I was also writing. I dabbled in essays, poetry, religious journals and musical analysis and I was thrilled when Mr Knox (probably at Mother's suggestion) sent me a manuscript to read. The book was called *Scottish Tales* and I remember it as a rather dull volume; the only notable feature being some rather bizarre illustrations, drawn by the author, that were placed alongside such exquisite Ballads as 'Auld Robin Gray'. When I wrote of my opinions to Mr Knox I pointed out that I did not think that many Scots would see the need for such illustrations and yet without them the book was very ordinary indeed. Following this review, I was pleased to receive further submitted scripts and I also started doing some sub-editing for the Firm. This had started in the summer of 1864 with a book on the collected works of George Herbert. I had great fun thinking up titles for the book and also cross referenced possible illustrations as well as submitted two sentences as possible mottos. Although none of my suggestions were actually used by Mr Knox I was thrilled to be asked my opinion and he must have been reasonably impressed because at the end of 1864 I was given a much bigger editorial job – compiling the *"Book of Dates"*.

This was really the turning point of my life in publishing as I enjoyed this job immensely and most importantly it was the first time I was officially paid by Charles Griffin & Co. It was a monumental task, particularly when I discovered that the *Book of Dates* for 1862 was full of errors and omissions and was quite unfit for publication. The only events listed were murders and other public horrors; there had been no mention of the International Exhibition or of any subject of scientific or literary interest and no reference to Parliamentary matters. I had to return it to Mr Knox to get him to send it back to the party who compiled it. Meantime I also had 1863 to edit and I spent many an hour poring over newspapers of the time and the *Spectator* as well as other publications to check for accuracy and omission. In August 1865, I also took on some translation work. My love of language and travelling meant that I had been keen to learn French and German – both languages which were to prove very useful in my business life. Not only was I given the job of translating books from French to English, I was occasionally asked to issue a French edition of one of Griffin's books. Not an easy task given their highly technical and scientific content.

During these early summer months I took advantage of the warmer weather and lighter evenings and often sat under the tree in our back garden wrapped up in my shawl, my limbs stiffened with cold, bent over my books. I had some peace as Mother took the little ones to the seaside in June for an extended holiday. The trip to the East Coast gave little Jessie some sea air and Mother was also in need of a break. I was happy to remain at home. I decided in Mama's absence to be rather prescriptive in my task of managing the servants. I now cringe at this diligence as all of our staff were more than capable of managing their day but so keen was I to appear to be the perfect mistress of the household, I wanted everything to be highly ordered. I came across my scribbled plan for the housemaid's duties the other day and I now laugh at the account. Sarah was, to be fair, the newest member of our household and was only 15 years old (not much younger than myself at this point remember). A willing girl, she was desperately homesick as her family were from Kent and she was the niece of one of our old servants when we had been at Swanscombe. Poor Sarah. She had simply nodded when I read out my wish list and I don't think she completed half of the tasks on my lists but the stairs had been washed, hot water brought for my bath and the grate in the drawing room swept. By the time she had aired the mattresses, cleaned all the brass and waited at the table she had looked flushed and exhausted and I had dismissed her after supper even though she had not turned down my bed or cleared away the supper dishes. I think she was glad when Mother returned to manage the house and she must have been very happy as she stayed with us for a number of years, sending money back to her Mother in Kent and making the most of her half day holiday to go out with the neighbour's maids who were of similar age.

Not long after Mama's return, in August, a saga began which none of us were expecting. Trouble with one of our most loyal authors, Papa's trusted physician and a personal friend of the family: Dr Aitken. I have on file copies of an exchange of letters written in August that starts with a letter from Dr Aitken to Mama complaining that he could get no money from Mr Knox. Mother replies to Knox: *"If Mr Ambrose is to blame, you should write to him at once and rouse him as Dr Aitken threatens legal proceedings."* Knox replies via a message from a clerk: *"we beg to assure you that our Mr Knox wrote to Mr Ambrose in the beginning of this month, urgently requesting a cheque for Dr Aitken to be here on the 10th to meet the latter gentleman on his arrival in London…. This week we wrote again"*. The 'Dr Aitken affair' as it became known in our house rumbled on and still it was Ambrose who held things up. On 2nd September 1865 Mother wrote again saying *"It is dangerous to trifle so with our authors. If we treat them in this manner we may as well shut up shop"*. (Perhaps this is exactly what Ambrose wanted!) Meanwhile, Dr Aitken had refused to send in any further copy until he received some money and we had sleepless nights over this embarrassment until the matter was eventually settled.

However, there was to be a bigger cloud on the horizon for Mama and one which caused her considerable personal grief. I remember this time very well, so traumatic was it for Mother and it was the first time I think both of us felt renewed fear over the future of Charles Griffin & Co.

Chapter 3

Richard went missing. This was not at first of great concern. We had grown used to Richard's disappearances but these were usually for a night spent with friends when he selfishly failed to keep us informed of his movements. He was probably reacting to feeling controlled by Mother and by the business: both certainly kept a very close eye on him and he showed signs of having a worryingly weak, unreliable side to his nature. This fickleness we could cope with but when he disappeared one weekend early in September and failed to show up at work on Monday morning we were naturally uneasy. By the end of the week Mother was worried sick and spent her days contacting his friends, family and work colleagues. How I cursed my brother! How could he do this to us and at a time when Mother and the Trustees had fought so hard to keep the Firm going? This was a distraction that none of us needed. I know this may seem harsh. For Mother it was the loss of her much doted on eldest son that vexed her so. My first thoughts were for the business. Not that Richard was a man of any influence at this time but his actions showed such flakiness of character I think even Mother became worried. Was he strong enough to lead a large publishing house? Whether such thoughts entered Mama's head, she never said. She just wanted Richard home.

The letter writing initially bore no fruit and then one morning in September Mother received a batch of letters that she hoped would shed light on Richard's location. I had woken that morning feeling tired and heavy of limb, and had only just emerged from the room I shared with Polly long after Mary had cleared away the breakfast dishes. Perhaps because of my pounding head, or because of Mother's agitation as she spoke, it took me a few moments to understand the implication of the letter's contents. The first was written by Francis Cotton from Belle Vue House, Chepstow:

> *"I can only inform you that I have not seen or heard from Richard for at least a year now and most certainly never therefore made any arrangement to go to Sheerness with him. Trusting you may have heard of him ere this".*

Outside the letter is written 'Coffee House, 29 London Road, and Liverpool'. That was in response to one of his office colleague's suggestion that Richard may have gone to Sheerness, but that was clearly a false lead. The second letter was more worrying. It was from a contact of Mr Knox's. Our manager had one day visited us at home and had tentatively suggested to Mother than Richard may have been persuaded to go to sea. Knox himself had written to a friend of his with whom he conducted business. A person whom Richard had met in London but who had since bought a boat and moved up North. The man was called Mr Hossack and he had met Richard at work before Hossack had left for Liverpool. Unfortunately, there was a misunderstanding and Mr Hossack clearly thought Knox was accusing him of kidnapping Richard! His reply was naturally hostile:

> *"I can assure you I am totally ignorant of his movement not having seen him since I made up my mind to leave home. He doesn't not even know the name of this Ship. If I see or hear anything of him I will telegraph to you at once. I am very busy at hard work as we sail for Cardiff tomorrow (Sunday). If you have time to write me a note I will be glad to hear from you".*

This letter concludes: *"...I must say I am surprised and annoyed at the contents* [of Knox's letter], *I was not aware I had very done any* [thing] *to warrant such action on your part".*

Mr Knox had forwarded several other letters – one from a business colleague in Dover who reported seeing a young tradesman (who did not fit Richard's description) and the other from a company called Stavely & Starr – an American Express Company of The Temple, Dale Street, Liverpool (the same firm incidentally for whom Mr Hossack worked for). Addressed to Messer's C Griffin & Co, it explains what their actions had been.

> *"Saturday is a half day holiday with us but as one of our young men had not gone home when your letter arrived, we set him to attend to it. He found Mr Hossack who is extremely hurt to learn that young Griffin has left home. He also found the W. H. Prescott which sails tomorrow for Cardiff. The lad is not on board of her, nor do captain or mate recognise him from description given to us by Mr Hossack as having applied for a berth".*

The letter finished by promising to call at the Sailor's Home – the place where people register for a ship – on Monday when the offices were next open. The ship in question, the William H Prescott, was an American boat named after a famous historian of the time who was an expert on the Incas. This American connection was what concerned us most. When Mr Knox first had a meeting with us to discuss who we might contact, Mother had voiced her greatest fear: that Richard may try to sail for America. All that summer the American Civil War had raged (Lincoln had been assassinated only a few weeks before) and Richard had followed events very closely and had shown great interest in the fighting. Richard, remember, was too young to recall the horrors of the Crimean War. I too was protected from such events, especially as the action took place on the border between the Russian and Ottoman Empire, exotic sounding locations far away from our cosy life in Scotland. But the horrors of how ill equipped, ill fed and mismanaged our soldiers were had been well documented back home. Mother and Papa would regularly exchange snippets of news about the appalling conditions of the soldiers, thankful at the time that their boys were too young to be involved and I remember Mama telling Polly and I all about Mary Seacole, and other inspirational nurses doing a hectic job. Of course I was only around 10 at the time but this was the first war that Britain had fought for some 40 years and it was a bitter, bloody fight. Mama had been scared that Britain may become embroiled in another battle which could involve her beloved family. Richard, like all the boys, was fascinated by any news of fighting or unrest but he was also born with a keen sense of his own fragility and I secretly felt her fears about any potential involvement in the civil unrest unfounded. I could not imagine Richard having the courage for such an adventure but I was as relieved as Mother when the letter from Liverpool arrived.

The angst continued as we were still no nearer locating Richard. I continued to condemn his selfishness. Mother became more and more distraught as the days passed and the effect of her depression was palpable. The younger children were either subdued in her presence or spent their time bickering over toys or whining for attention. I abandoned all hope of writing, and instead helped Polly to distract the children, instruct the Governess and direct the servants.

Finally we had news. Richard was safe. He was in Scotland and it was Mr Ambrose (of all people) who was Mother's saviour. Apparently Richard had travelled north and spent time with friends before ending up in Glasgow at Mr Ambrose's office in search of money. Richard was coy about his exact movements when Mother received him home like the prodigal son, with only the briefest reprimand for all the trouble he had caused. However to be fair, Richard was much subdued on his return and appeared to be repentant. He certainly acknowledged that he had been wrong to disappear without explanation and Mr Ambrose had clearly laid into the boy. Perhaps this authority was what he needed in the absence of Papa? Mama was right about one thing. Richard was resolved to go to America and he used this ambition as the main reason for leaving home. For all his business ineptitude Mr Ambrose was a great personal support to the family at this time and it was on his suggestion that Richard applied to the Trustees for money to fund such a trip. The money he wanted had actually been left to little Jessie by Uncle Stewart (Aunt Eliza's husband). Mother wrote to Mr Collins in support of this application on 18th October 1865. She added:

> *"I feel that after what has occurred he will not settle well but I have that confidence in him to believe that on his return he would apply himself most diligently to make up for lost time and with a man who would take a proper interest in his advancement. I have no doubt that he would turn out a good businessman. I think it's due to Richard, as his father's eldest son to give him this chance".*

As if Mother did not have enough to deal with at this time, there was another monumental event that required her full attention: the replacement of Mr Knox. Knox and Griffins were to part company (by mutual agreement) and the search for a replacement was under way. As well as sorting out Richard, Mama spent hours poring over applications and references and at first she favoured a gentleman called Mr Marsh. I remember her commenting to me that he was worth pursuing as she felt that he was a man of experience and education who would be a good influence on the boys and give 'a good tone' to the house. As well as passing on her views on the application, Mother also had to take time to thank Mr Ambrose and I have just re-read the letter she sent to that effect, written on the 24th October, which finishes with a reference to Mr Marsh:

> *I ought to apologize for not having written before to thank you for the kind and judicious way in which you received Richard. When he returned he spoke most gratefully of your attention to him, and seems to be deeply impressed with your powers, for he told me that he had not been five minutes beside you before you had got from him the*

whole history of this escapade, although he had a strong desire to keep
this to himself. I am thankful for this, as it is very important that the
boys should feel they have someone over them.

He came home, poor fellow, resolved to do his duty and make the best
of the situation in which he has placed himself, but I soon perceived
that it would be better to let him go away from the Warehouse until
the change has been made.

According to Mr Collins's desire I made enquiries after several
applicants, none of whom were at all suitable except a Mr Marsh,
who for integrity and experience seems all we could wish...

The Trustees wanted a greater choice of applicants before they decided who would manage the business and, following the initial advertisement in *The Bookseller*, Mother placed another in the *Publishers' Circular*. Four people applied, two had already answered the first advertisement, the other two Mother sent on to Mr Collins. One of these was from a man called Bohn and Mama was immediately hesitant to see him in case he was in some way related to Henry – Papa's previous business partner. On the 10th November, we received a new application from a Mr Crafter of Cassell, Petter & Galpin. A man, it turned out, who was a relation of the firm's owners, (this I remember immediately impressed Mother who was all for family connections). Mama was excited about this candidate and she visited Cassell's to meet personally with the partners there. They were open in their opinions of Mr Crafter and said they would be sorry to lose him. So there were two men in the running. Mr Marsh – Mothers' initial favourite - and Mr Crafter. On reflection Mother voted for the latter in light of his age (Mr Crafter being just 34, where she guessed Marsh to be at least 60).

Still there was no firm decision made and this delay was typical of how the business was run at this time – inevitable really considering the location and workload of two of the Trustees. Mother was the only one who devoted all her time (in tandem with running her household of course) to the business and again it was left to her to push things along. In December, there was still no final word on Knox's successor and Mother wrote again to her co-Trustees stressing the need to recommend one over the other to guarantee financial security for the Firm. Ambrose put a fly in the ointment by vetoing Mr Crafter since he could put up no money himself (the underlying problem being that Mr Knox would have to be paid off). In exasperation, Mother placed another advertisement, this time in the *Athenaeum* and *The Times*. A week later, she followed this with a further letter to Mr Collins stressing that Crafter remained the best candidate despite his lack of funds. His age and experience she did not see as a problem and she pointed out in her letter (astutely I feel) that Griffins would not be able to afford a ready-trained manager, as such a person would require at least £500 a year and the Firm could offer at most £300.

Mother played a clever game over the management appointment. I know how important she felt it was to get the right man for the job. Polly and I were subjected to hours of debate and Alex was also consulted after being made to read through the applications. Despite this fervour, she played her own role down in the decision-making process, particularly with Mr Ambrose. Mr Collins was a different matter. He encouraged Mother to express her views and I have a letter that she wrote to our Scottish solicitor in which she subtly reinforced her choice. Having stroked the egos of her two male Trustees by stressing that they were the experts, she first comments *"I have had so little to do with the business that I could not presume to do this"* and then goes on to explain that she has talked to our author, Mr Southgate *"who is an old friend of Mr Griffin's and knows our business well, and he thinks so highly of Mr Crafter's ability and integrity, and said that it was a most fortunate thing, that we had the choice of securing such a man".*

On the 19th December Mother went to the City to follow up Crafter's references. She also wrote to Mr Collins telling him that she did not have the experience to sell off stock herself and desperately needed help. She pointed out that Uncle John had spent much time with Mr Knox but to no avail and she was not able to ask him again because he was busy at this time moving his own business to the West End.

Meanwhile Richard had made it to America. We had word in November 1865 that he had arrived after a bad voyage in which he had spent much of the time feeling very seasick. He followed this up a few weeks later with another glum letter lamenting the state of the economy in New York and complaining of an uncomfortable bed and poor quality food. Mr Knox sent a further report to us at the beginning of December with similar news as Richard had warned that the booksellers were struggling due to the Civil War and we were not to expect large orders. Still the Firm had received a few smaller orders from America, so he must have had some success. Mother fretted about her eldest son and she predicted that he would be home by Christmas. Call it Mother's intuition but Richard was indeed home by the Festive season, looking a little thinner, with longer hair and a slightly hang dog expression. He spent all of the Christmas holiday relaxing in Papa's old chair by the fire or lying on his bed, claiming to be travel worn and bone-weary due to over work.

Mother's troubles were far from over and having her eldest son back in the fold did little to stabilise the situation. During 1866 both Ambrose and Collins said they wanted to leave the Trust and that if they could not they would wind the company up. I think both men considered their Executorial obligations a burden; an extra complication in their lives that they could do without. One can imagine their wives nagging them to slow down as they advanced in age, but ironically their unwillingness to allocate sufficient time to the task of decision making meant that Griffins became a larger burden; a more time consuming problem for them. Mother was naturally frustrated. She could make no progress without their consent. In despair she wrote once more to Uncle John for help. Again, her letter is worth quoting in full, as so much was at stake.

> *I cannot again personally ask you to become a trustee, after the repeated refusals you have given me, but I am compelled to apply to you owing to a letter which I have received from Mr Ambrose and which I enclose for your perusal. You will see from it that he, as well as Mr Collins wishes to resign; and if obliged to remain in the Trust, it is evident that they intend either to wind up or sell off the business. This you know, my dear Sir, would be fatal to the prospects of the family, and as it is necessary according to the Will to have two or more trustees, it would be impossible for me to take matters on my own responsibility and act alone. I do not know any one except Mr Landale* (her sister Isabella's husband, a wealthy mining engineer) *and yourself whom I could ask to take us up, and if you would but kindly consent to do it for a year or two, so as to take it out of the hands of Mr Collins and Mr Ambrose then by that time perhaps some younger friends would be able to help me. If you would take the direction of affairs as Agent instead of Mr Ambrose, both myself and family would gratefully pay whatever sum the estate would afford, and you would consider necessary for your services. I entreat of you, my dear Sir, to give this your kindest consideration, as if you turn away from us there is no alternative but submitting to any measures these gentlemen in their weariness of the Trust may think proper to take. With so many boys and young children, it is a very very serious matter to me, indeed I feel intensely anxious. You know, my dear Sir, according to the Will you run no risk. I could leave everything in your hands with the utmost confidence; with your judgment and prudence nothing would go wrong.*
>
> *With kindest regards…*

Two days later on 6 April 1866, Mama wrote at length to Mr Collins clearly desperate to keep him on her side.

Mr Griffin having been ordered off to the country for his health, I have corresponded with him on the subject of his taking up the Trust, but he has again refused, saying that he feels totally unequal to the work, though he still promises to give his valuable assistance in the event of our selling off a portion of the copyrights and stock, a course which both he and I regard as <u>necessary</u>. I know of no other responsible person whom I could ask to become an executor, those who would have done it three years ago not being willing now that others have had the affairs in their hands for so long a time.

In your favour [i.e. his letter] received yesterday you refer to the probable amount of Messrs Ambrose and Murray's charges – you may remember that I spoke of it two years ago, and asked you to bring it forward at our Meeting, for it was impossible that I could do it, being so delicately placed. – I don't think Mr Ambrose will claim so large a sum as you mention, seeing that the greater portion of the work to be done had devolved upon you. I look upon Mr Ambrose as a just-minded, honourable man, and one who has our interest at heart, but he has not knowledge of publishing to fit him for the duties of factor, and therefore could not take that position. If anyone is to be paid for factorship, I think it only just that it should be you, my dear Sir; and if you will only consent to take the office upon you we will be all right, I cannot tell you how thankful both myself and family would be.

You warn me to be prepared for any contingency – I cannot see what you mean by that except a winding-up of the business; this I will not consent to. I look upon the business as the only real property my husband left his family, and we <u>are bound</u>, as trustees and executors, to carry it on for their benefit. You know that it would be impossible to bring them up on the sum left after payment of the liabilities, - selling off the business would be nothing short of ruin – it is fearful to speak of it with five lads growing up, two of them already no *longer children. If Mr Ambrose proposes anything so absurd, what is there to prevent you and me working together? – We are both of the same way of thinking. You seem to forget (judging from what you say – that "you could not go on against Mr A.'s views") that I am a trustee, appointed by the Will, and besides Mother and guardian of the children, and therefore that my opinion must have at least as much weight, on such a subject, as Mr Ambrose's.*

If a trustee resident in London is necessary, I am on the spot, & with the sanction of my co-trustees would gladly give my constant attention to the business. It is true that I have not had a business training, but I have Mr John Griffin always at hand to consult with. I do not see why the business should not continue to pay as it has done for the last 50 years, provided always that it is put into a more healthy condition by getting rid of some of the liabilities.

My own opinion is that Mr Ambrose should not be troubled with the <u>working</u> of the business; he himself owns that he has no knowledge of it; and the damage already done by delay shows us that the system pursued hitherto has not been the right one, and that now with a new manager we ought to try some other plan, such as I have suggested.

This is a truly brave letter for Mama to write. I remember the anxiety she felt and the relief when both men were persuaded to stay, boosted by the eventual appointment of the new Manager, Mr Crafter, in April. Griffins had survived to fight another day by the skin of its teeth.

Richard and Alex both went up to Stationer's Hall Court each day on the train but neither seemed to embrace their working life with any enthusiasm. Richard used his wages on drink and socialising with friends; Alex seemed to be on a similar path and returned home each day with a frown, responding to Mama's enquiry about his day with a sullen *"acceptable"*, *"average"*, or at worse *"dreary"*.

Mother overcompensated for their lack of interest and became more and more involved in the intricacies of running the Firm. She had greater confidence in Mr Crafter and quickly established a working relationship with him that left him in no doubt as to the extent of her involvement. She was the only visible Trustee and as such she took her duties very seriously and in truth began to enjoy her working life. As the younger children settled into their new fatherless routine at Canonbury Park Square, and the business entered a period of relative stability, she began to discover more about what made for a successful Publishing House. Like a faithful puppy I was hard at her heels and I was also becoming increasingly ensnared by the world of Griffins. This was, after all, Papa's legacy and for a young woman who was at the time more interested in books than her looks, this rare window into a man's world was hard to resist.

By the summer of 1866, Mother began to have some involvement in what the Firm published, even questioning a suggestion from her great Mentor Mr Collins, who put forward the idea of publishing a three or four volumed work on Jewish Antiquities. I don't recall this event at all but was amused to read a letter written by return in August in which Mama states *"We have already a work in one pretty large volume"*. What I do remember was a discussion she had with Mr Ambrose during one of his rare visits to our house. The gentleman arrived dressed for Scottish weather in a thick frock coat and bowler hat, looking much older than when I last saw him, his face like a Cairngorm crag and complaining of poor health. He was rather short with a broad face whose one redeeming feature was his lofty expansive forehead, and he had acquired by this time a slight stoop as though he was permanently bent over his desk, loath to be parted from his beloved papers. After brief platitudes and a light luncheon to which I was invited, the discussion turned to an application for the position of traveller. Mother was vocal in her dismissal of Mr Ambrose's favoured candidate, a man called McDonald who, as his name suggests, was a Scotsman by birth. I tried not to smile when I observed Mama's technique when dealing with our esteemed advocate. After appearing to hang on his every word she steered the conversation around to McDonald and cleverly delivered her verdict as if it were a widely held view. *"I have heard that his manners are brusque, coarse and not such as would take in England"*, she slipped in between the soup and the main course, and followed this with an astute reminder of previous employee trouble: *"I know you will agree it is absolutely necessary to have a gentlemanly representative. We have suffered greatly by having such a traveller as Mr Warner; what we require is a high class man..."* Of course a high class man was unlikely to apply for such a lowly-salaried position, but I could see what Mother was aiming for – as indeed could Mr Ambrose, who left our house with a full stomach and a similar view.

In the autumn, Charles James left the City of London School. He was a very bright boy with a strong aptitude for mathematics. A favourite party trick at family gatherings was to get Charles to add up large sums in his head, and when we checked on paper he always had the correct answer. Mother had pinned her hopes that he would show strong business aptitude like his father and grandfather before him (and like his Mother as it turned out), and he was duly sent to a first class business house for an apprenticeship in the publishing trade.

The months passed, and Mr Crafter settled in well as manager of Griffins. Mama relaxed a little and spent less time bent over the desk agonising over the books. Jessie had just turned 15 years old, a young lady who, although very stiff in her movements, had determinedly practised the art of walking with two sticks and was able to move between the rooms in our house allowing her some privacy and independence. Although Mother kept a watchful eye on her health, Jessie's fighting spirit was a huge relief and allowed Mama to focus her attention on the younger children. John Joseph (named of course after our uncle) at nearly 13 years old had followed in his older brother's footsteps and was attending the City of London School, as was Henry Brougham, named after his Godfather, Henry, Lord Brougham, a prominent member of the Government in King William IV's time and a friend of Papa's. Griffin's published all of Brougham's writings, something we are all very proud of given he had risen to the rank of Lord Chancellor in 1830 and he had done much to facilitate the Reform Bill of the day before retiring from politics in 1834 and concentrating his attention on promoting technical education, which was when Papa got to know him well.

I digress. Left at home with the two little girls – Helen, now a sturdy seven year old, who we all knew as Nelly – and five year old Alice Edith, Mama spent more time reading, sewing and drawing with the girls. Then, in February 1867 Mother took the little girls on a trip to Scotland. She had been feeling quite tired and struggled with a nasty cough that had started after Christmas and lingered for several weeks. Her sister Eliza's invitation to convalesce with her in Roseneath, near Helensburgh was not hard to resist and they had spent a month in the Scottish air before returning in March. Whilst in Scotland the girls were sent to the seaside with another Aunt – Helen Rae, Mama's immediate elder sister. Inverkip in Renfrewshire, was a regular holiday destination for the Rae family and a place where we had often begged to be taken to when we had lived in Scotland. Inverkip is four miles South West of Greenock on the Southern shore of the Firth of Clyde. A beautiful location that seemed a million miles away from the smoke and congestion of Glasgow and yet it was a mere sixteen mile journey from my Grandmama's home.

Even when they were away Mama could not resist a few letters to Mr Crafter, mainly to check up on Alex who was showing worrying signs of unreliability. Sadly I had been the one asked to pass on the news from Mr Crafter that Alex had failed to turn up to work a couple of times and was regularly arriving late in the mornings. Given the trouble we had had with Richard, we were naturally worried. Fortunately by the middle of 1867 the reports from Stationer's Hall Court were favourable in terms of Richard who appeared more settled after his American adventure, and the fact he had much more respect for Mr Crafter than he had ever shown Mr Knox seemed to be keeping him on the straight and narrow path. Alex was another matter. His behaviour was becoming increasingly unpredictable, and his drinking was a serious issue. He often returned from work intoxicated and Mother was at her wits end. She confessed to me during one of our conversations about this difficult period that she had been concerned that he too would one day do a disappearing act. For this to happen to two of her sons would have been humiliating to say the least and with that thought at the forefront of her mind, she desperately sought a solution to Alex's wanderlust.

Perhaps because of the impact of Richard's transatlantic trip or maybe at Alex's own request, I was never sure, the solution suggested was a trip to the other side of the world – in this case New Zealand. Not a visit or holiday but to live and work. This was a brave decision by Mother given Papa's desire for all the boys to enter the Firm. It reflected an acknowledgment on her part that Alec's heart was not in the publishing world. The evidence for this was plain to see. He had barely progressed from his initial role as office junior and had sat behind his desk like a caged animal snarling at all who approached. His favourite time of day was when he was asked to take the letters to the Post Office and he told me he used to linger there, claiming a long queue at the desk, savouring his freedom and happy to observe the hustle and bustle of porters, men, women and children and other office boys as they attempted to finish their transactions. When his misery began to impact on us all, Mother took action and plans were made for him in March 1867 to come before a meeting of the Trustees to ask for £50 and permission to go to New Zealand. He too needed to dip into the funds left by Uncle Stewart for Jessie and required the Trustees' permission for such a request. Luckily they agreed and Alex was give the money 'until say the period when he would come to majority' (i.e. in 1869). In addition William Collins kindly gave him some introductions to some of his own customers and correspondents in Dunedin where Alex proposed to go.

I clearly remember the flurry of activity that accompanied his departure as Mother rushed around to kit him out with the clothes and other essential possessions he needed for his travels. He left for New Zealand with a light heart and an even lighter purse and my admonitions to behave himself ringing in his ears. Alex was one of life's good time boys. He loved to enjoy himself and hated to work and I'm sorry to report that he failed to settle in New Zealand despite moving up the East Coast from Dunedin to Canterbury on the Eastern seaboard of the South Island. No, his letters home were rare and full of his attempts at finding work. He did try several jobs, including tutoring and working on a newspaper, but both involved sticking to regular hours and showing responsibility: neither tasks my little brother found easy. We shall leave him for the time being languishing in the Antipodes for we all had another more pressing worry much closer to home.

Just when Mother had sorted out the boys, young Jessie's health deteriorated. Having enjoyed a healthy winter, the spring of 1867 left her weakened after a series of different ailments. The Doctor was a regular visitor to our house and various potions were prescribed, none of which seemed to help. Her invalid status I often felt gave the medical profession an excuse for poor diagnosis and we were all worried sick by the summer that any further infection in her weakened state might have killed her. Mama was frantic and in July she wrote to Mr Collins in desperation. The only solution offered by the new Doctor who saw Jessie on recommendation from a friend in the city, was for a 'change of air'. The reason for the correspondence with Mr Collins was to request funds to make this happen. She wrote imploringly:

> *I fear that unless she can get this the coming winter will tell much upon her, but with my present income it is impossible for me to bear the expense of taking her away from home, which could not be done under £15. If you do not see your way to advance this sum at present, I think that, in so urgent a case, we would be perfectly justified as Trustees in appropriating for the purpose a proportion of the money left to her by her Uncle Stewart. Perhaps you will kindly give the matter your early consideration, and let me know your opinion. Jessie is now past fourteen, and could write to you a letter on the subject, if you thought it necessary. It is now several years since she has been out of London – all that time confined to her couch. She says often that if she could 'only feel the sea-breeze' she would get strong at once, poor child.*

The reason of course she mentions Jessie being past 14 years of age is because as recognised by Scottish Law, this is the age of pupillarity after which a child has a say in the disposal of his or her income. Whilst Mother had undoubtedly exaggerated the time Jessie had been stuck in London, in truth it seemed to them both a long time since they had taken a 'proper' holiday and Mother lost no time in planning their excursion. After consulting Mr Crafter on the train timetable, Polly and Mama left for the East Coast taking Jessie and the little girls with them. On this occasion, I chose to remain at home and, as I was a young lady of 22 years of age, Mother was happy to leave me in charge of our depleted household. At first I relished the peace and quiet after the family had left. Of course one is never quite alone in the house due to the servants; and Richard and Charles were also at home at this point although they were rarely around. In the evenings I pretty much had most rooms to myself and this at first seemed the ultimate luxury. As the days passed I began to feel differently and after the first week I remember feeling quite lonely and felt a pang of regret when I received updates from Polly in a series of letters. She reported that Helen had been daring enough to paddle in the sea for the first time under the eagle eye of Mama, and on the second day Polly herself had taken to the water, encouraged by a pleasantly warm day, lack of spectators and proximity of a 'decently sized' bathing machine which deposited her right into the sea for a leisurely dip. I was jealous when I read of her swim as this had always been one of my seaside pleasures. It must have been perfect conditions for Polly to take to the water; she was normally worried about spoiling her hair or catching a chill! I was even more jealous when she told me of the books she had obtained from the circulating library we frequented when we visited the seaside. It was only open during the Season but it provided a welcome list of popular fiction and often the proprietors looked out for the kind of books they knew we loved and recommended them when we returned, which we did often, given our passion for reading.

We were all delighted when young Jessie came home from her holiday with colour in her cheeks, light in her eyes and a return to her usual happy disposition. The highlight of their trip for her was all the activity at the beach: the minstrels performing magic tricks and the boys with mouth organs whose music transcended the chattering masses on the promenade. Later, Mother swapped her parasol for her umbrella as the rest of the summer turned out disappointingly wet, forcing us all indoors. Time to pore over the Griffin ledgers; trawl through the many prospective manuscripts that now often came our way for approval; and an opportunity for us to wade our way through the pile of correspondence that was a constant presence on Papa's desk. As usual, many of the letters Mother wrote were to her fellow Trustees. Mr Ambrose continued to be a great source of irritation, as he was so slow and unreliable when it came to settling bills and returning the necessary paperwork.

The final straw came at the beginning of 1868 and, as I was asked for my advice over the matter, I can accurately report the sequence of events. Mother was much vexed over Mr Ambrose's procrastination regarding the Probate Duty as she had been served with a Writ for contempt of court for not appearing to answer a final summons. She vented her frustration at me over the unnecessary additional expenses the Firm would incur because of Mr Ambrose's inefficiency and then followed this by writing a note to Mr Collins and then visiting Messrs Vallance (our London Solicitors) whom she asked to communicate at once with Mr Ambrose to get the matter sorted out. She had lost patience with his excuses and (as she quite rightly pointed out to me), felt that he should give the factorship over to a competent party if his health was to blame. Moving forward, her strategy was to increasingly get Mr Collins to act as 'go between' as she felt he had more influence over her Scottish solicitor than she herself did and I found one letter on file in February 1868 that is typical of Mama's guile. She was enclosing a bill from the tailor who provided Alex's clothes before he went off to New Zealand; she was concerned that it still hadn't been settled. The tailor in question being, as she put it: *'in a small way of business and cannot afford to stand out of his money".*

I cannot help to smile now as I read out the remainder of the letter:

> *"I would not have troubled you but it is of no use my writing to Mr Ambrose as he takes no notice of my letters. God knows, I have enough to do with my small income, without being worried about debt I did not contract for myself. I have not received a farthing of the money I laid out for Alexander. I cannot understand Mr Ambrose's conduct, it seems so strange: he calls out, that funds are low, and yet through his negligence we are put to so many extra expenses. The Probate Duty is a sample".*

Poor Mother and poor Mr Collins who must have been mightily fed up being stuck in the middle of our tangled web. Remember he was himself running a highly successful publishing house, a firm that he had inherited when his father retired in the mid 1840's. Our debt to him is immeasurable. In recognition of this fact and in the knowledge that our friend was not getting any younger, Mother was anxious to add to the number of Trustees. By May 1868, she wrote to both her co-Trustees with her suggestion that Richard – now 21 years old – be appointed. Unfortunately, Mr Ambrose was not happy to agree to this and the matter threw up an unsettling debate over who should be at the helm of the business. Mother was happy with the manager, Mr Crafter, who was showing strong leadership skills and a solid foundation in the publishing world. However Mr Collins brought up the subject of appointing a Mr Blackwood – a man he suggested for the position of Manager because of his experience in running a business. However, Mother resisted his appointment because he had wanted a share of our company as part of the deal, something she had always resisted especially after the Bohn partnership; and she enlisted Uncle John's advice in her quest to settle the matter once and for all. At the same time, she was managing another pressing matter: the long overdue stock sale. In February Mother approved the go-ahead of a sale of surplus stock at Stationer's Hall Court and in May the Trustees had finally all agreed that such a sale was necessary to be converted into money to relieve the Company's debt. However, by now the stock was older (and therefore less attractive) and the delay from the time of Mother's first suggestion that this should be done, some five year's previously, meant that the value of these assets was much reduced. Mr Crafter found a bulk buyer but still the Trustees procrastinated and the matter rumbled on. It was left in Mr Collins hands to agree the final sum and the letters flew between the Trustees and Uncle John asking his advice.

In May Mother received a letter from Mr Crafter that caused her extra stress. She had come up with a possible solution hoping her sister's husband David Landale, a man of much repute in the world of mining, might be persuaded to become a Trustee. She had mooted the idea some years previous to Mr Collins but no formal approach had been made. Her plan was to send Richard to his home in Scotland to persuade him to consider such a position. Unfortunately, Mr Crafter had other ideas and it is to his credit that he felt able to stand up to Mother and refuse the request which he had assumed was just a social visit. He did not feel he could single Richard out for special privileges like extra leave just because of his family connections. Mother accepted his decision but wrote of her regret pointing out that she had been particularly anxious he went on the trip without elaborating on her reasons. Mr Crafter did not bow to pressure and the matter was dropped. Uncle David could not be persuaded to join the Firm when asked by letter and Mother changed tack. Anyway, her eye was quite taken off the ball by Polly.

Chapter 4

It all started when Polly returned from a short holiday in Germany where she had been visiting her favourite haunts from school days with an English friend. She had been introduced to a gentleman at a concert, who had immediately become very attentive, singling Polly out in the crowd of young ladies like a fox chasing the plumpest hen in a crowded pen. A few months after her return from England in the summer of 1868, during another short break, this time with the family in Felixstowe, she had arranged to meet with her suitor following several months of letter writing and much swooning (on her part) over the contents. After a pleasant week at Walton on the Naze we had moved down the coast to stay at our usual guesthouse right on the seafront. We had been visiting the same guesthouse for years and the owners were delightful folk who went out of their way to please. It was there that we became acquainted with Polly's gentleman friend, a Swedish man by the name of Victor Abraham Svensson – the man who was later to become Polly's husband. I was not at all sure about Victor but I never once confided my unease to my sister. It was the first major secret I had from her and my heart ached at the wedge it drove between us. It was not that I disliked Victor. Far from it, he was courteous, intelligent and not a bad looking man, with a straight nose, a good set of teeth and large brown eyes that were a little too close together for my liking (bringing the fox analogy back to mind), and at times unsettling in their directness. I remember commenting to my sister on my surprise at his swarthy complexion, and neatly curled black hair, as I had expected a stereotypical blond, blue eyed Nordic specimen, and she wore her delight at her 'catch' like a badge of honour for all to see. I could not quite put my finger on what it was about Victor that made me a little uneasy and I dismissed it at the time as jealousy and sorrow at my sister's removal from our lives. Of course this sounds dramatic but I was under no illusion, (despite being a family who were happy to travel) that we would see little of Polly after her marriage: Sweden was, after all, over two days away from us.

None of us was immune to Polly's mounting excitement however and it was a pleasure to see Mother taking such an interest in something other than the family business for a change. The younger girls were in heaven, spending long hours planning how they should wear their hair and giggling ecstatically when Polly insisted on dressing them in matching gowns, with straw hats that just about contained their cascade of ringletted hair. Jessie and I chose to wear our hair in large buns hidden beneath our poke bonnets, the strings decked with artificial roses, and for once neither of us grumbled about the time that Mary spent lacing up our corsets, as we both felt beautiful, although naturally it was Polly who outshone us all. Resplendent in a pale pink dress which floated around her like a shimmering cloud, held in place by a bustle so enormous, that young Henry crawled under her skirt and hid there from Mother when she called for him to get changed. She positively glided down the aisle followed by a beautiful pearl edged train that must have been all of a yard and a half long. The wedding ceremony took place on 26th June 1869 and I still have the cutting I placed in *The Times*: '*On Saturday the 26th June at the parish church, Walton, Suffolk, by the Vicar, the Rev Charles Maunders, Victor A Svensson of Gothenburg Sweden, to Mary Anne, eldest daughter of the late Charles Griffin esq.*'.

It was such a special day for Mother and, apart from shedding a tear in acknowledgement of Papa's absence, she had a happy day, laughing and joking with her children and enjoying the glorious surroundings of the beautiful Suffolk church. There were only two members of Victor's family present at the ceremony: his Mother Maria, a widow, and his younger sister Hulda, a shy teenager with a shock of fair curls which she spent most of the day trying to contain within her cap. Poor child, she spoke only a couple of words of

English and spent the day with a permanently baffled expression on her little pale face. Thinking back to that day it was evident that Victor had total domination over his womenfolk. Perhaps I am reading more into this memory with the benefit of hindsight but both Victor's Mother and his sister were very quiet and submissive. The fact they were both small and fair and seemed happy to fade into the background seemed to please Victor who rather cruelly dismissed our attempts to draw them into the conversation. Although their English was very limited and our Swedish non-existent, we found a common language in German and were keen to make our guests feel welcome. Victor was quick to break up any attempts we made to converse and I'm ashamed to say that after several attempts throughout the day I gave up and concentrated on enjoying myself. Mother was more persistent but the language barrier and obvious agitation whenever we sought Maria's opinion meant we all resorted to smiling and handshakes and gave up on the idea of forming any family bond. Mother was satisfied that Polly would be looked after, materially at least. Victor's occupation is 'rentier' (which basically means he lives off his income from rented properties), but the family also owns a profitable brewery and in financial terms Polly appeared to have chosen a secure and comfortably middle class lifestyle. The only problem of course was that it was in Gothenburg.

And so it was with more than a little trepidation I waved off my elder sister, friend and confidante as she set off for a new life in Sweden, leaving me as the eldest child remaining to help Mama. This was definitely another turning point in my life and a time when I took on more responsibility for organising and managing the household as well as becoming more involved in the Firm. This period also coincided with a deterioration in Mama's health. Perhaps due to the excitement and stress of the wedding, or maybe because of some infection or other, her bronchial problems worsened and she consulted her physician at my insistence. His remedy – yes you guessed correctly – was a spell at the seaside. In fact, her Doctor suggested the South of England but Mother rejected this idea but did consider his second recommendation: the West of Scotland. The pull of her homeland proved very strong but in the end she decided on the warmer climes of France and started immediately to organise the trip, packing all the documents and contact details she would need to ensure she stayed in touch with the business. She was not the only one suffering ill health. Mr Collins had also been unwell and once again stated his desire to retire as Trustee. Mother wrote from France to stall him, as Uncle John was also away at the time and therefore unavailable as an advisor. One of the problems of course was the number of Trust members who could be assembled if she herself was away. Two were needed and with Mr Ambrose being incommunicado, it left her and Mr Collins alone to keep the ship afloat. Mr Collins was once again persuaded to stay for the time being but the idea of Richard becoming a Trustee was repeated, and this time my name was also suggested to the Board in addition. Mr Collins at least was in favour of the idea and I can remember feeling a mixture of pride, eagerness and anxiety at the prospect of taking on such a role.

Meanwhile I was trying to adapt to a new life without Polly. How I missed her in those first few months. We may have been very different in many ways (Polly being much more interested in shopping, gossiping and sewing than I for a start) but we had been very close. Most importantly, we shared our concerns over Mother and Jessie's health, over the boys' behaviour and the little ones' education. I grew up considerably during this period and inevitably became closer to Jessie. The seven year age gap between us seemed to narrow with every passing year and the fact we shared a love of books, art and music brought us even closer. Jessie herself was an accomplished pianist and had plenty of time to practise her skills. She was also showing signs of being a good writer: a talent I was to harness later in life. Sadly, her physical disabilities meant she was unable to accompany me on all my jaunts to various classical concerts. This remains a huge pleasure in my life. We were about to enter the 1870's, a time that saw a musical revival in England and I loved every minute of it. At least with Mama away, I did not have to lie awake at night listening to the deep, dry cough resound from her bedroom and I was comforted that she was now in cleaner air. Before she had left her breathing was quite laboured even after a minor excursion. Remember we lived in a bustling, but dirty city. The capital was still mainly a walking city but with more and more people moving out to the suburbs the need for buses, trams and eventually trains connecting them to their work increased. Fire was a big threat to buildings and clouds hung over the rooftops as coal smoke could not escape and formed a thick blanket over the city's grimy buildings. Although we were not in the worst of the built up areas, even we found that gas lamps had to be lit early in the afternoon to combat the gloom, and escaping from the smog was sensible advice. One of my favourite passages from Dickens's *Little Dorrit*, written in 1857, demonstrates what much of London was like in this period: *It was Sunday evening in London gloomy, close, stale.....In the city* (the rain) *developed only foul stale smells, and was a sickly, lukewarm dirt stained, wretched addition to the gutters.*

Of course we were not living in such conditions as our house in the square wasn't cheek by jowl with the neighbours and we were well placed to enjoy some of London's finer open spaces, with Finsbury Park within striking distance and Hampstead Heath within walking distance, with its acres of green space overlooked by Kenwood House. Highgate Woods, Regent's Park and Victoria Park were all near enough for Mama or the nursemaid to take the children for a stroll or picnic (although playing games, drinking alcohol or playing music were all strictly prohibited, making these much less attractive locations for the older boys).

Just after Mother had left on her travels, both Richard and I were successfully co-opted as Trustees. With Mother struggling, I had to immediately increase my responsibilities to the Firm and I was keen to appear in control. Unfortunately, the first major issue I had to deal with was a problem with my newly appointed co-trustee - my brother Richard. Mother had received a letter in November 1869 which detailed a very serious matter. She did not feel strong enough at the time to reply and the matter was passed on to me to deal with. The letter I wrote and Mr Crafter's reply are worth detailing as it shows the level of the problem. Richard, as eldest son, should have been the natural choice to eventually take over the Firm. These letters give a clear indication as to why this did not seem likely...

November 1869. *"The intelligence in your note of Friday has vexed me much – I had hoped that you and Richard would have been able to work amicably together. Of course, I can see that this is by no means easy for you, as Richard's position is not exactly defined. He is no longer a boy, and at the same time not on the footing of the others in the Warehouse, but notwithstanding I thought you would see the necessity of being on friendly relations with him, and keep it in mind in your intercourse with him. I know that Richard respects you highly for your business qualities, and would be perfectly willing to meet your views in every way, if there were only a proper understanding between you. With regard to his being "the last to come and the first to go", he is only acting on an opinion expressed by Mr J.J. Griffin long ago, which I give you in his own words – premising that no-one would dream of laying the sin of laxity or over-indulgence to my Uncle's door: "It is absurd that a youth in R's position should be allowed no more latitude than a mere paid clerk. The Manager ought so to arrange that he can leave as a general rule about 5'oclock, so as to have his evenings free for study or amusement – and moreover if he wishes to go out for a few hours in the course of the day to dine with a friend etc., no objection should be made". I consider that R. has not had justice done to him. As to appealing to Mr Collins – unless you have very strong proof that Richard has neglected his work, you had much better do no such thing, as I am not at all sure that he would take your view of the matter, and in fact would, as I do now, decline to interfere between you, seeing, as all must do, that if you and Richard have come to loggerheads already, what will it be as times go on?'*

To this Mr Crafter replied – in an undated letter – as follows.

Dear Miss Griffin

Though I am sorry for it the line your reply to my recent letter would take I quite anticipated. In what I am about to say you must be so good as to leave my personality out of the question as my course is dictated not from my personal feeling – your Brother, I am sorry to say, does not see this – but solely by the interests of the business which are not only yours & his but your Mama's and the rest of the Family. I would not have troubled you again on the subject but to correct an erroneous view as I consider you in common with your Brother hold as to his duties and the mode in which he should perform them. Your view would be quite correct if this was a wealthy Banking House but as from circumstances to a certain extent it is a struggling concern with the staff reduced to the extreme minimum, for any member of it to think it possible to act as though it were otherwise is, to put it mildly, a great mistake, it being an absolute essential to its prosperous existence that each one should put his shoulder to the wheel (irrespective of position), and I have yet to learn that there is anything infra dig in industry and labour. I may mention in passing that on the day I wrote to you I had, at 6 p.m., to take myself from more important matters to personally superintend the delivery to Simpkins and Hamilton of their Sale orders which had been lying ready for delivery the whole day and which a day or two previously I had requested your Brother to see were executed and on my expressing surprise at his absenting himself for 4 hrs in the middle of the day when he knew the transaction had to be completed he took it as a personal matter, forsooth, and intimated he was not my servant. From the moment I entered this Firm I have always treated your Brother, excepting perhaps an occasional hasty expression not meant offensively and forgotten five minutes afterwards, not only as a Gentleman but as a man and by my own example compelled a more respectful demeanour towards him by the subordinates than from what I saw he had been in the habit of receiving prior to my advent, and my constant desire has been to work hand in hand with him, instructing him in all that my greater experience might suggest or he might desire to know; therefore I can conscientiously say the present difficulty is from no act of mine. With respect to Mr Collins, he is unfortunately ill and I am averse to trouble him at present but if I am compelled to put it before him I should leave the matter with perfect confidence in his hands as I am sure his decision would be dictated not only by worldy experience but also from businesslike and common sense point of view. In the meantime I will act according to circumstances.

Reading these letters now I feel far more sympathy for Mr Crafter than I had done at the time. Whilst I could acknowledge the seriousness of Richard's lack of work ethic, I had at this time not had first-hand experience of what it was like to work alongside my brother and had a natural inclination to favour Richard's account over our Manager's. Nevertheless, it left me distinctly uneasy.

Meanwhile my thirst for knowledge kept me reading widely. I was like a sponge, eager to soak up any information about the world that I struggled to make sense of. On Saturday 4th December 1869, I picked up a copy of a new newspaper to hit the London shelves called *The Graphic* and this became one of my favourite weekly reads. How I would have loved to have read this to Papa as he had been a subscriber of the *Illustrated London News* since we had moved south and I know he would have appreciated *The Graphic* with its twenty or so pages of fine-toned paper of beautiful quality, crammed full of articles and pictures covering all sorts of topics from music to science. What I liked most about it was the fact it did not shy away from showing life as it really is. Who could not fail to be moved by the engravings showing scenes of working class life from the slums to the Workshop? We have always known how privileged we are to have been born into a family of relative wealth. I used to think my brothers sometimes took their privileged lives for granted, even after Papa's death, and I too cannot pretend to understand the daily struggle for survival of all too many families, but I was not immune to their fate, and I liked to think *The Graphic* kept me up to date with the real world. Life beyond our publishing cocoon – keeping my eyes open to the street beggars, elderly bonneted women bent double in the rain, the queues outside the Workhouse or the sorry sight of a black coated widow surrounded by a scruffy ill-fed brood as they wait outside the butcher waiting for scraps. For these were regular sights on my trip to the office seen from my horse drawn cab and it was a source of amusement to my brothers when I recalled with tears in my eyes the latest tragic being I had spotted enroute to work.

With Mother in the south of France, at Mentone - a coastal town on the Mediterranean Coast to be precise – for the first half of 1870, the day to day discussions over the business fell to Richard and to me. Richard, perhaps feeling more freedom and a loosening of Mother's apron strings at last, showed more interest in the Firm and yet I dealt with the main correspondence between the Trustees. This I could continue to do from home, whilst Richard travelled daily into the office. Although not visiting daily, I did attend meetings at the Warehouse occasionally. For example, around this time Mother had asked me to report on how the long awaited stock sale went and I was disappointed when Mr Crafter failed to attend an agreed meeting with me about the matter. To be honest I was annoyed at his manners, and much inconvenienced having travelled from home on a particularly crammed omnibus having decided that without

Mother a private cab seemed rather too decadent. Mr Crafter obviously felt he had more pressing matters to attend to and meeting a woman was clearly not a priority in his eyes, even given my own impending Trustee status.

This was to be a monumental year on a personal and professional level. For the Firm celebrated its Jubilee in 1870 and Griffins, under Mr Crafter, continued to publish many important volumes, including the last four manuals written by Macquorn Rankine, the Professor of Engineering at the University of Glasgow, (Papa had been appointed the University's official publisher from April 1853 until February 1871 and the association with Glasgow University is immortalised to this day in the use of part of the university Arms, the oak tree, in our company logo). As with Rankine's other three manuals, *Machinery and Millwork* (published in 1869) was a classic of its time. His earlier works remained best sellers in the world of engineering and physics cementing Charles Griffin & Co's growing reputation as publishers of technical and scientific work of the highest quality, a specialism that has stood them in good stead over the years.

Sadly in January I had some less favourable news to report to Mother as we reviewed the results of the long awaited stock sale. On 7th January 1870, I wrote the following letter to the faithful Mr Collins…

> *The mortifying result of the Sale – just disclosed, has completely upset our plans for the present.*
>
> *We see nothing for it but to inform the Creditors that in consequence of the extreme depression in trade, we have been obliged to postpone making any great effort for another year.*

You will see from Mr Crafter's account that he was compelled to buy back all the principal things that had been offered; only 7 out of the 100 stereos were allowed to go; and the amt. gained represented a loss of about £1500. In the present stagnation I think he was wise not to sacrifice more – the very best books do not realise anything like what they would have done a year or two ago, and our old stuff goes like waste paper.

It is most unfortunate, but what is to be done? We cannot compel circumstances.

I see no possible way of raising the sum required by any other means, and if Mr Bell and the other gentlemen are not willing to wait, I wd. suggest the following plan.

Have a clear, definite statement of our financial position made out and submitted to one of the great Capitalists in our trade (Spalding for instance). He might be induced to advance the funds to clear off the Scotch liabilities receiving a lien or bond over all our property.

I do not consider this impracticable – Strahan, Ward & Lock, Routledge, and many others, are notoriously in the hands of their Printers or other backers. If we have any difficulty in Scotland, this ought to be tried. From what I can gather the business itself is doing well for the state of the trade.

Mr Bell, I should point out is the principal of Bell and Bain, printers in Glasgow and one of our Scottish liabilities and Spalding is the principal of our Paper merchants Spalding and Hodge. Despite our concerns over the Firm's financial status, it was not as fragile as our own personal financial position and Mother continued to fret over our outgoings. After hours of consideration I came up with an idea that if the Firm sold some copyrights to Macmillan's and made enough money to pay off the demands of the National Bank, but not enough to apply to the liquidation of any other debt, then the family could perhaps keep the proceeds? I know it did not seem like a good idea on the surface, given the Firm's own debts, but Papa would not have wanted his family to be in such a perilous position. He left Mama an annuity for her own use and funds were to be given as required for the family. I saw this as a way of acquiring such funds. Mr Collins wrote in agreement, and his letter arrived the same day we heard the sad news that Mr Ambrose had died.

Despite her vocal opinions on her Scottish solicitor, the news sent Mother into further decline. This was nothing to what happened when she received the bill from his firm, however, which detailed work that Ambrose claimed to have done in London. She sank deeper into depression. She wrote to Mr Collins from France and sent me a copy of the letter. As well as pointing out that somehow the work he claimed was in fact done by our English solicitors Vallance and Vallance (who were dealing with our business in London) and by Mr Smart, the Accountant who was paid to audit the books, she went on…

> *I have often deplored that we had no active Co-trustee, so as to relieve you of some of the anxiety and toil which you so kindly took upon you at my poor husband's death, and I need only refer to the immense amount of correspondence which has passed between the Manager of our Business and yourself to show who has done the laborious part. So keenly have I often felt on this point that I have more than once wished that I was a man, so as to take upon myself a portion of the work.*

Mother ended this letter by stressing her own poor health and I knew then that I would be acting in loco parentis for some time to come. Her letters were a comfort to me, and arrived with reassuring regularity. It's a shame really that the picture postcard was not more widely available, as I'd have loved to have received a series of beautiful cards with pictures of France but, even though they were introduced on the Continent around this time, Mother was at first scathing of their suitability and took many years to accept this method of correspondence. *"Why would anyone write private information on an open piece of paper for all to see and read?"* she questioned when we received our first card, sent I may say some five years or so after her French trip , by a relative visiting the Alps. I on the other hand grew to love postcards, and rather wickedly I know, took great pleasure in sending Mother several during my later visits to Germany, although I did of course confine my working correspondence to my usual letterhead, concealed within a firmly sealed envelope. Anyway, I was delighted when the tone of Mama's letters became more positive as the weeks progressed. Towards the end of her stay she had visited a friend of her father's who had a vineyard not far from where she was based and her letter about this day trip was a particular delight to read. Her description of the long undulating journey made us laugh as she told us of having to alight at regular intervals at the coachman's insistence to ease the path of the old horse. We could imagine the hillside speckled with female workers as they tended to the vines in their tight fitting jackets, short petticoats and high white caps. Mama went on to tell us of the picnic she had attended with the family at their vineyard, where newly erected trestle tables were laden with bowls of salad, great hams accompanied with mustards, large fruit tarts with lashings of cream and all washed down with plenty of wine. The feast was clearly eaten with great gusto and Jessie and I were jealous when we imagined the merriment of the affair, on that sundrenched hillside.

Despite my inevitable pre-occupation with the Firm, I still managed to sneak some time for creative writing – a pleasure that I saw as essential for my own personal wellbeing. Not to be outdone when it came to amazement at our solicitor's fees, I was astounded to receive a huge bill from Vallance and Vallance when in fact I was expecting a modest one of around £5 or less. I had called on them about 'the Deed' and saw a partner (not either of the Messers Vallance I might add) and left a copy of Father's will. I had to get the matter sorted out as this was the official document required to allow me to act for the Trust – a matter of urgency considering Mother's convalescence in France and Mr Ambrose's demise. To my surprise, Vallance and Vallance asked me to call again which I duly did, accompanied this time by my brother in law Mr Svensson who happened to be in London on business. This time, I saw Mr John Vallance, but no business was transacted other than him enquiring about the particulars of Mr Ambrose's death. Mr Vallance then went on to make a strong bid for all of Charles Griffin and Co's legal business, suggesting that all the papers ought to be in one place, not split between Scotland and London. To be charged so highly for what I saw as a sales pitch for their own company was a disgrace and Mother agreed, suggesting we move to another firm of solicitors. (However, my experience since this occasion is that such a move would not necessarily have reduced our bills).

After showing some signs of stepping up to the mark in Mother's absence, Richard slipped into his previous bad ways and in February I had to write to Mr Crafter to tell him that Richard was not at home after he had yet again not turned up for work. To be fair, his health was not good that winter. He seemed to have inherited Mother's weak chest and had to stay in bed for several days in late February and early March confined to the house due to a heavy cold. It was not only Richard who was attending Stationer's Hall Court at this time however. Charlie had started work at Griffins having finished his apprenticeship as had John – the latter unfortunately showing no desire whatsoever to be employed in this way, but it made sense for him to start work given that his education had come to an end. Henry, who was not yet 14 years old at this time, was the only one of the boys not working at the firm (other than poor Alec of course).

Mr Collins, despite being quite an old man, remained our most valuable Trustee and continued to be as supportive as his age and location allowed. For example, in March he wrote to Mr Crafter suggesting the Firm consider publishing a new series of cheap Elementary school books for England given that in 1870 an Act by Mr Forster created the School Board and had established a national system of elementary education. Mr Crafter had forwarded the suggestion to me and whilst at first I thought it an excellent idea, on reflection, I was unsure how much autonomy School Boards would actually have in ordering their own text-books. I duly wrote my concern to Mr Collins pointing out that the Compulsory Education Bill would follow as a necessary consequence and a Minster of Public Institution would in all probability adopt the French and German plan of a uniform series of books chosen by himself, to be used in all those schools receiving Government aid (as in fact was the case). However, this suggestion by Mr Collins demonstrates his thoughtfulness and generosity in wanting Charles Griffin and Co to succeed. We were after all rivals in the publishing world and he sought no personal financial gain from our success.

Mother returned from France on the 11th July feeling much refreshed and considerably excited as Polly and Victor's first child was due and she relished the thought of becoming a grandMother. She arrived in the nick of time because just two days later on the 13th July, Polly produced a son. After placing an advert announcing his arrival in *The Times*, I was desperate to tie up loose ends so that I could travel to Sweden to be with my sister and new nephew. I had business to attend to before my journey however and the children to sort out and it was not until the end of July that I left for Gothenburg. I spent two very happy months with my sister and her gorgeous baby – Charles Oscar Rae Svensson. Polly had changed considerably in the short time since her marriage but seemed happy enough and was clearly devoted to little Charlie. The fact that Victor was a distant figure who barely visited Polly's rooms during my stay did not strike me as odd at the time. It is perfectly normal for the baby to form a closer bond with its Mother and her nurse than the father in the early months but by the eighth week of my visit, when Polly was dressed and more integrated into the running of the household, it did begin to occur to me that husband and wife seemed a little distant, even awkward in each other's company, Victor using a similar tone to his wife that he adopted when talking to the servants. Of course, the benefit of hindsight is a wonderful thing. At the time I was not unduly concerned about Polly and reported her glowing happiness in becoming a Mother to Mama and my other sisters on my return to England.

Over the years it became apparent that Polly's marriage was not made in heaven. Two years after Charles, Polly produced a second son: Ernst Victor Rae, after a difficult birth that prompted another extended visit to Sweden by me. Childbearing did not come easily to my sister, for, after successfully bearing a daughter Jane a year after Ernst, she lost two babies in early infancy. Both had been born too soon. Alf survived for a few months and Polly was devastated when he caught influenza and little Ellen was so weak at birth she only lasted for a matter of weeks. All of this took its toll on Polly's mental health. She had been pregnant with Ellen when Alf died and when she lost Ellen, we were desperately worried how she would cope. She was fortunate to have a couple of years' respite before she gave birth again (I suspect Victor was banned from her bedroom for sometime after Ellen's death). Luckily, she went on to produce two healthy girls – Hedvig Elisabeth in 1877 and her youngest child little Blenda Victoria some four years later, in August 1881 – when her eldest Charlie was eleven years old.

Ironically we had seen as much of Victor in those early years of Polly's marriage as Polly herself, as he was often over in England on business and always made a point of visiting us wherever we happened to be living at the time. Polly was far too busy child rearing and her letters rarely mentioned her husband at all. By all accounts it was not a very happy union. After Alf had died, Polly was ill for several months – a worry for us all as she was by that time four month's pregnant. Mama and I both visited but we were not made to feel welcome by Victor when we were under his roof, probably because we failed to conceal our shock at his treatment of his wife. Whilst polite and courteous to his visitors, he adopted a clipped formal tone whilst speaking to Polly in public: in private his raised voice could be overheard in nearby rooms as he chastised her for some perceived misdemeanour or blamed her for any problems with the children. After 33 years of marriage Victor's unkindness became too much for Polly and she did a most courageous thing and left her husband. The final straw for her was her husband's relationship with Anna, one of the maid servants. Polly had long turned a blind eye to Victor's straying eye, his list of mistresses had been common knowledge to her throughout her marriage, but when he started carrying on with one of her own servants – a 20 year old lowly housemaid at that – Polly's pride took a final battering. She told me that during their affair, the housemaid Anna was nothing but a mischief maker. She would tell Victor all sorts of untruths about her which made Victor very angry and she even found that when she was not around Anna would go into her drawers and try on her clothes!

Finally she could take it no more. In the summer of 1891, Polly left Victor to his new mistress and came to England with Hedvig and Blenda for a break, staying with us for several months. We were delighted to have her of course, but the weary, cowed woman who moved back home was not the carefree, frivolous sister I remembered and we struggled to regain the closeness of our youth. Not surprisingly, to be fair, after what she had been through. Whilst I had devoted my life to the Firm, she had tried so hard to be a good wife and Mother. Victor by all accounts complained about everything she did over the years, including getting pregnant so easily (ironic then that when he married Anna, it was only a matter of months before his next child arrived), and this undermined her self belief to such an extent that she sought a second opinion about the most mundane of tasks. She finally plucked up sufficient courage to leave her husband and divorce proceedings started whilst she was still with us in England and they were not pretty. Victor's lawyers were ruthless. Polly became more and more angry and upset as official looking letters arrived from Sweden telling her that Victor was planning a fight. On her return to Gothenburg the process began in earnest and Polly wrote telling me that Victor's line was that she was to blame as she had 'of malice and disgust left and runaway from her husband and gone abroad'. Polly's despair was obvious; she finished her letter with a question: *"Can you think of a greater lie and unfairness?"* In truth I could not, and we all felt angry and betrayed by Victor whose head had clearly been turned by his nubile new mistress.

Polly survived this horrible process and has remained in Sweden to this day. She changed her name in the end from Svensson to Rae, Mama's maiden name, rather than Griffin. Before I leave Polly in her new life I must report that she has become a changed woman. Dusting herself down after years of being put down by her husband, she has blossomed in her independent state. So much so that she has recently founded the Gothenburg Girls High School and she seems happy now with her children growing up fast and a busy life devoted to nurturing young minds. We are closer again, sharing a common interest in education but I have jumped way ahead in telling you Polly's tale and I must now return to the months following the birth of Polly's first born, Charlie, back to the autumn of 1870.

I was personally very busy at this time. Not only preoccupied with my new nephew, but also working on an exciting venture – my biography of Beethoven - a man who was to me like intellectual wine, a hero whose life is a fascinating story of artistic brilliance. Although I fully accept there have been other great composers (I do have a high opinion of Mendelssohn who had after all, the option of leading a life entirely in accordance with his fancies irrespective of the pecuniary circumstances that dictate the course of most of us, but who scorned this easy life in favour of a life dedicated to art), it is Beethoven whom I most respect. I was timing the publication of my memoir to mark the centenary of the composer's birth in 1770. The exact centenary date was the 17th December and I cut the submitting of my final manuscript very fine indeed. Poor Mr Crafter. I confess he had to chase me several times and it was not until the 12th November that I was able to send him final copy. Part of the reason for the delay in getting the work finished was the possibility of including a most valuable and much prized contribution from Mr Ferdinand Hiller, a composer from Cologne who had recently come over to England for the Birmingham Festival. He was to submit an essay on Beethoven but I had to translate it and it did not arrive with me until the 10th November. After many a late night and early morning, the work was finished and it was with much excitement that on the 17th November I received the final copy. The 'getting up' was first rate, the general feel of the final design a pleasure and the type top notch. I remember suggesting that Hiller's Essay stood first (as I saw this rather than my writing as the main selling point) and I did not want to risk my name before his. Not that I wrote the book using my own name. Like another heroine of mine George Eliot, I knew that writing as a woman would mean that my work would get largely ignored by literature critics and male readers throughout the land. No, I chose the name Elliott Graeme. Not only did I think it rather a pretty name, I had other reasons for using it: Elliott is a family name and Graeme is Scotch and finally the initials are the same as my own.

After my initial excitement at seeing the book on the 17th, there followed some anxious weeks whilst it was printed. Would it be ready in time for the centenary in December? The system adopted was that I was sent the proofs to check over as the papers were printed but the printers were very slow and I urged Mr Crafter to pay the extra charge for night work. Even though the business of printing books had become increasingly mechanised (something Henry was to get involved in later in life as you will learn), there was still a number of time consuming stages after the final copy had been sent over. The text had to be set in metal type; then, following the first printing, a metal plate was cast from that type, which could be stored for reuse if another printing was needed. This was only the start of the process. For, once the pages had been printed, the paper then had to be folded, sewn into a book-block, trimmed, pressed and glued before the spine was inserted and the cloth or leather cover produced. I knew enough about the business to appreciate that they needed time, but I was fighting against the clock. On the 4th December, I sent all of my manuscript, preface included, back to the printers and prayed that they would pull out all the stops and produce the memoir in time. I received a letter from Dr Hiller hoping I had reserved the right of translation (something at the time I felt seemed an absurd precaution but one we did attend to). I had secured a capital portrait of Beethoven (that I had seen prefixed to Lady Wallace's Translation of the letters published by Longmans) which we had used, and I inserted the following motto from the man himself on the title page:

"How glorious it is to live one's life a thousand times!"

Mr Crafter continued to question my pseudonym. For some reason he disliked the name Elliot Graeme and suggested I dropped a nom-de-plume on the title page altogether. I was forced to defend my decision for it to remain, as I felt if it was omitted then Dr Hiller would get the credit (or indeed the discredit) for the whole. On the 14th December, just three days before the centenary, I sent Mr Crafter a list of all the people I wanted to receive a personal copy of the book. I was secretly delighted with the outcome, even more so when

Mother said how proud she was of me, describing the book as a *"chaste and elegant volume"* or words to that effect. She insisted we kept a copy on display on the mantelpiece at home for visitors to admire! The book is octavo in size and fits beautifully in between a picture of Papa and our treasured copy of the Old Testament. Mr Crafter sent it to various newspapers for review and the ensuing publicity was useful in generating public interest.

My relief at the book's publication was magnified by the fact I was under increasing pressure to help Mama with the business. I had spent weeks before I had submitted my manuscript at my desk in the shiny pool of light provided by my little bedroom window, fine-tuning the contents and all of my spare time for most of 1870 had been spent researching, translating Mr Hiller's work (which was of course in German) reading other reviews of Beethoven and writing my own account. But for me, this was leisure. I loved every moment I spent in Beethoven's world. I had even managed a quick visit to his hometown of Bonn. I loved that old town which in many ways has not changed much since Beethoven's day. There are the same churches and cloisters, the same quaint flying bridge, the same ruins of Drachenfels and Godesberg towering above the same villages. The Seven Hills look quietly down on the same classic Rhine but of course this majestic river is now desecrated by puffing tourist-laden steamboats and shrieking locomotives. My visit that year had been brief but I had spent many hours playing and listening to Beethoven's music, and the work of other great composers. To spend time immersed in the music of such composers as Handel, Ries, Wageler and Marx and to scour through my texts on Milton, Goethe and other poets so I could add quotes where relevant was nothing but a joy to me. After I'd caught up on some sleep, following the book's completion, I felt quite bereft and at a loose end for several months. The initial excitement of receiving some favourable reviews (my favourites being from the *Spectator* who described it as *"A gracious and pleasant memorial of the centenary"* and the *Observer*'s critic who wrote *"We can ...... recommend it as the most trustworthy and the pleasantest memoir of Beethoven published in England"*) spurred me on to contemplate my next writing project. Perhaps because of these reviews (and of course the timing of the book), the first edition sold out within a few months of publication and I replaced it with a reprint using the work of Alexander Thayer to update it. I will leave Beethoven for now as I want to return to what Mama and the Firm were up to, but suffice to say that after the first 1000 copies were sold, a second edition of 1000 or so were printed in 1876 and even a third edition was needed but it's not clear if all of these will be sold as there are currently plenty still available! I mention these sales figures not to boast but to point out that my efforts appeared to have been worthwhile and I received modest royalty payments, a portion of which I proudly handed over to Mother to pay towards the household expenses.

John Joseph was the next of my brothers to need 'sorting out'. He had left school in the summer of 1870 and, after a few weeks enjoying his freedom rather too much, the matter of his future was openly discussed and he had reluctantly followed his brothers into the Firm while Mother debated what do to with him. Past experience with Richard and Alex had made Mama cautious about assuming that her sons would enter the Firm and John had long expressed a desire to become a farmer. Once again, Mama had to go cap in hand to the Trustees for money to help him realise his dream. She wrote to Mr Collins in August telling him of the opportunity she had to place him with a friend of the family who had a farm in Canada. Re-reading the letter now it would appear that Mr Collins had at first refused the request to dip into the money left to Jessie by Uncle Stewart. To be fair, he was probably worried that there would be none left for Jessie herself given the amount that had already been distributed to her brothers, but young Jessie was a kind and generous soul and with no pressure from Mother or John, she was keen for him to get the finances he needed. Mr Collins withdrew his objection and John left as planned on the 15th September. I remember having to write a letter to a Mr Stark, the Manager of the farm on which John was to work, introducing us as a family and confirming the agreement made between Mama and Mr Stark's employer, a gentleman by the name of Mr Van. The agreement was for a two year stay and the farm was located on an island to the South West of Montreal called Lachine. In many ways we were all secretly relieved when John left home (perhaps this was why Jessie was so keen for him to get the money he needed). Not that we didn't love him dearly. He was a generous spirited chap, quite lively and very personable with an open friendly face under a thick mop of unruly dark brown hair, chocolate brown eyes and a rather large nose, flanked by two dimples which emerged whenever he smiled. Weary of his sociable nature, Mother was also worried he had a tendency to be *"very easily led"* and was aware that he was also rather too fond of the bottle and the high life. We used to get letters sent from his school telling us of his tomfoolery, and he was often getting in some kind of scrape, playing hard rather than concentrating on his studies. How different he was in every way from his namesake, our obsessively hard working uncle. This is why Mother thought it wise to encourage an outdoor life for him where he would be free to roam, and you couldn't get more open than Canada.

Unfortunately Canada did not suit him although he did enjoy the farming aspect of his new life. He sent regular letters home (a signal of his homesickness to be sure), in which he told us all about the beauty of the island, the cattle, the impressive yield from the various crops they grew and the invigorating extremes of the climate. There was little or no mention of any people in his letters, a matter of great disappointment to Mother and I, and it appears that Lachine Farm was so huge and the neighbouring farmers a close knit bunch who were, in his words, *"very Canadian"*. I think the shock of moving from the high life in London to the back of beyond was too much and he became increasingly miserable as time went on. I have to say I felt proud of him for sticking it out for the full two years as arranged, and in part take some credit for keeping him there as I wrote religiously once a fortnight in an attempt to jolly him along. He did stay at the farm as planned until the August of 1873 when he worked his passage back to the UK arriving on the 27th November 1873 in Liverpool. He was penniless and had written asking us for the rail fare back to London and I remember sending him the money and reminding him to arrive clean and tidy. I even had the audacity to suggest he had a hair cut before he presented himself! I know Mother was anxious to see her fourth son but I also knew she was worried how he would be after his Canadian adventure. It did appear to have tamed our wild child up to a point as his manners, though in some ways a little coarse, had generally improved and he was more appreciative of home comforts and showed more concern for his loved ones. Peeling off his carefree cloak had revealed a much more sensitive, careworn creature but despite his new maturity, John didn't settle into life in the big smoke. The pull of the outdoors was too much for him and he looked at the map and planned his next adventure. Not wanting to follow Alex's footsteps, he chose another continent and South Africa beckoned.

I'm pleased to report that he is still there to this day, happily settled. It took a while though, as he first married a lady called Rebecca – the daughter of the hotel owner where he first went to work in Tarkastad, and they had two sons and two daughters before divorcing (he claimed she was 'unreasonable'). We never met Rebecca so I cannot comment on whether there was any truth in his accusation, but I can only assume that she had tried to rein him in as he described her in letters to me as a *'hectoring'*, *'bossy woman'* who was *'very keen for me to stay at home'*. I had some sympathy with her, knowing John's weaknesses especially when it came to socialising and I could imagine her frustration at her husband's absences. But he is, after all, my brother and for that reason I just wanted him to be happy and he seems more settled with his new wife, a lady called Eleanor. The couple first settled in the Cape of Good Hope and then East London and they had one child together, a little boy called John Arthur. We hear all the news regularly and John seems at last to have matured and is happy to build a home with his wife and son. He remains in close contact with his other children and we are all very proud of his success, not only as an hotelier but as a farmer too. He used to come back to England to see us periodically and he really did look the part of a prosperous gentleman and Mother was suitably proud. Sadly he missed the recent run of family funerals. I just hope he gets over again soon as none of us are getting any younger and he will notice a sharp decline in Mother's mental health after the year we've just had. But I'm jumping ahead once again. I need to return to 1870, the year our John was first sent to Canada.

Just before we celebrated another Christmas in 1870 Richard was given a boost by Mr Crafter. It started when Mother received a note from our manager on 22nd December in which he stated:

> *"I have long felt that his salary was too small for his position, therefore I will be glad if you see your way to advancing it a little".*

He then went on to wish us all a happy Christmas and New Year. Richard was indeed very grateful for the extra money. He was showing signs of increasing restlessness at the speed of his advancement up the managerial ladder and his salary increase kept him happier for a short time at least. It also enabled him to start saving for his future, as he had to prove he had excellent prospects and a solid financial backing before he stood a chance of asking a lady for her hand in marriage. Richard, like Alex and in time Charlie, was not in the habit of openly courting and Mother and I preferred not to think about the time he spent after work when he visited various taverns and brothels before catching the last omnibus home. The boys' journey was not an easy one. The route was constantly disrupted by some kind of building work. Streets were often blocked as buildings were being demolished and either rebuilt or cleared in preparation for the railway. One consequence of all this work, other than a frustrating increase in journey time to and from Stationer's Hall Court, was the displacement of thousands of poor folk from their homes. When Mama travelled with me, she used to press a lavender soaked handkerchief against her nose to counteract the aroma of horses and she'd avert her eyes as we swept past some poor unfortunate, who had been left on the street contemplating the rubble of their former home. Although I comforted her with the thought they would be rehoused elsewhere, we both knew that in truth the railway companies were slow to sort out these evicted occupants with alternative accommodation. The building of the Metropolitan Underground Line was just the start of years of demolition and slow bus journeys and the initial novelty at gazing at the vast trenches that emerged in the streets and marvelling at the glimpses of tunnelling as huge shafts were sunk into the ground, soon gave way to irritation at the grind of daily commuting into work took its toll. But there was always a price to pay for modernisation and in many ways I felt privileged to be living in the city during such a massive transformation. Meanwhile, Mother and I quietly celebrated Mr Crafter's promise and the stability it brought to Richard's life and he at least, seemed to relish his extra salary, showering Christmas gifts on the family much to the delight of the younger ones. We saw out the year by toasting Papa, marking Charles Dickens's passing, and raising a glass to our absent siblings before a few moments silent reflection, when I for one, remember offering a prayer for prosperity for our much beleaguered family.

Chapter 5

And so we reached 1871 and the Firm and the family had survived a decade without Papa. To recap, Mama was eight and forty years old, still active but prone to bouts of ill health and keen to slow down. To this end, I assumed more letter writing duties and was fully involved as a fellow Trustee.

Thinking back, 1871 was another important year for us although for the first half of the year nothing exciting seemed to happen. I continued to get more involved in the Firm's publications, encouraged by my own success at writing; and Richard was more empowered due to his salary rise, although his health was a concern and he continued to have days at home when his chest was troubling him. I think it was a gradual build up throughout the year between the family and our manger Mr Crafter that brought matters to a head. Perhaps Mr Crafter's suggestion for Richard to earn more money was in fact a veiled attempt to point out his own financial position, for he seemed to get more and more disgruntled as the year progressed. Finally in June we had an open demand for a rise in salary and he requested a meeting with the Trustees to discuss the matter. As usual, such a meeting was not speedily arranged and I felt that once Mr Crafter had made his demands he simply rested on his oars until he learnt of the final decision. This situation had to be resolved and Mr Crafter forced us into action by finally giving us an ultimatum: 'improve my salary or I'm leaving'.

With this hanging over our heads, Mother sought a distraction and it came in the guise of another house move. We had lived in Canonbury Park Square for nearly ten years and she just fancied a change of scene.

She also needed to reduce our rental income now that she no longer needed such large accommodation. By this time, it was still the horse drawn tram and buses that provided the best commuter service but the railway network was growing each month and this allowed us to widen our search and we considered moving slightly further away from the Firm. We settled on the cheaper, but still respectable, district of South Tottenham. The house we found was number 4 Osborn Villas, Westgreen Road, and it had the advantage of a larger garden even though it had fewer bedrooms. Richard decided at this time to move in with a friend, leaving us with young Jessie, Henry, Helen and Alice at home (although Mother had plans for Nelly and Alice to be sent abroad to be finished at the same school that Polly and I had attended). Charlie was still boarding close to the business where he was gaining valuable work experience, learning the publishing trade, although his placement was about to come to an end. He regularly came to see us in the evenings and Henry was particularly pleased when he came home and saw Charlie's hat and boots in the hall way. While Mother spent many an hour planning our move, the boys had more pressing matters to attend to. A key memorable 1871 moment was the first Scottish-English International Rugby match which prompted quite mixed loyalties on our household! In the event Richard and Charlie supported Scotland (as did I) and Harry played devil's advocate and backed England. It was with great delight to us Scottish supporters that the Scots won the match and weeks of crowing prevailed. Charlie was more interested in cricket if I'm honest - a game he excelled at when first introduced at school. A mean fast bowler, he went on to become an ardent follower of the County Championship when it was first established in 1873 and kept a keen eye on Kent's progress throughout his adult life.

Anyway sport and our house move could not distract us from our business concerns for long as the problems mounted. Mr Crafter was still not happy and the solution we came up with was designed to reduce his workload. We felt he could continue to act as overall manager, with Richard dealing with some managerial duties and it was suggested that I work alongside my brother to oversee things and to offer advice and assistance when needed. Whilst Mr Crafter was happy to try out the new management structure, sadly this arrangement fell apart almost as soon as it was established because my little brother started abusing his position. To be fair, Richard had been working in the Firm for 9 years and he did not feel it right that I should come in as an equal or even above him. By November, the situation had become critical and he gave his formal notice to the Trustees. I have a letter on file that Mother wrote to Mr Collins on the 25th of that month that I think you should read in full.

I thank you very much for your letter… regarding this affair with Richard.

Southgate's matter is simply this. Richard sent me an unfilled-up bill to sign, which I returned to him to get the name of the Drama added to it, as I have all along made it a rule to do. He has taken offence at this, and declares that I have no confidence in him.

I am not at all pleased with the way in which he has acted. He got into the position at S.H.C. with the express understanding that Lizzie was to work and act with him. However, when it came to it, he would not have it, alleging that if the Trade knew she was there to help, they would at once say we did not trust him, and that he was not fit for the position. Lizzie went into the Warehouse repeatedly to do her part of the Agreement, but he would neither give her information nor work to do. So, after the first week, we have left him to take his own way.

So far as I can judge, he has been doing his duty faithfully since he took it up. He is the first at the business in the morning, and the last to leave it at night; but he is so close that I never know from him what he is doing, and he even does not think it necessary to consult me about anything. I, of course, naturally feel anxious, as he is very inexperienced.

I would feel much more comfortable if Lizzie acted with him, as she is thoroughly reliable, zealous, and energetic but in his present mood, any attempt at co-operation on her part would be a mere farce.

Perhaps you would kindly correspond with him, and place the matter in a proper light before him. If he still persists in his resignation, I see no alternative but taking him at his word, for I feel that we have shown the greatest forbearance towards Richard, and he requires a lesson.

Don't be fooled. I was secretly terrified at being given such responsibility. It was, after all, almost unheard of for a young Victorian woman to hold such a position. But like Mother, I had one goal and that was to keep the Firm going; to continue Papa's legacy and to ensure that we had a stable income for the rest of the family to live on. I also felt more secure knowing that Mr Crafter was nearby and willing to act as my advisor and that Charles (a brilliant mathematician remember) was now employed by the Firm as our Bookkeeper. Richard did not go quietly.

He insisted on staying until the 23rd December 1871 – the full month after he put in his resignation. Sadly, his conduct during this time was nothing to be proud of. He paid no attention at all to Mother and I when we went up to the Warehouse, he had drawn out money for himself using the private ledger and he acted totally independently of me. Remember he was still one of the Trustees. We needed his signature on official documents and his lack of cooperation was not only worrying on a personal level, it was potentially damaging to the business. Now I think back over this time, with the benefit of experience and hindsight I realise how difficult it must have been for my brother. He was, after all the eldest son, working in a man's world, and yet he appeared to be dominated by women. He had not cut the ties of his Mother's apron strings and in many ways lived up to the role of indulged son, playing hard, misbehaving in meetings, taking time off work at any opportunity. Perhaps it was no surprise that he found it hard to assert his authority and when it was so openly challenged he reacted in this extreme way? I do now think that we made the wrong decision. When Mr Crafter threatened to resign, we should have all backed Richard as the new manager. I could have continued as I had been doing as part of the team. As it was, we effectively forced him out and I was left to manage alone. I have to say my view is not shared by others, who felt that Richard was too immature and unstable to take over, and that without my intervention the business would have been even more vulnerable to closure. Who is to say? The damage was done. Richard left the Firm and disappeared from our lives for the next few years. Mother was naturally devastated but we both had more than enough on our plate to keep us occupied. The survival of the Firm was now firmly in our hands. At least the sale of the stocks (albeit at a lower level than we would have liked) kept us going for a while and we were able to siphon off some of the profits to bolster the household account which had become dangerously low. This salvaged some of Mother's pride and enabled us to live comfortably without going cap in hand to the Trustees every five minutes.

Mother made a monumental decision in December 1871. At the end of the year she would 'retire' from writing official business letters and I would take over completely. I was looking through the letter books in my name the other day when I was at the Warehouse. The sheer quantity that accumulated over the years still staggers me. A whole series of leather bound volumes dated 1872 to the present day.

I really don't want to go into detail about my business life at this particular time. Suffice to say that the first few years were very busy.

This period of my life is quite a blur. I was so busy it was all I could do to keep my eyes open in the evening. After supper Mother and I would sit with Jessie, Helen and Alice chattering about our day and we deliberately kept the business out of our conversations. This was not only to prevent my sisters' eyes from glazing over with boredom, but more importantly to prevent Mother from continuing to be bogged down with the trials and tribulations of office life. In truth I built a double existence in the interests of self preservation. The short journey home was my 'in between' time, when I allowed myself half the trip to mull over events and compile a list of tasks for the following day and then let my mind drift for the remainder of the journey so that by the time I reached number four, I was firmly in 'family mode', eager to leave my work attire in the hall and slip back into the role of dutiful daughter and attentive older sister.

This period of my working life was by far the hardest for me on a personal level. The office staff took a long time to adjust to my leadership. Some never did, but I accepted and respected this attitude (particularly from older members of staff) and learnt to play the game. When I was dealing with other businesses I was careful to bring a senior male colleague to meetings and I decided from the first that my strategy would be to ignore any hostility and win over support through my results as a business leader. I had learnt the need for forcefulness; diplomacy and resourcefulness from my Mother and a love of books and strong leadership skills from my father. The perfect combination for the manager of a growing business. It was just coincidental that I was a woman.

I never stopped my own writing and it was a great relief to me to escape the office and spend a few hours in my little bedroom - my sanctuary, including my treasured writing desk. Here, the old mahogany bed had been smartened up recently with red hangings to match the red vase I keep on my dresser. How I love to escape to the comforting silence of that room, to sit at my desk scribbling away at my latest venture: at this time I was working on a novel. I decided to call it 'A novel with Two Heroes', and I was delighted when Mama and the girls gave it a positive review and the work was published, in two volumes on 16th March 1872. I loved writing the book which I set in Germany and even managed to sneak over to that beautiful country for some 'so called' research. In fact, I stayed with family friends and made sure I had the time to attend a few concerts whilst I was there. The visit, I remember, was all too brief. I was, after all, a working lady and I never allowed myself more than one week away from the Warehouse in those early days. I was determined that nothing would undermine my authority and, perhaps driven by the fact that Charles was showing worrying signs of adopting his older brother's rather lackadaisical attitude to some aspects of working life, I was a stickler for routine and punctuality. Charles was a brilliant bookkeeper but as already mentioned, he too was rather too fond of the bottle (I think the boys must have each inherited some trait that made them susceptible to this demon) and so occasionally he would arrive into work late and a little worse for wear. He did me the favour of accompanying me to a number of plays and for this I am eternally grateful especially as my favourite show of all time was one that I shared with him, on a night he had planned in celebration of my novel's publication. The production of Henry V was not only very moving and well acted, but ended in a spectacular 'shower of gold' scene where gold dust was sprinkled down on the conquering heroes and I have kept my programme and ticket to remind me of this wonderful night.

I meanwhile had a plan. It was always my intention that I would straighten out the management structure of the Firm and then I would leave to carry on my domestic and literary life. I had every confidence that Richard would come back to us. Driven primarily by lack of funds but also, I felt, by a deep rooted desire to do the right thing. He was, after all, the eldest son and the responsibility of the family and the Firm also seemed to draw him back like a magnet.

He had tried to sever links before and failed, and I felt it only a matter of time before he would return. In my plan, Richard and my other brothers would then take over the helm once again. I had 1878 as my end goal. That was when I would officially 'retire' like Mama before me, and leave things to the boys. By then they would be more than capable of managing the business between them with Richard as Manager, Charles as Company Secretary and Henry as Head Traveller. That was my vision at least.

I must just tell you before I go on, about my little brother Henry. Harry (as we often called him), or to give him his proper name: Henry Brougham Griffin was a chap who aspired to achieve great things. Perhaps because of his almost unnatural interest in material possessions, Harry was the only one of my brothers who seemed keen to enter the Firm: if only to earn some money. He never ceased to relish an opportunity to explain to strangers how he was given his illustrious middle name and he made much (rather too much if truth be told) of the family connection with the famous statesman. To be fair, as I have already mentioned, Lord Brougham's association with Griffins can be traced back as early as 1828 (not long after he was instrumental in founding the University of London in 1825), when his book called 'Natural Theology' was published in two volumes by the Firm at the price of 18s. Griffins then bought the Copyrights in as many of Brougham's other books as they could, thereby collecting together a more or less complete set of his works. The Firm continued to publish a number of new books and editions until Papa's death. Papa became quite friendly with Lord Brougham. I remember him visiting us at home a number of times around the time of Henry's birth, and I clearly recall the excitement when he agreed to become Godfather to little Henry in 1856, just before Christmas, which added considerably to the festive frivolities. I believe it was Papa who attracted a range of eminent intellectuals to publish their work through Griffins (Brougham was in esteemed company with the Reverend John Eadie, a senior figure in the Anglican church and a prolific author of religious works, another MP Sir Henry Craik and, Macquorn Rankine, Professor of Engineering at University of Glasgow to name but a few). Their addition to our list undoubtedly boosted our reputation in the publishing industry. Who knows what might have happened to the Firm had Papa lived for longer? Sadly Mother and I were rather too busy staving off insolvency to spend much time wooing new literary talent but we did prioritise in keeping our existing authors happy.

Anyway, the problem with Henry was that he was not all that keen on books. As a little boy, whilst he had enjoyed being read to, he rarely read alone and I suspect that his insistence of 'one more story' before lights out was more to delay his bedtime rather than a desire to further his literary education. As an adult, if you saw him reading, it was usually a nonfiction book, often about engines, engineering or science: some kind of account about the latest technological advances that seemed to be happening almost daily.

Perhaps because he spent so much time amongst women from an early age, (his older brothers being away at school), and as his upbringing was largely shared between Mother, Polly and I, together with various nursemaids and governesses, (at least before he was sent to the City of London School at the age of 9), he was very gentle in nature, very intuitive and sensitive to the feelings of others. He also had a keen sense of humour and would lighten any atmosphere, although his love of teasing his younger sisters by 'stroking the wrong way', was not always taken as a joke. The downside to Henry's character was that he had a worrying tendency to allow others to organise him all the time. In fact, as a young man, he was passive to the point of being lazy. Whilst John would charm the birds from the trees, Harry's skill was to sit quietly, smile sweetly and do nothing in the hope that others would do it for him. He also knew when to keep quiet. Whilst his older brothers would argue and bicker, vying to have the last word, Henry would stand back, observe and silently do his own thing. His final skill: he was a great listener. He would look directly at you as if you were the most important thing in his life, nodding intently, as if avidly interested in what you had to say, before softly contradicting you, or totally ignoring your view point and charmingly offering one of his own. These skills, I had noted in him from a very young age and I am pleased to say they never left him, even after the rigours of boarding school.

We were all terribly upset when Harry reached the grand old age of 9 and was ready to progress to 'big' school. Polly and I were secretly fearful that his sensitive nature would be taken advantage of and deep down I knew that unlike Charlie and Richard he would not excel in the classroom academically; and he would almost certainly lack Alex's and John's prowess on the sports field. My sister and I decided we needed to discuss our fears with Mother and I clearly remember her response. She had been sitting in her usual place at Papa's desk in the parlour when we broached the subject (Mother was struggling it transpired, to politely decline yet another request to attend a neighbour's 'at home') and she seemed glad of the interruption. That was until she had listened to our concerns. Far from dismissing our comments outright, she promised to speak to young Henry, who at the time could be heard playing a noisy game of soldiers with his sisters, marching through the kitchen with Helen in command. I observed her strategy over the coming weeks and marvelled at her cunning.

She started by getting Henry to perform more tasks on his own. He was sent to the local shop on various errands, to give a message to a neighbour or to organise a taxi on the pretence that the servants were otherwise engaged. He was allowed to stay up alone a little later than his sisters in order to read aloud to Mama as she sat with her embroidery, and he was encouraged to show us his school work and bask in the resulting praise. But it was only really after he had spent the summer preceding his entry into the City of London school playing almost exclusively outside either with his brothers or with Jacob, the son of a second cousin of Mother's, who perchance lived just a few streets away – that Polly and I began to relax. Those two months were enough for him to toughen up and mature sufficiently to cope in a man's world. The night before he left Mother did what she had done for all her boys, she showed them the letter that Papa had written to his own parents from boarding school in Scotland. As with the others, she emphasised how it must have been for Papa – pretty much an only child (if you don't count his brother Richard who had died in adolescence and his illegitimate half sister Sarah Bond who of course never lived with the family). The letter was duly sent for. I have it here with me now. A much prized family possession as it is one of the few items that we have from Papa's childhood; it is becoming quite fragile around the folds. It is such a sweet letter, written in beautiful copperplate writing (not bad for a 9 year old) and it never failed to comfort and inspire. If nothing else it gave the boys an indication of how hard they used to have to work 'in the olden days' at school. Papa himself had told the older two repeatedly that they had never had it so easy, and it was a standing joke in our family to refer to 'the letter' when the boys used to moan about their own daily routine in school. Indulge me please as I write it in full, exactly as written – it is not a long letter but one that means so much to me, and even now has the ability to bring a tear to my eye…

New Kilpatrick
July 24ᵗʰ 1829

My Dear Father

I now begin to fulfil a promise to you which I made sometime ago, namely, to write you a letter but as I never have written a letter before, I do not know very well how to begin, what to say, or how to finish it. It is more difficult to do, I think, than my Delectus. Mr

Waker says he will not help me. Well then I must try it myself. How did you and my Mother and Miss Aitken get home on Sunday night I was pretty tired when I came back to kilpatrick. Mr Walker and M^rs McColl and all the boys are well. I am at present learning English Grammar, Geography, English Reading, Writting, Latin and Arithmetic. I hope Mr Malcolm and Mr Aitken are quite well. I am fourth dux in the Delectus and second in the Arithmetic Class. We rise at seven in the morning, then we go to school till nine, then we have breakfast, and play till ten then we go to School till one, we have dinner between one and two O'clock, then we go to school till half past four, then we have tea and play till six, then we go to school till eight then we play till nine then prayers, then we go to beds.

I remain,
My Dear Father,
Your Affectionate Son,

Charles Griffin

I must just point out to those unfamiliar with the word, that Dux is the name given to the head pupil in class in Scotland. The boys were of course used to hearing the Delectus – a task that few of them relished, although I secretly loved translating passages from Latin and from Greek and was regularly asked by one or other of them to help with a particularly tricky word or phrase.

And so it was that Henry was sent off to school and it was with much relief all round when he settled in well and more importantly made a group of like minded friends. As predicted, he never excelled either academically or in the field of sports, arts or music, but he had an aptitude for science and engineering and he spent his leisure time taking things apart or making things from scratch. His childhood ambition to become an inventor was, however tempered by his growing desire to earn good money. He was interested in the latest gadgets. He of all the boys aspired to own a large home and employ an army of servants and it was Henry who was desperate to ride in the first underground train, who relished travelling by overland train and who in later years, urged Mama to look to moving to a house with a proper bathroom. He was the first to suggest we buy the latest oil lamps and ranges, even electric lights when they first came available. To fund his passion, Henry could not wait to leave school and enter the Firm.

He started off in the Printing Department – or at least that is what he told everyone, even though the Firm had no Printing Department at this time. I have to say that it was really only when I started going up to the Warehouse on a regular basis in the early 1870's that I realised that Henry was in effect drawing a salary for doing nothing. So I sent him to Brunswick to study printing with a view to him opening an official Printing Department on his return. I remember being appalled when I realised how young Henry had been taking advantage of his position by quietly taking long lunch hours, arriving late and leaving early. I know his older brothers were no great example, but I had expected more from Henry and told him so. He was duly chastened and seemed happy enough to learn a new skill. In 1873 I accompanied Henry to Glasgow to see the new horse-drawn tram and he was spellbound, standing for what seemed like hours watching with envy as the trace-boys (who took the cars up the hill), mounted on their saddled horses. He continued to be inspired by the great inventors of the age, particularly those who had a Glasgow connection like himself – men like Thomas Telford, the builder of Glasgow Bridge, Henry Bell and most famous of all, James Watt and he dreamed of one day becoming famous.

Luckily he settled down and enjoyed his time in Brunswick and ended up staying there until the end of 1882, principally because we shelved our plans to open our own Printing Department, it being more economical for us to outsource this elsewhere. So Henry stayed on until he wanted to progress up the ladder and was keen to earn more money. I tried to get him a better position in the printing world, approaching Bell & Bain – a Scottish firm of much repute – but sadly they had no vacancies and refused to employ him. Instead he rejoined Griffins in a different position. I made sure he had a proper role this time and he took over the London travelling from Charles and also nurtured our relationship with many of our best authors. He was good at both tasks, his ability to listen and to persuade being ideal characteristics of a salesman and a 'relationship builder' but I could not afford to give him the kind of salary he desired. So I tried to add to his responsibilities to justify a wage increase, by giving him proof reading to do but if I'm honest he wasn't very good at it. His own writing skills were frankly not up to the job and so it was mutually agreed that Harry should look elsewhere to develop his career.

Charles James (who at the time was travelling in the UK), was brought back to London and Henry left to set up a small printing shop of his own. He went on I might add, to have a reasonably happy life, but it is a great sadness to me that he never married. Henry remained very close to his sisters and protective of Mother and for that I'm grateful, especially as he stayed at home the longest of all the boys, moving with us from Osborn Villas in South Tottenham to West Kensington and then after only a short time (for reasons I will discuss later) to Criffel Avenue in 1886. He did eventually move out of the family home, choosing for reasons of ill health to relocate to the Sussex coast – an area that Mother and I came to know well. He moved to Bexhill on Sea, into a smart house that was far too big for him but one befitting his status as a successful business man and he filled the top floor with a small army of servants who tended to his every whim. He had at least fulfilled many of his dreams – even if he left no son and heir to inherit his spoils – the most precious of which was the makings of a motorised carriage. To my mind this was a funny looking machine, open to the elements, it looked a bit like an ordinary carriage but had massive wheels and was hugely uncomfortable to travel in. He had persuaded me on one occasion to have a ride but I refused to go further than his drive and I secretly felt that it was as much the gentle slope that propelled us forward as the complicated, smelly contraption underneath our feet.

So I must leave Henry for now as he quietly forged his own life in the midst of, but slightly removed from the hustle and bustle of family life, and return to the late 1870's, near the time when I had hoped to 'retire' from the Firm. Sadly, we ended 1877 on a sombre note when we learnt of Alex's death in December 1877 from alcoholism. Always our 'wild child', Alex had been a peripheral member of our family for a number of years if I'm honest and was a constant nagging worry to Mother, who had long feared for his safety. As I have mentioned, he had always been too fond of the demon drink, and since his return from New Zealand, he struggled to settle, sleeping on various friends' floors, sometimes disappearing for days on end. He never reached a position where he could offer a lady his hand in marriage as neither his financial position nor social standing were suitably attractive. Instead he turned to the bottle for comfort and I know for a fact that he visited the many brothels that seem to have sprung up all over London. It was one thing imagining what he was up to in New Zealand, quite another when his 'friends' and acquaintances would report his sorry state or he would turn up on our doorstep inebriated and begging for money at various times of the day or night. After years of excess, his liver finally gave up at the tender age of nine and twenty, and it was surprising how few of his friends attended his funeral – an event that prevented any festive spirit that year, despite Mother trying to put on a brave face for the sake of the younger children. Nellie and Alice remained unsure if they could openly express their excitement at the festivities due to our black attire and Mother's red eyes, and it reawakened in us older children the nightmare period following Papa's death.

Chapter 6

With Henry out of the frame, Alex dead and John Joseph abroad, this left Charlie and Richard as the only Griffin men left to help take the business forward. So much for my grand plan of retiring in 1878. Richard was at least back, after five years or so in the early 1870's spent doing not very much. Drinking too much for sure. Only one positive event that came out of his 'lost' years was that he found and married his wife Ruth. The couple wed in 1877 and settled in Stamford Hill. Sadly, neither Richard nor Ruth were in the best of health and seemed to take it in turns to report some malaise or other. We had regular updates as Richard had matured and mellowed and had rebuilt his relationship with Mother. Marriage clearly suited him. He was drinking less and acting more responsibly. He re-entered the Firm, albeit for a shortened week, as he negotiated a half day off each week in order to rest. The arrangement suited me to be honest because I also decided to take a different half day off, as did Charlie, in order to have more leisure time (in my case) but more importantly this job share saved the Firm money. The problem for Richard was that Ruth's health was even less robust than his own, and I can now rather guiltily share with you (given that neither party are on this mortal earth), that I had no time for such wallowing in ill health and considered their preoccupation with their own wellbeing rather distasteful. Whilst Ruth was in many ways the perfect wife for Richard as she pampered and Mothered him, I also felt at times frustrated by the couple's self interest and secretly blamed Ruth when Richard took regular days off sick either for himself or to tend to his wife. Certainly it did not correlate with the needs of a strong businessman and a manager of a leading publishing house.

Poor Ruth. I now realise I was being unfair. She was genuinely afflicted with very severe pain in her joints, poor circulation and a weak heart. Mother visited more regularly than I, and supported the couple after their move to 11 Manor Road, Stamford Hill. She even bought Ruth a new bed in 1879 when her legs became so painful that she could only lie on her back for days on end. I think Mother relished having the time to visit relatives and to concentrate on Alice and Nelly after years of fretting over the business. Helen was about to finish her education and Alice was not far behind, at nearly seven and ten years old, but both girls were still having tuition with Miss Lindner and both were preparing for a stint in Germany to be finished at the same school that Polly and I had attended in Frankfurt.

With Mother ever more distant from everyday events at the Warehouse, she was able to play the role of dutiful Mother-in-law and fussed over Ruth. I confess I felt a little jealous of the attention given and was also cynical of the sickness that presided in Richard's home until that is, the moment we got news that Ruth had died. Quite suddenly in the night on Boxing Day 1879. Richard was naturally devastated as we all were for him and Mother spent hours consoling her weeping son. The funeral on the 27th was a sombre affair, just days after Ruth had sat opposite me enjoying the festive feast prepared by cook, we watched in silence as her body was committed to the ground. I go to Abney Park Cemetery still to pay my respects to my sister in law. A lady who I was never really that close to in life, but for her positive influence on my brother, I remain eternally grateful.

Richard was naturally never the same after Ruth's death. He was at that time the Company's Accountant having taken over from Charles, (who was still travelling), and he went into deep mourning. He wrote his letters on the black banded paper that Mother had used following Papa's death, dressed entirely in heavy dark suits to match his sombre mood and refused to be comforted. For months we tried to cheer him by offering concert tickets, day trips or seaside holidays. All such offers were refused.

I was not without chaperone however when it came to enjoying evening entertainment. Charles often came with me to Crystal Palace and the pair of us regularly took Alice and Nelly (who were still only half ticket price at this time). A particular favourite concert that sticks in my mind was the Halle Festival but nothing for me compared to the Wagner concert I had been fortunate enough to attend with Charlie in 1877. Holidays in this period included regular trips to see relatives in Scotland and we also visited France to give young Jessie some warmer air.

The year after Ruth's death, 1880, was an eventful one for the Griffin household. We were all really excited to witness a romance blossom between Charlie and one or our employee's sisters. Daisy Barrett (or Alice Emma Barrett to give her full name) lived nearby in Stoke Newington. Whilst the rest of the family worshipped at the local Anglican Church, Charles became a member of the congregational church, a small but fervent establishment whose key attraction for Charles was the sight of Daisy in her Sunday best studiously ignoring his adoring gaze.

Throughout my life my faith has been my guiding light. Christianity was instilled in all of us from birth and we all attended Church without fail every Sunday. In Scotland we had attended St Andrews' by the Green, like Papa's parents before us; indeed, my late paternal grandfather had played a key role in the church and devoted much of his precious spare time to fundraising and improving the fabric of the building. For me, attending the Sunday service was never the chore it so clearly was for my younger brothers. For it allowed me to sing. Like Mama and Papa, I loved the chance to listen to the organ being played and when we moved to Kent I joined the church choir and enjoyed many an hour practising with the rather motley selection of villagers who made up our ranks. Mother was very pious and as she grew older she spent an increasing amount of time in silent prayer. I suppose in many ways it made her feel closer to Papa and it certainly meant she was not afraid of death. I too am not frightened of meeting my maker and confess to becoming more interested in the spiritual uncertainties of this world as I get older. Ghosts, fairies and spirits may seem far-fetched but I am increasingly curious about the afterlife and I suppose this comes with the territory after witnessing so many funerals and given the creeping pull of the Grim Reaper. I have a keen interest in many paintings and work of literature produced on the subject. It's one thing enjoying a fantasy like the little ones (they used to love *Alice's Adventures in Wonderland* written by Lewis Carroll and I lost count of the number of times we used to have to read it to them), quite another to believe in the notions of fairies and spirits. I think my interest in scientific and technical advances has led me to question any unproven theories about the scientific world, but equally I, like Mother, remain just as sceptical about Charles Darwin's blasphemous publication of *The Origin of Species.* How could such a man question the accepted view of the creation as depicted by God's holy book? I still shudder at his arrogance. I have after all, seen many a creature who would refute Mr Darwin's theory of Natural Selection. Take the neighbour's son for example, Mr Clayton, a man with features so peculiar he might have evolved out of anything, from a hedgehog with startled bristles to a trembling chimpanzee. Anyway, back to Charles and Daisy.

Daisy's brother Ernest worked for us at Griffins. Daisy was a lovely girl, petite in stature, with a sweet nature and kind heart and Mama and I were delighted with the match. Following a blissful summer in which the pair courted (in between Charlie's obsession with the first International 'test' match against Australia which he managed to get tickets for on both the opening and final day), the wedding was planned. Charlie was a fine figure of a man with smooth limbs, neat white hands and a quiet yet assured face. He took great care over his appearance and grew a luxuriant moustache and kept his hair neatly trimmed as you will see from the splendid picture I have included in this book. It was taken by the Artists Association of Tottenham Court Road around about this time. He is resplendent in a very wide winged collar and is dressed in casual clothes. He looks like the cat that has got the cream and well he might. Daisy was quite a catch, and the wedding, which took place on the 18th November 1880 at Hare Court Chapel in St Paul's Road in Islington, was a fantastic day for us all. Mother was very relaxed and young Jessie was going through a better period in her health, having spent much of that summer at the seaside at Cawsand in Devon, and there was not a dry eye in the house when she played the piano for us at the small evening reception held at Daisy's parents' house after the ceremony. Alice and Nelly had relished the opportunity to buy new dresses and were clearly hoping to attract some male attention and Mama looked very elegant in a full length lace trimmed gown with matching shawl, a bustle so tight it took inches off her waist, her face the picture of maternal pride. Funny really, I can remember what the others were wearing but have no recollection of my own attire that day.

Charles was 30 years old by the time he married. Perfect age to be fair, as he was well established in the Firm and Daisy came from a similar background to our own; her father Samuel was also a publisher by trade. After the wedding the couple settled in Sutherland Villa, 19 Bethune Road, Stamford Hill and I felt we all gained hugely from the union.

There is so much to report from this time that I fear I am missing out key events and I'm aware that I am glossing over my working life as if it was unimportant: far from it. I barely had time to draw breath between meetings, reading manuscripts, liaising with potential and current authors, promoting our books, chasing orders, chivvying printers, overseeing accountants and of course one of the hardest tasks of all, managing our own staff. My routine was punishing but hugely rewarding and (although it was a struggle at first), most of the team grew to accept my authority as overall manager and to be fair I don't think my being a woman was an issue for them. It was a different matter outside the Firm, although our regular authors had grown used to my involvement and were also accepting of my position. Conducting business with other suppliers, competitors, and legal or financial companies was far more challenging. I lost count of the number of awkward be-suited gentleman I met who insisted on addressing all their comments to Richard or Charlie. They would stare over my head if forced to respond to one of my direct questions and even at times refused to acknowledge my presence altogether. I took no offence and to this day bear no grudge. I accepted that the extraordinary circumstances that had thrust me into such an unusual position were just that: out of the ordinary and therefore hard for many to accept. We may have made some progress in terms of gaining a right to be educated but women are still far from equal in the eyes of men. The Griffin girls were not typical. Most men fear that an educated woman will take away the work of men and I have to admit that it took years for me to prove my worth as manager of Griffins.

I have only two unmarried friends, one in employment, the other occupied in another fashion, both experiencing a very different life to my own. The one in paid employment became a governess and went on to move between households, sometimes happy sometimes sad, always a little lonely due to her 'in-between' status – the jam in the sandwich between the family and the rest of the servants. My other friend Sophie is from wealthier stock and she is also the only girl in a family of boys. That meant she was the natural successor to her own

Mother to run their large and sociable household, a position she saw as her duty as her parents became infirm but one she took little pleasure in. *"I'm bored, Lizzie"* she would often write and, before her parents became too dependent, she would often come to stay with us in London just so she could escape the daily grind of stretching her few tasks throughout the day. *"A waste of a good brain"* Mother would say when Sophie returned home and I agreed, sorry that she did not have the opportunity to study and to work as a growing number of women are being allowed to these days.

Charles' marriage and the stability it brought to his life meant that I began to harbour thoughts once more about my own retirement. It was now 1879, and I was still firmly entrenched as Commissioning Editor and overall manager, working every day (albeit with shorter hours every Thursday) with little or no leisure time. My main frustration was that I was keen to continue my own writing but it was hard to find enough hours in the day to do so, and I also longed to travel, to spend more time with Polly in Sweden and to indulge my other passions of art and music. Selfish though it may sound but I had come to accept the fact that I would never marry and by 1880 at the grand old age of five and thirty years, my child bearing years were slipping away. This was a relatively stable year for the Firm. The country was in quite good shape economically, the UK being responsible for 41% of all manufacturers entering world trade, far exceeding Germany's 19% and the United States' 3%.

In 1881, I offered to retire on £50 0s 0d a year and grant to Charles the managership at his own salary plus £100 0s 0d from my own which I would then give up. The matter was considered and Charles was ready for the challenge but in the end the timing was not quite right as the Firm was about to go through yet another turbulent period.

For twenty years – from the time that Papa first brought the business to London, the Warehouse had been at number 10

Stationers' Hall Court (SHC). We also had addresses at numbers 7 and 12 Ava Maria Lane between 1864 and 1869 but those were additional offices rented by Mr Crafter at extra expense and we reverted back to only having our Stationers Hall Court address in 1869. I should point out to those readers unfamiliar with SHC, that this is almost exclusively a street of publishers and booksellers, the perfect location for Papa to choose when moving down from Scotland. Firms such as ours and companies like Warren the Packing Case Maker at number 8 and Cameron & Fergusson the wholesale stationers at number 13, were cheek by jowl. At number 4 was a close friend and colleague of Papa's – Mr Whitaker (publisher of *Whitaker's Almanac*) – who you may recall had initially agreed to become an Executor for Papa's estate but after his death refused on the grounds that he was too busy. Anyway that was SHC, our business home for 20 years or so but in 1881, we decided the time had come to move as the rent at the property was due to rise far higher than we had expected and we also required more space as the intention was to expand the business.

We chose a location further west at number 12 Exeter Street, Strand, and have rented offices and warehouse space there ever since. The move was exhausting and it took months of preparation and even longer to re-organise the space to suit our needs. I was determined to start afresh and took hours planning the layout of each space to maximise the storage potential and minimise the time people spent searching for relevant material. In between times, I continued with my day to day work of proof reading, sorting out the advertising, ordering paper and other stationery, getting books in hand ready for publication and wading through the mountain of letters that poured into the business several times a day. All needed reading, replying to or disposing of depending on their contents. All of this took its toll and in 1882 I fell ill and consequently missed the Trustee meeting in February for the first and only time in the 13 years I had held the post. I had caught a chill in the cold weather that gripped the country in early January and I seemed powerless to shake it off. Mother insisted I spent some time at home and in May, following my Doctor's advice, I decided that if I was unable to retire altogether from my post, then I should at least reduce my working hours. I made plans to go to the office only on Mondays, Wednesdays and Fridays – an arrangement that suited me well. One of the key benefits for me was the chance to spend more time with young Jessie. We had grown even closer over the years with Polly long gone and the younger ones away for long spells in Europe. Jessie had a sharp mind and gentle nature and was very gifted musically. Despite spending long periods of her life on the couch, she made the most of her restricted mobility by reading vociferously and she often voiced her frustration at not contributing something to the household coffers. To this end, I encouraged her to write, and she proposed ' *A Dictionary of Handwork for the Use of Ladies – to comprise knitting, crochet and all departments of work pursued by the gentle sex'*, although sadly this was never actually published as the boys at work were not convinced of the potential market for such a book.

I also wrote in my spare time and remained fully in touch with the business on my days at home but I felt much less exhausted due to not having the daily travel. I must stop and make a little confession here about my travelling arrangements. In the early days when I went with Mother to SHC, we usually took an omnibus with the boys if we were up early enough, but Mother disliked the crowded conditions, especially if she was crushed beside a 'bowler hatted' city worker. Indeed the final straw for her came one journey I remember when she had had her skirts crushed as she was squashed between a Mother and her small child on one side and a rather unkempt looking man who smelt faintly of rotting leaves and wet grass on the other. In the end her bonnet had been dislodged by the troublesome child who refused to sit quietly on his Mama's lap, despite a myriad of disapproving stares from all directions. Poor chap, I felt sorry for him and passed him my fan to play with and that occupied him for part of the journey before he grew tired with this activity and started to pull the ribbons in his sister's hair. The journey was slow and tiresome and Mother had become very warm, her breathing quite laboured in the end and it was a relief all round when we had been deposited at our destination, a short walk from the Warehouse. After that, we always travelled by private carriage, a luxury I have continued throughout my working life.

Despite the use of a private Hackney, I still found the trip very tiring and I put my extra hours at home to good use. Most of my 'spare time' was spent bettering myself, bent over various books gathering material for my next writing project. I also whiled away many a happy hour at the piano and continued to go to as many concerts as possible and Mother and I had even attended a couple of Gilbert and Sullivan's new Savoy operas, but neither of us were that impressed. I was particularly affronted by their ridicule of female higher education and their dismissal of feminism as some kind of a joke, something that may have been reflective of the mood at the time in certain quarters (male of course) but was not a view we shared. We were more excited to read of the windows of opportunity finally being prized open for educated young women. Gilbert and Sullivan may have been appalled at such events as the first Medical School for women that opened in London in 1875 or even more exciting, the admission of women to Oxford or Cambridge universities, but Mother and I rejoiced. I say Mother rejoiced; she did celebrate such advances but has been slower to embrace change the older she gets and now has little time for politics, just when I am becoming increasingly interested in such matters. Whilst she recognised the need for reform on many levels, it was I who read out snippets from the paper about Lord Shaftsbury's (and others) attempts to eliminate at least some of the gross social injustices of the time whilst she quietly treated her own staff with respect and fairness, paying them a decent wage and ensuring that their living conditions were good. It is testimony to her kindness that our cook stayed with us for many years and Mother herself has had a great track record in keeping her maids. I despair of women ever getting the chance to vote. All adult men have not long been franchised after all, and I rile against such injustice. I have witnessed much male incompetence in my time at Griffins and conversely know of many intelligent, well informed and sensible women who simply do not have a voice. I know I have been lucky to have commanded the position I enjoy at the Firm but believe me it was hard fought for and as you know came about more by circumstance than by personal ambition.

Interestingly, despite her love of all things domestic, my sister Nelly became increasingly interested in woman's suffrage. Encouraged (Mother thought) by a distant cousin from Scotland, she joined the London Movement in about 1889 and it was a subject that caused such disagreement in our small household that we finally agreed not to discuss it at all, although in Mama's absence it was a regular topic of conversation between Nelly and I. Mother was of the opinion that men were physically and mentally superior to women – a view I once held myself, but I have changed as I have advanced in years. Perhaps I'd feel differently if Papa had lived as he had certainly been the ultimate paterfamilias when he was alive – ten children and a large household kept Mother busy enough and she was happy in this role. You might think that Mother would also have changed her view of male domination given her own business competence and dealings with men, but she never swayed from her view that deference and respect were essential features of any male-female relationship. She had after all, been born in 1823, the fifteenth child of a Sheriff substitute – a strong male head, who had enjoyed considerable authority both inside and outside the home.

Anyway, back to my request for shortened hours. There was another reason for it. Mother had grown bored with Tottenham and had planned our next move. To be fair, Tottenham was not the place it once had been. Although it was not until several years after we moved out that the Cheap Trains Act (of 1883) opened up Tottenham and other suburbs to the working class commuter (as they have recently become known), there had, during our time in the area, been an increasing diversity of residents moving in, and our part of Tottenham began to be transformed. I am not proud to report Mother's reaction at such an occurrence. She was fearful of the unknown and as a result she chose to decamp to West Kensington. Anyhoe Road to be precise, a new development away from the pocket of poverty in the northern fringes of Kensington, where many poor families teeter on the verge of destitution in the winter months as their main occupations end with the break in the London Season. Henry was instrumental in the decision of where to move, urging Mother to rent out a brand new property. He was attracted by the fact that Aynhoe Road was part of a development that benefited from having a more advanced sewage system and he enthused about the indoor bathroom. We were all excited by these indoor facilities having witnessed the extraordinary engineering and building project that was required as a vast network of drains and sewers were constructed to supply London with clean water and a reliable system of waste. Cholera stalked the city and we were initially very taken with our state of the art drainage system.

Henry kept us all up to date with the latest technological advances and this was helpful not just on a personal level but also given the Firm's speciality. For example, he had insisted we were among the first to witness the spectacle of the Embankment being lit by electrical street lights in 1878. Charles and I managed to look sufficiently impressed but Mother was dismissive, questioning the advantage over gas lamps which *"served the purpose equally well"*! Gas lighting had been the great innovation of her own childhood remember, and she was reluctant to relinquish its marvel. She may have grown up in Scotland but Mama still talked of the first gas lighting to be seen in public in time for the King's birthday in 1805, an event of such magnitude that it was a regular topic of conversation in her family throughout her childhood. Of course she grew up reliant on the soft glow of candlelight and even my early memories of Provan Side in Glasgow are shaped by the dim pool of flickering light (albeit fed by oil) illuminating certain images in my own memory – from the little table next to the bed I shared with Polly to Papa's favourite chair next to the fire in the drawing room. I loved that chair, mainly because it was from deep within its comfy depths that I would snuggle up to my father for our evening stories, fighting Richard or Polly for control of the much coveted 'page turning knee' on the nights when they joined this bedtime ritual. Of course we were all thrilled when we moved down South to The Lindens, Lawrie Park in Beckenham as there were gas lights in the house making piano playing, embroidery, reading and even eating one's meals at night, a more enjoyable experience. By their soft light we illuminated our lives quite happily, although I for one worried about the threat of leaking pipes, fearful of explosions that were not uncommon. Papa was after all a daily newspaper reader.

Henry also pressed for a telephone to be installed in the Strand offices, after he had purchased one for his own home. Although first invented in 1875 none of us had actually seen or used such a contraption. The first London telephone exchange had opened in 1879 in Coleman Street and by the late 1880's there were seven exchanges, but even by then, the connections were poor, the system terribly expensive and of course only of use if the recipient also had a telephone with which to answer our calls. Indeed Henry's excitement at having one fixed inside his house was initially tempered by the realisation that he couldn't ring anyone as none of his friends or family had a telephone to receive his calls! However, we did eventually have a telephone installed in the Warehouse and I must say Henry did benefit from being able to communicate directly with staff when he was so far away at Bexhill. I must admit that after extreme trepidation on first having a conversation with someone not in close proximity, I relish the freedom and convenience it offers. I particularly enjoyed speaking to Henry but the connection remained poor and we were regularly cut off many times and had to wait for the operator to reconnect us. I still cannot understand the technology behind this invention and am tempted to have one fixed in our house, although I know that Mother and Helen will be wary of such a miraculous and mind-baffling contraption, even though it had been invented by a Scot!

Interestingly, Henry was less interested in the bicycle and it was Charles who was the keen cyclist in our family. It was only the distance he travelled to work each day that prevented him from trying to use his Ordinary to get to the Warehouse. This I have to say looked a most uncomfortable contraption, with its large front wheel, tiny back wheel and high seat but Charles was always quick to point out his padded seat, well away from the dust kicked up by horses and carriages, and he was one of the first to upgrade to a new model when they added springs to the seat. In reality Charlie cycled at weekends and on lighter summer evenings and passed on his love of cycling to his son Charles, who has benefited from the far more streamlined models of later years. Not that I would ever be seen on a bicycle, although I know I'm old fashioned in my view that one cannot be ridden with propriety. In the last year or so there have been a far greater number of female cyclists on the roads. I believe that Alice is thinking of buying a bicycle but at the moment she is taken up with her latest social pursuit: tennis. When first introduced to the game when she was living in Wales, (for reasons I will come to explain a little later), she immediately took to it and she has recruited a group of friends with whom she plays, although she insists that none of them take it too seriously, and all struggle to run after the ball even in their special tennis attire. I think it's the excuse she has been waiting for to restrict the number of layers of corsets and petticoats she has to wear under her frock, although of course the new silk tunic she bought to play in is still worn over a long skirt and cream bodice.

They are all disadvantaged by the heels on their shoes and I once watched a game and it was amusing to see them all trying to run across the court without losing their footing and their dignity. It was fun to watch and they all seemed to be having a jolly time, but I have never been tempted to join them. They always accept my excuse of age and infirmity but in truth I've never been a sport lover and I certainly have no desire to partake in any organised physical activity. Once my sea bathing days were over, my only other form of exercise is walking and in my defence, I do ensure that I take the air at least once a day and when away on my travels, I always cover quite a few miles on foot getting to know my surroundings.

I certainly took my time exploring the new area to which we moved around Aynhoe Road in Kensington, but after only a short time, it soon became apparent that Mother was not happy with her new location. For a start, the street was much busier than Westgreen Road with more traffic and street noise than expected which did not diminish at the end of the working week. The weekends were noisy too, as Saturday shoppers could be heard enroute to the West End. Another problem I remember was the smell. Our 'state of the art' sewage system was in fact defective, often overloaded and, added to that; the busy roads were liberally spread with manure from horse drawn vehicles. The result: an unbearable stench that prevented us from opening the windows at the front of the house, especially on warmer days when such ventilation was most required. There were other teething problems with the house itself which were, to be fair, minor issues that Mother and I sorted out early on. The main problem was that the houses were so recently built when we planned to move in that the newly constructed walls were still wet. This not only meant that the wallpaper which Mother had spent weeks choosing for the hall and parlour could not be hung, but we also had to delay the date of our move for fear of inflaming Mother's bronchitis. We were patient of course and the walls duly dried sufficiently for the new wallpaper to be hung and the remainder of the walls painted. We were proud of the interior of that house and in many ways it was the smartest of all our family homes, if not the largest. *"The girls"* as I continued to call them were by now young ladies. Each had a say in the new decor and I left it to Nelly to liaise with Mother about the choice of soft furnishings. They concentrated on the front parlour, installing rich dark carpets and curtains covering the chairs in matching fabrics and adding selected porcelain on the newly polished furniture. Jessie and I were happy as long as we had room for the piano and space for our many books. Nelly was the only one around at the time of this particular move and she was still harbouring a broken heart.

I should just tell you that following her time in Frankfurt in 1881, Nelly returned to live with us and was a great asset to our household. Her organisation and practical skills were put to good use and she chose to take on much of the household duties from Mama; instructing the servants, deciding what we were all going to eat, organising our social lives (although in this she was never very successful, as Mother, Jessie and I had our own ideas on how to spend our leisure time and were not concerned by social convention or etiquette when it came to entertaining). Nelly was perfect 'wife material'. Her organisational skills could have taught Mrs Beeton a thing or two and she was as adept at keeping control of the household budget as she was managing the staff. She took pride in a scrubbed doorstep, polished windowsill and blazing hearth whilst sadly young Jessie and I overlooked such domesticity and our tendency to leave our books, tumblers or needlework wherever they were last used was a common cause of angst for our younger sibling. Not that she had to do any tidying herself of course, but she simply loved order. *"Everything in its place"* was her motto and we learnt to respect her wishes at least in communal areas, on the understanding that our bedrooms were out of bounds. How she longed to organise Jessie's room which was full of ornaments. Shelves with delicate carvings on the edges and sides flanked her dressing table (itself crammed with brushes, powders, gloves and perfume) and on her shelves a range of bottles, vases and porcelain collected since childhood. She had started being a collector at a very young age, largely in response to the gifts Papa used to give her on return from his travels. We each continued this trend, keen to offer some compensation for her lack of mobility and her nature was such that she delighted in such presents, relishing each treasure whatever its worth as if it were a piece of gold. There was one item in the communal rooms that was 'out of bounds' to Nelly and that was our piano. A sacred object that Nelly would have loved to hide beneath a silk drape *"for neatness sake Lizzie"* but one that the rest of us fought to leave unadorned.

Nelly's intention was to set up her own home one day and she took great pride in her appearance in the hope that she would woo a suitable suitor. Her patience appeared to have paid off when, on her return from a trip visiting a friend in Ripon in Yorkshire, she was positively coy in her description of the family (other than to establish the magnitude of their wealth) and, in due course, a romance developed between herself and the elder brother of her friend, a gentleman by the name of Samuel. Mama and I thought nothing of the fact that he rarely travelled down from Yorkshire. Hetty (Nelly's friend) was forever writing, and regularly proffered invitations to my sister to travel up North. Perhaps we should have seen it coming but it was not until after a courtship of some 18 months (where not a great deal happened to be frank), that Nelly's beau came to stay and finally asked Mother for her daughter's hand in marriage. Sadly no ceremony ever took place. Just when Nelly and Alice had worked themselves up into a lather of excitement and a date had been set for 19th January 1887, the wedding was called off when a rather curt note arrived from Samuel informing Nelly that he had fallen in love with another girl: a girl who, it turned out, his family favoured due to her Yorkshire roots and the small matter of her father's thriving Mill in nearby Knaresborough. Poor Nelly was devastated. She had just secured a cheque for £30 from the Trustees to buy the 'necessary' requirements of a young bride and she was inconsolable. I secretly rejoiced, having not taken to the cowardly Samuel during the courtship, but as time went on and Nelly's mood failed to improve even I came to hope that he would change his mind. No such luck. Instead it was a sombre Christmas that year and we all looked to Alice to lighten the atmosphere with tales of her *"little ones"*.

Not her own little ones I hasten to add for Alice also remained unmarried. No, Alice had found her vocation. After forever being the 'little one' in our family she had expressed a desire from a young age to become a Kindergarten teacher. This did not surprise Mama or me in the least. Whenever friends or family had visited with young children, it was Alice who entertained them. Like bees to a honeypot, they would swarm around her, holding out their chubby hands and, with trusting eyes and a shy smile, they would disappear to her bedroom to play. Alice could also be found on such occasions sometimes kneeling in the garden inspecting a ladybird, occasionally stooped over a palette of messy paints at the kitchen table and often on all fours careering around the house with a squealing toddler clinging to her back. All the while she would be singing, chatting or laughing and so it was no surprise at all when she expressed a strong desire to become a teacher. Alice, like Nelly, had been sent to Germany but to a different establishment – to a Froebel Institute. Unlike Nelly and me she did not enjoy the experience one little bit. She had been infected with a nasty stomach bug en route to Frankfurt and it took its toll on her at a time when she should have been establishing herself and making friends. Instead she never settled and confessed to me on her return that she disliked her fellow students. More importantly for Alice she disliked the food. So she had returned much thinner and with painful memories of her time abroad but she had at least enjoyed the subject she had been sent to study. She enthused about what she had learnt

and Mother enrolled her in a new school in Sussex, near Arundel. She then went on to teach at Bedford Kindergarten and Training College. It was there that she developed a new Apparatus for teaching young children based on her love of singing and on her observations over the years about how engaging and instructive music could be in teaching very young children. I am very proud of Alice. Whilst she never knew Papa, she looks the most like him with her thick dark hair, eyes the colour of treacle and ready smile. She is kind and generous, although quite highly strung and emotional and she has certainly brought plenty of fun and laughter to our household. The singing apparatus she developed was taken on by several kindergartens and was particularly keenly adopted by Miss Sims, the headmistress of Bedford Kindergarten. Sadly the apparatus never became widely available due to poor publicity, a tragedy considering that those who did buy into its system – based on the Tonic Sol-fa and Cliè
ve Methods aimed at encouraging correct intonation and purity of sound from the outset – were effusive in their praise of it and reported excellent results with their youngsters. Alice herself had taken it to our local school in South Kensington and they embraced it, encouraged by its simplicity and by the fact that groups of children could be taught together.

Anyway, enough of the sales pitch. The fact was that Alice was showing another of Papa's characteristics, an entrepreneurial streak and Henry helped her to market her product by drawing up a compelling prospectus to sell the system to prospective clients. A great idea, but not really suitable for Charles Griffin & Co to publish. We did find another interested party – a small publishing house in Soho who specialised in educational material for the very young, but they never achieved the distribution that was promised before the deal was struck – hence its limited success. After this excitement, Alice settled down to her teaching and she worked in a variety of institutions ending up in Swansea in 1892 as I will tell you later.

Back to 1886 – the year after poor Nelly lost her beloved. After our miserable Christmas, Mama thought we all needed a change of scene and, having never fully settled in our house in Aynhoe Road, she suggested yet another move. This time she chose to venture further afield and (rather bravely I thought at the time) planned to rent another new house. There were plenty to choose from. The mid to late 1880's had witnessed a rapid growth in suburban development and by the time of this latest move there were much improved transport links between the banks of the River Thames making south of the River more accessible. There was now no toll on the pedestrian traffic on Southwark Bridge, special suburban surface lines had been built in the area and most of the left bank termini were in operation. However, it was not just the improvements in transport links and the disappointment with the quality of the building work in Aynhoe Road, or even the desire for a change of scene that prompted Mother's decision for another house move. We had long discussed a feeling of unease about the environment around our home as the area in which we lived had changed and our mainly female household started to feel a little vulnerable.

If you will allow, it is worth taking stock of the economic and social conditions of the time, just so you can understand our feelings of unrest. 1886, after a bitterly cold winter which had put many Londoners in the building trade and the docks out of work, was the year a crowd of about 20,000 demonstrated – at first peacefully in Trafalgar Square and then more violently. The crowd smashed shop windows and turned over carriages as they walked to Hyde Park and the reports of this mob violence were truly terrifying. As had been the case in Tottenham, we had other problems as our sanitary conditions seemed to be getting worse and our corner of West Kensington was becoming increasingly congested and noisy. And so it was that Mother and I decided between us on a move to Streatham Hill. After a few weeks searching we had come across a new development being built by Sutton & Dudley: an estate called

Telford Park. This particular estate appealed to Mother because it was relatively low in density and height. After our teething problems with Aynhoe Road we were naturally more cautious about signing a new lease until we had assurances the new house would be ready for us in time. Not surprisingly, Mama was particularly wary about the sanitary condition of the property and wrote to Sutton & Dudley in May for assurance that they would be responsible for repairing any damage to pipe work caused by frost etc. On 12th May – the day after we had received a letter with such an assurance, an agreement for tenancy of 15 Criffel Avenue, Telford Park, was prepared.

I remember everything about this house quite clearly because Mama was so careful before signing on the dotted line. The tenancy agreement was to run from Midsummer 1886 for three years at a rent of £55 per annum with an insurance payment of 12s 0d per annum. The beauty of renting a brand new property (and one asset we had not been able to utilise in Kensington as the house was finished when we moved in), was the ability to get the developers to work on the finer details and prepare the house to our particular taste. For example, Mama and I asked for the floors to be stained and varnished in the dining room, drawing room and front best bedroom and we were able to arrange for a length of carpet to be laid as required in the dining room (the room was well proportioned and there was still plenty of space for our large sideboard). Mother naturally had the largest and best bedroom with Harry occupying the smaller room at the back (for he had yet to move to Sussex at this point), and Jessie and I the other room on that floor which overlooked the small walled garden. The girls were to share a room on the next floor (this was really Nelly's room with Alice joining her when she was home in the holidays), and there were two tiny servants' bedrooms in the attic. Mother was kept very busy planning the move and she enlisted Nelly's assistance with the arrangements. This seemed to help take my sister's mind off her romantic interlude and I recall many an evening when I returned from the office to find the pair once again huddled over house plans, or flicking through a drapery catalogue arguing over the best colours for the curtains. I was far too busy to help, as any spare time I had was directed at my latest venture, a new book I was near to completing.

I had long been fascinated by the trends in church attendance amongst different strata of society and like others at this time, was alarmed by the growing tendency for some groups to stay away from the Church. Even in rural parishes, there has been an upsurge of alternative religion and far more worrying a growing trend of nonattendance. Once seen as an essential part of life, the Church had for some become a less compelling attraction and I was keen to find out why. My book was in fact a series of chapters, each of which presented one of London's ordinary men and women producing an excuse as to why they didn't attend church. I then went on to explain what may be done to attract each one back to the fold. What made me feel I had any insight or qualifications to make such suggestions you may well ask? Well I, for many years, had been a lay helper in the Anglican Church. I have spent years every week attending whichever was our nearest Church of England house of God and I consider myself, as you will recall, a deeply religious person. In addition, I have not been blind to the extreme poverty that surrounds me in London and shudder still at the sights I have seen around me of destitute children in rags begging for food, women with drawn pinched faces hardened by years of 'making ends meet', men with deeply lined skin, engraved in the filth and dirt they are forced to live with. Squalor is one reason why the poor have turned away from the church. How can they believe in a God who gives them so little and how can they spare a Sunday when they could be out searching for food, shelter or the chance to earn a few extra pennies? I do think that many missionaries, priests and preachers are increasingly divorced from the plights of the working man. I am in support of the Church of England Working Man's

Society that was founded in 1876 in St Alban's Church, Holborn,
where the priest there – a certain Father Alexander Herriot
Mackonochie (there's a good Scottish name if ever I heard one) –
specifically aims his preaching at the poor. His particular form of
religion – he is known as a Ritualist – is quite high Church – and
involves himself and his church taking on the mantle of poverty
themselves. I have to confess as a very privileged member of the
upper middle classes, I could never become a Ritualist myself, but in
my research for this book I was interested to find out more about the
different sects within the church and I do think we cannot ignore the
challenges ahead. Without the moral, spiritual code of the church
surely anarchy lies?

I spent many months researching for my book and I lost count of the
number of hours I read and re-read the Bible and, as ever I drew
inspiration from my beloved Beethoven and added quotes from
various philosophical works. I discussed in length George Eliot's
Adam Bede – a book I find totally fascinating – as well as quoting
from other literary work such as John Bunyan's *Pilgrim's Progress*,
Miss Ellice Hopkins's *Work amongst Working Men* and the poems of
Robert Burns. I also added facts about suicide rates and other census
data to back up my arguments. It was a great personal challenge to
me but one I am particularly proud of, even though it only made it
into a second edition (in 1887) after publication. Coming from my
own position where the church is central to my life (as with Mama I
attend three services every Sunday as well as a discussion group on
Sunday evenings), I felt it my duty to consider such a worrying
decline in church attendance. Not for me all the pomp and
ceremony of the Roman Catholic Church or the peculiarities of the
various sects that have sprung up on the edge of the Church of
England. No, I try to live my life according to the Good Book and I
thoroughly enjoy my time in Sunday school, working with the
young people as they are shaped and moulded ready for the wider
world. In my book I extol the benefits of foreign travel, although I

realise that I am privileged to be able to partake of such a spiritual and mentally stimulating activity.

Back to the house move to Criffel Avenue, which inevitably came with costs and we had to budget hard for the soft furnishings and also the blinds, the curtains and the bookcases that were to be newly installed, let alone the physical cost of moving. We employed a first rate team for this task. Very cheery fellows from Pimlico who charged us £4 18s 0d for removing all our general furniture. I found the bill the other day (that's how I can be so exact on the price) and I can still remember Mama insisting we all packed our own china, glass and ornaments in case of damage. The reminder of her precious glass vase that was broken in our move to North Kensington being sufficient evidence that *"these men are strong but not careful"*. And so we moved in May and settled into life south of the river. Henry and I quickly adjusted to our longer journey to work. I was by then of course working fewer days in the office and took to working at home one day a week if possible.

Whilst the others were busy with our new house, I had other projects on the go. I was translating a number of books from German to English and it was about this time (until the present day I might add) that I started my work on *Hellas*. This is a mammoth task as it not only involves translating the work of E Doering; it also entails delving into the fascinating world of Greek Mythology. I love everything about the art, culture, religion and history of old Greece and this project has been one of my most challenging and time-consuming studies to date.

Meanwhile, the boys had brought some stability to our family Firm and despite his poor health; Richard was doing a good job helping me with the day to day management of what was becoming a thriving business once more. Charlie was really shaping up as a top traveller and his solid family life was a huge benefit to him. Daisy had brought the family great enrichment. The only tragedy in their otherwise blessed life was the death of their beloved second child Leonard. After their first born – a delightfully robust and cheerful boy called Charles Rae (born on the 2nd November 1881) – Leonard had followed some two years later. He too appeared at first to be in rude health. A good weight at birth, he had quickly followed his brother's milestones and by the age of one he was staggering behind his big brother, a huge grin on his face, arms windmill-style to keep his balance, legs slightly bowed as if sagging under his weight. I do remember Charlie telling me around the tragic time I am recounting of the agony that the little chap was suffering with his teeth coming through and I often remarked how tired my brother looked some mornings on his arrival at the office, even though it was the nursemaid and Daisy I might add, who got up to the fractious child in the wee hours. Charles insisted he was disturbed and he had even moved downstairs on several occasions to sleep on the chaise longue in the hope of getting some rest. We joked about this, Richard and I, but in truth were secretly a little jealous that out of the three of us, he had little ones to keep him thus occupied. And then disaster struck.

Just nine days after his first birthday, on the 23rd December 1884, a date etched forever in my mind – little Leonard died. His nurse, presumably exhausted after several sleepless nights, had made the fatal mistake of taking the baby into her bed. There he had tragically suffocated after being overlaid by her extensive girth and Charlie is haunted to this day by her screams as she discovered her cold, motionless charge. How the family suffered from this tragedy, myself included. We wept as my brother carried the little coffin into the cemetery and with help from the grave digger, lowered it into the frozen ground of Chingford Mount Cemetery at 2pm on Saturday 27th December. Daisy and Charles refused to have a church service and we stood in silence as the earth was scattered over his coffin, accompanied only by the agonising sound of Daisy's sobs.

Charles was naturally not the same after losing his little boy but the fact that Daisy was pregnant at this time with their third child, and the presence of three year old Charles Rae helped him to cope. I know that child mortality is commonplace but, just as memories of my little sister Helena's death are forever locked in my mind, no parent or sibling is untouched when they lose a loved one, however young. Charles threw himself into work, spending an increasing amount of time away from home travelling for the Firm. Daisy (not surprisingly in my opinion) refused to employ a nurse again, even after her third child – a fragile looking little girl named Doris Mary – came along on 19th July 1885. I adored my little nephew and niece and with Polly's and John Joseph's children so far away, I lavished all my attention onto Charles's offspring, and relished every milestone of the children's development. Daisy was generous in allowing me such access and, as I sit here all creaking bones and stiff joints, I recall with a smile the many occasions I would run after the little ones in the park or accompany them on trips to feed the ducks. I even visited them on several occasions when they were on holiday at the seaside, just so I could witness the delight on their faces. Daisy naturally fretted about Doris when she was very tiny but, whilst petite in stature, the infant was strong and shrugged off the usual run of childhood illnesses and grew into a delightfully feisty, quick witted toddler.

A highlight for me came in 1887 in the form of Queen Victoria's Golden Jubilee celebrations. It was June and Daisy and I took Charles Rae (then six years and very grown up for his age) to join the crowds watching the Queen's carriage as it was drawn to Westminster Abbey and then we took him to Hyde Park where he had the time of his life at the children's party there. I have to confess feeling a little less enamoured with the noise, which was deafening, as the children waved their bunting, sang and cheered their Queen. I am very patriotic however, and am a great admirer of the Queen. It may have taken her until Disraeli came onto the scene in 1874 to resume her public duties, but no-one can deny her dedication to her subjects throughout her 50 year reign. The banquet held in her honour at Buckingham Palace was greatly talked about across the whole of the Kingdom. Invited guests included all the crowned heads of Europe, most of whom were related to Victoria in some way. I may have the greatest admiration and respect for our Queen but I know she would not approve of my working status. She has made it no secret that she frowns upon the idea of women holding professions even though she also strongly objects to the conditions imposed on women and children in the mines and factories that thrived at this time.

After the excitement of the joyous Golden Jubilee celebrations, we settled into a new routine as we became accustomed to life south of the river. Being further from Charles's family was one of the biggest penalties of the move but we kept in regular contact. As 1888 unfolded and the terrible reign of Jack the Ripper gripped the nation, Mama was mightily glad of our relocation. We were left to fret over Daisy's safety especially when Charlie was away, as Whitechapel, the Ripper's hunting ground, was not that far away from their home in Stamford Hill. The newspapers were full of the gory details of throat slitting and seemed in my opinion to elaborate, even glorify, events, treating the story like a real life detective adventure, not unlike Arthur Conan Doyle's new Sherlock Holmes' novel *A Study in Scarlet*, a book that had become a firm favourite in our house, particularly with Henry.

The next couple of years are a little blurred in my memory, as I was so busy, either at work, researching my book, attending church, or taking the occasional trip to a concert. Mama continued to congratulate herself on our move south of the river after an uneasy summer in 1889, which was remembered for a growing sense of unrest amongst a huge section of London's poor classes. It all started in West India Dock - a strike that within a week had ground the

London docks to a standstill. Three weeks later and it was the bosses that caved in, significantly shifting the power to the underdogs. Never in my lifetime did I think I would see such a thing and it left Mother and I and members of the upper and middle classes uneasy and a little scared of the potential repercussion of such a shift in power. There was no evidence of any of this in our growing establishment however and the late 1880's signified a period of relative stability for the Firm and was certainly a time of few staff leaving us.

I did manage some weekends away to family or friends but I seem to have fewer letters of significance to refer back to for these years, and, as I grew more confident in managing the business, I began to recognise the need for more leisure time. The Firm had consumed my every waking hour and I decided it was time for more balance in my life. I loved to visit art galleries in town and marvelled at the work of Constable, Turner and Gainsborough – so gifted and each so different in style. My favourite however were the Pre-Raphaelites with their romantic, rather beautiful images; but I also loved the pictures that told stories: pictures that depicted real life as never before. Artists like Gustave Dore, a French painter who's *London: A pilgrimage* we published in 1872, depicting an image of Victorian life I recognised completely – at least in terms of the city I had viewed from my carriage window. And if I craved escapism, I'd look for the work of the Cranbrook Colony, men who immersed themselves in rural life and depicted a somewhat rose tinted view of life there. Paintings by artists like Thomas Webster who invoked happy memories of my siblings' childhood (if not my own), during our short stay in Kent – even though we were not living a particularly rural existence in Swanscombe, being well within the village boundary. I never tried to paint myself. I left that to Alice and Nelly who were both much more gifted than I in that way, although neither would agree if they heard me say so. Appreciation of art was something I had in common with Nelly and she would often join me when I travelled up to Town. We used to memorise every last brush stroke of our favourite paintings and play a game on our return with Jessie. We both had to build up an image of our choice using elaborate descriptions of the paintings so that Jessie could visualise each masterpiece and make her own preference. I have a tear in my eye as I write of this game, as Jessie was such a cheerfully willing participant, despite her inevitable frustration at not being able to travel with us to see such masterpieces at first hand. I think of all of us young Jessie was the strongest and most stoic of the family and I am so very proud of her.

The years slipped by with surprising speed and we all focussed on 'getting on with our lives', although in my case Griffins still took up most of my time and I fully intended to leave the Firm when the Trust expired. However when the business finally incorporated as a Limited Company on the 22nd December 1891, I was persuaded to continue as Managing Director. We formed a new company under the guidance of Vallance and Vallance, enabled by a ruling in the High Court of Justice Chancery division on 23rd November 1891. This agreed that the Trustees could wind up the Trust and sell the Firm to a new limited company. This we formally named Charles Griffin and Company Ltd and made sure that provision was made for Mama according to the terms of Papa's will. The case was formally made between us three Trustees (Mother, Richard and I) and the other members of the family (namely Charles James, Henry Brougham, Mary Ann Eliza, Jessie Jane, John Joseph, Helen and Alice). In addition, Charles' son Charles Rae was named as was Helen Rae. Each of these direct family members was issued with shares.

I was six and forty years old and because of all the extra work surrounding the creation of the Limited Company, I had been working practically full time, and this began to take its toll on my health. The added pressure of these additional hours really took it out of me and in the spring of 1892 I became unwell. I seemed unable to shake off the illness. Mother suggested I take some time away from London to recuperate. Germany was my natural choice. I loved everything about this progressive country, relishing its language, heritage and people and I knew that a trip there would be the ideal tonic to my flagging mental and physical health. I left for the continent in such a hurry that one piece of my luggage was overlooked and I had to write to Henry to arrange for my little box to be sent on. I could not resist taking work with me of course, and spent a good part of my time in Germany responding to various letters regarding the business. I had to keep in touch and would not have agreed to take this leave had I not made Richard promise to keep me informed and provide my forwarding address to relevant clients and suppliers and the business I conducted when I was away has stuck firmly in my memory. For example, I remember having various correspondence with Messrs A & C Black (from whom we were buying electros) about some illustrations needed for Dr Le Neve Foster's *Textbook of Mining* and I kept in touch with my work as Commissioning Editor, writing to prospective authors about their proposed work as well as encouraging our existing list of authors to write further for the Firm. I also insisted that Richard kept me up to date with the company's finances. I was sent details of Charles' earnings so I could keep a track of how much commission he was granted on sales made in the town (i.e. to London booksellers). In addition, I had to keep an eye on the expenditure of producing *Hellas* as I was concerned about the spiralling cost of typesetting especially after making my many changes. I felt much happier keeping abreast of events and it eased my conscience no end as I was otherwise having such a pleasant break away from London.

Chapter 7

My chosen location was a small town in Germany called Gottingen and, having arrived on 31ˢᵗ March 1892, I did not return to England until the summer. I reported my safe arrival to Mother and mentioned the snow which made such a pretty scene for me to describe in my long letters back home, and I stayed in that town for a month or so. Gottingen was almost as familiar to me as my own home in London and I had visited the little town so many times I was becoming quite well known amongst the local townspeople. My hosts were long standing family friends, with whom I had stayed before and who regularly made the trip to England. Frau Agnes was Scottish by birth, and is some distant relative of Mamas by virtue of a shared maternal cousin and she had married Herr Muller just before my parents were betrothed. Agnes had over the years developed a slight stoop, meaning that her eyes were permanently cast to the floor, but this failed to dampen her enthusiasm for life and she was so devoted to her husband even after all these years that she smiled like a fox with a bellyful of chickens whenever he came into the room.

They were the perfect hosts, despite having to attend to Herr Muller's elderly Mother who had lived with them since his father's death many years previously. Frau Muller was a typical elderly German lady, big boned; she had thickened over the years around the waist giving the folds of her neck and her disproportionately small head a bird-like air. Unlike Agnes, she remained upright and strong of limb despite her snow white hair in its customary tight bun and row of bristles on her chin and she was rarely seen in the evening without needles in hand working on a worsted stocking. Her mind remained sharp after a lifetime devoted to setting an example for others to follow and yet she spoke very little English, it not being considered necessary for girls to learn any other language than their own when she was growing up. She did know the odd phrase – her favourite being *"me 'ope you are well today"* and *"sorry I no spik English vell"* – but otherwise we conversed entirely in German, and I had learnt to love her dour, gentle nature. The house was much quieter these days, as all of the Muller children had long since grown up and left the family home, but two had married local men and I always made a point of visiting them when I was in Gottingen, particularly Hetty the eldest of the Muller children with whom I shared many common interests. My visit that year was deliberately designed to coincide with Easter, as I know no other place to celebrate the conclusion of Lent as elaborately as this quaint German town. As is customary in Germany, much was made of the start of Lent, which was marked with a fair amount of pomp and ceremony, but it was the Easter Possession that kept the weary townsfolk on their pious path during Lent. Confectioners spent a good part of the year planning their magnificent displays of chocolate sculptures, sumptuous coloured bon bons and extravagantly wrapped candies. Meanwhile the Easter Festival was the talk of the town. No sooner had I unpacked my case and carefully hung my velvet emerald gown on the hook in the guest bedroom, than had I been sucked into the minutiae of the pre-Festival build up.

As I sit here pen in hand recalling this event, I can still feel the knot of anticipation in my stomach and hear the noise of the drums from the marching band still ringing in my ears. I had sat with the family and their close friends on the first floor of their townhouse, at the window overlooking the market square. Hetty's boys, high on a mixture of anticipation and sugar, shrieked with excitement causing many a 'tut' from the elder members of the group as they wove in and out of our legs, brushing their sticky hands against 'best' dresses as they went, at least until a spilt drink and frayed nerves led their Mother to fretfully pull them to one side with the false promise of impending activity. To be fair there was a palpable air of anticipation on the streets. Sadly the weather was not kind that year and the snow had given way to drizzling rain, which filled the paving stones with an inky fluid forcing the country folk to huddle on the steps of houses and shops to the great annoyance of those within. At last the first of the carriages rumbled past and we were all transfixed with the visual feast that followed. Clowns and knights of the Middle Ages jostled with overgrown school boys and my ears were assaulted by a cacophony of uncouth sounds heard through the open windows – baying trumpets, beating drums and the grind of hand organs mixed with the squeak of tin whistles and shouts from the festival revellers. I was reminded of a much earlier time when Polly and I had joined the family for another celebration, that time to mark the start of Lent. On that occasion we had had the perfect view as the weather was fine and warm allowing us to sit on the balcony. Polly was almost sick with excitement as we were joined by a couple of handsome German cousins and she spent much of the day trying to engage in conversation with the taller of the two (I forget his name) who I secretly found rather vacuous. I remember Mama had sent over our prettiest dresses for the event – mine a primrose yellow with a soft fur mantle, which I had hardly needed despite the February date. I could have done with that mantle during the Easter Festival in 1892, for I remember feeling chilled, my limbs stiff with cold (and age I suppose) as I stood behind Frau Agnes watching the rain which fell in torrents, dampening the skin, if not the spirits of the carnival revellers in the street below.

That earlier Lent parade had seemed an altogether livelier affair, perhaps because of my youth when I think of it now. Far from being aware of my aching back or tired legs, I was caught up in the madness of the moment, made all the more exciting as this was Polly's and my first experience of a German carnival. The minutes seemed to fly by while we stood together, drinks in hand, admiring the transformation of the town from grey to a riot of colours, as flags and banners fluttered in the wind bearing a design emblematic of some bygone civic triumph.

Finally the strains of the military band could be heard in the distance signalling the approach of the cortege and, as the last morsels of cakes and sweets were crammed into the mouths of the festival revellers below, the joking crowd gradually ceased their chatter and the Carnival King made his appearance flanked by a number of trumpeters on horseback attired in gay pink and white striped jackets. There followed a feast for the eyes: carriages of flowers a gift of flora to the Festival, a company of be-powdered bewigged soldiers, cages of apes, bands of hunters clad in green each led by the hand of a peasant girl in the picturesque traditional costume. In the middle of the procession were four ancient ladies, all rouge and crinoline, singing at the top of their quivering voices the most elaborate of operatic songs supported by a rather off-key orchestra. The following array of private carriages filled with maskers of all ranks and ages in every conceivable disguise provided plenty to view, in between ducking the shower of bon bons that poured from all sides from the balconies, the carriages and the crowds in the street. At last the climax of the possession came into view. A fifty foot high gilt chariot drawn by six horses mounted by postilions and high above all, on a level with the roofs of houses or so it seemed was the young man – the Lord of Misrule – who scattered bonbons from his great height laughing at the crowds below. The evening ball was Polly's favourite night of her entire stay in Germany, but I preferred the daytime celebrations. Whilst it was fun to plan our costumes in the weeks preceding the famous Masked Ball, I viewed it as a light hearted fun event, whilst my sister saw it as another opportunity for husband hunting.

There was no ball after the Easter Festival, just a celebratory church service which was so packed that people spilled out of the door onto the steps and the doors had to be left open so that snatches of the service could be caught by those unable to gain a seat inside. How I wish our church had similar pressures each Sunday! Instead the back pews are often empty, especially during Evensong. But that is another story, and one I have already attempted to tell; but for now, I shall continue with my tale and return to 1892, to my last ever stay in my beloved Germany. I feel very strongly the similarity between England and Germany. The same mistakes made, plus neither better nor worse lives planned, promises made and broken and I felt a renewed closeness to my host nation. Of course it helps that I speak the language and understand their customs. For those unwilling to educate themselves in the ways of their fellow continental neighbours ignorance can surely bring fear and mistrust?

I look back on my final visit with happy memories. I had spent a few weeks in quiet retreat, strolling round the pretty gardens of my friend's property, reading endlessly, and sleeping a great deal. Not that it had been all rest and no play. I had attended a number of concerts when in town. There was always plenty of private choral and instrumental groups that thrived in this corner of Germany and I have the greatest respect for the musicality of my German brethren. I believe they are more willing to extend the right hand of friendship than we in England, possibly because the life-blood seems to flow more calmly through Teutonic veins. Certainly, I have never felt lonely or threatened as a single woman in this country and have found the locals very welcoming and keen to engage in conversation. I was lucky enough to enjoy a period of weak spring sunshine a few weeks into my stay. This had allowed me time to stroll along the river, where I found the rhythm of my steps unleashed my thoughts and I was able to 'switch off' from my surroundings, allowing memories to flood back, past conversations played out in my head to the sound of my feet on the grassy banks. I would then rest awhile to enjoy the present – the beautiful winding of the river twisting like a serpent among the hills until the eye, water and sky finally merged into one. I also liked to visit one of the many street markets with rows of brightly covered stalls selling anything from cotton goods, blankets and stockings to pots and pans or hampers of cheese, before stopping at one of the many outdoor cafes along the route to enjoy a coffee, something I would never have even contemplated drinking in England. I preferred to take my refreshments outside, as I was at least able to breathe in some fresh air, something that was not always possible given the thick fog of smoke that hung round many of the cafes, concert and dining halls in German towns. Cigar smoking is now becoming just as popular in England these days something I very much regret, and it's increasingly hard to avoid its insidious odour in any social situations.

Mama wrote urging me to take the air and my only anxiety about staying in Germany came in April when Jessie sent a letter to tell me that Mother's leg was troublesome and Alice had been taken really unwell. Both of these pieces of news worried me greatly. Mother's leg (something you will note she herself failed to mention in her letters) was a concern in case it became infected, and I was mightily relieved when I had word of improvement from Daisy who was also kindly keeping in touch. Alice was more of a worry. Clearly overworked, Alice was at this time, in the spring of 1892, teaching scripture in a school in Swansea. The headmistress of the school, a Miss Vinter, did by all accounts leave much of the work to my sister and when Alice basically collapsed from nervous exhaustion, Miss Vinter refused to send for the school doctor. Alice's theory was that this was to cover up Miss Vinter's poor treatment of her employee but when she fainted, the school doctor had to be called in and Alice complained of a terrible pain in her side. I spent many a sleepless night worrying about my sister until Daisy's letter arrived telling me that she herself had travelled to Swansea to fetch Alice and on the 9th April our Doctor – Dr Davis – examined Alice and I was sent his report.

Fortunately, his diagnosis – of overwork causing an attack of the nerves, rather than any physical disease - put our minds at rest. His report also highlighted the fact that Alice had a nervous temperament something that surprised us somewhat. Although undoubtedly highly strung, we assumed that this attack of the nerves must have been the result of her time in Wales. Our man suggested she saw another Doctor – John Williams of 63 Brook Street, London - a specialist in the kind of nervous complaint that Alice had developed. Dr Williams mapped out the following regime for her. I have written it down, which is why I can accurately recount it now: a/ She must stop taking afternoon naps, b/ she must get up for breakfast, c/ she must go out three times a day and d/ she must drink five tumblers of milk a day. There was more. The Doctor went on to suggest that she must take no stimulants at all and she must interest herself as much as possible in needlework and light household duties. On no account must she return to Swansea and the family were advised that her recovery could take some time.

I feel at this point that I should let you know about two letters written by Alice that were forwarded on to me in Germany so that you can fully appreciate the state she was in at the beginning of April and how much she had improved by the end of the month. The first letter was sent to our sister Jessie and I was shocked at the childish writing style. Believe it or not, this disjointed letter with its oversized writing was supposed to record Alice being 'a little brighter'. By the 20th April the second letter she wrote was in so normal a style and content it is not hard to see why the earlier letter had worried us so.

I was glad that the family were rallying round in my absence. Charles and Daisy were really supportive as I have mentioned, Henry less so but at least he was present in the house and Richard was a regular visitor. Jessie junior was fantastic at keeping me in touch and I have kept all her letters sent to me in Gottingen. Almost as soon as Mama's leg was on the mend and Alice was on the road to recovery, there were reports that Richard's health was deteriorating. Although well used to such an occurrence, I picked up on Mama's concerns and grew uneasy. Richard was, after all a Director of Charles Griffin and Co, he was also by 1891, four and forty years old and had a long history of ill health.

Meanwhile after a delightful Easter service in my usual church in Gottingen, where the locals were as attentive and welcoming as ever, I moved on to a little place called Freiburg near Baden where one of my friends from school had settled. My stay was short, Mary having aged terribly since my last visit. I too was struggling with pain in my joints and some breathlessness I might add, but otherwise was the picture of health compared to my friend. Never before had I been as aware of the passing of time as I left Germany with the distinct feeling that I would never return.

I have indeed never been abroad since this trip but like the rest of my family, I have had regular spells at the English seaside whenever I have felt the need to boost my health. This became easier for all of us when Henry (also a director at Charles Griffin and Co, but a very infrequent visitor to the Warehouse by this time) decided to relocate to Sussex. He had recently acquired a new companion: a chocolate Labrador named Nelson, who could usually be found at his master's heels and whose utter devotion and loving temperament brought much pleasure to my brother in his advancing years. As I have already mentioned, the house he chose (in typical Henry style) was large and imposing. The redbrick establishment was distinguished as its handsome portico and substantial walls were in direct contrast to the two timber framed cottages on either side. Directly opposite the house was a superb Emporium which sold a wide variety of stock from waterproof overalls to sou'westers - essential protection from the many windswept coastal days – together with a dusty display of parasols and tartan rugs to capture the day trippers who passed en route to the beach. Not that Henry had ever had the need to step into the Emporium but he did like to admire the historic building and gaze upon the eclectic range of customers who frequented the store. His house, St Trinians, had at some point in its earlier occupancy been a small guest house, and the rooms were all large and there was a spacious hall with a separate lobby for parasols, bathing costumes and all the other beach paraphernalia. It also had a well equipped kitchen with a shiny double range which gave out a welcoming heat all year round – ideal to thaw in front of after a spell in the sea. Not that any of us swam any more sadly. No we left that to Charles and Daisy's children but we were not averse to paddling on warmer days. I always tried to engineer a visit whenever Charles Rae and Doris were staying. They had both grown up into such wonderful little companions. Charles was a serious boy whose self consciousness was at its peak now he was nearly thirteen, and little Doris who at seven more than made up for her brother's moody silences, by chattering ten to the dozen.

I had a particularly delightful holiday with the two children in the late summer of 1892. Slightly melancholy after my return from seeing Mary in Germany, I had struggled to settle back into my old routine. Mama was looking increasingly frail and Nelly and I were beginning to get worried as she was becoming rather forgetful. Certainly we had long since had a role reversal with us girls more like parent than daughters and Nelly, I am delighted to report, was an excellent carer, giving just the right amount of support without making Mother feel too dependent. After several months in London and following Henry's move I suggested to Daisy that Mama, Jessie, Nelly and I take the children on a short break to the seaside in Bexhill on Sea. We were incredibly lucky with the weather and, undeterred by a stiff East wind and misty mornings, when the grey sky merged with the angry leaden sea, we spent every day on the beach delighting in those magical moments when the sun broke through the cloud transforming the murky waters by casting prisms of sparkling light onto the rolling waves.

I can hardly believe that this holiday I refer to was barely two years ago. I have spent less time at Bexhill during these last couple of years. As I have aged I really cannot face the journey, despite its relative ease, and I do find that our favourite haunts are changing and not for the better. Perhaps my nostalgia is misplaced but on my last couple of visits we have been dismayed at the crowds on the promenade, the queues in the coffee houses and the rather distasteful sight of so many bathers in such close proximity. I can still remember the feel of the salt water on my skin as it slipped over my body like a cold glove, but the memory is fading fast because I've not swum for years. I used to be happy swimming with the other ladies in my long flannel shift well away from the men and boys, but I could not entertain the idea of mixed swimming. No I am happy to leave all that behind, although Nelly did persuade me to accompany her to Broadstairs shortly after our Bexhill on Sea break, and to be fair we spent a delightful couple of days, the highlight of which was a surprisingly accomplished symphony concert that followed the minstrel show. We had left Mother and Jessie with her maid Caroline and whilst at first we fretted for their well being, we both benefited from our little break and came back much refreshed. I may not take to the waters any more, but I love nothing better than a spell on the beach, even though my preference now is to visit out of season. The wind may howl and the dash of the waves on the cliffs sound like the sullen roar of a caged beast, but the beach is often deserted then and I feel like a young girl again, itching to run towards the turbulent sea, cheeks pink and glowing on my return to the guesthouse.

So much has happened since then. Imagine our surprise when on Christmas day 1892, three months after our seaside trip; Daisy announced she was pregnant again. Eight years after the birth of

Doris, little Jessie Alison was born on the 9th May 1893. Knowing how much Daisy and Charles yearned for more children we all shed tears of joy at her safe arrival and Mother was particularly ecstatic with the birth of her namesake. Even now that Jessie has taken her first tentative steps; Mama is obsessed with her little granddaughter. As her own mind becomes increasingly befuddled, like a muddy pool with moments of lucidity when the sediment settles, she is becoming increasingly child-like in many ways. Her short term memory is very poor. She is beginning to forget names, simple instructions and recent news and yet if you ask her about her own childhood, her Scottish upbringing or the early days of her marriage, her memory is crystal clear. That is why I was moved to document our story. As I sat and watched the white haired old lady with eyes so faded they look almost translucent, only occasionally flashing into life, her mind empty of much that she had achieved, I knew it was my duty to put pen to paper. In order that future generations like little Jessie (who incidentally adores her crooning, sedentary Grandma) is left in no doubt of the struggle she endured to keep the Firm and the family afloat.

These were my thoughts when I first started to formulate the idea of writing this book but there was one final catalyst which left me in no doubt that I had to get on with my task.

When I have finished my tale (which I can assure you is imminent) I shall be delivering my own will and planning my funeral. We have gone through the most terrible year, which has left Mama's mind shattered and when I am gone I do not want to overburden Nelly and Alice nor indeed Charlie with sorting out my affairs. Not that I have a lot to leave but I have my personal effects and a modest sum to distribute. We have been fortunate, us spinsters, that we have lived as comfortably as we have done, given the absence of a father or husband to support us.

We moved house last week. We had hoped this might help Mama's state of mind. None of us could bear the look of frantic panic on her face as she searched for Jessie. A daily occurrence that was beginning to drive us all mad.

1894 was our *annus horribilis*. The year that London celebrated the opening of Tower Bridge was a particularly sad one for us as Mama lost three of her children. I don't want to dwell on those terrible events as they are still far too raw for me. Suffice to say that we had no sooner buried Richard in March (who incidentally had gone into a nursing home in Bromley after Christmas), when Jessie became ill. We dispatched her to the seaside to stay at Henry's house in the vain hope that the sea air would do the trick. Sadly her illness became too much for her frail body to overcome and she lost her fight less than two weeks after Richard. Unlike her older brother who had written his own will and sorted out his affairs years ago, including instructions for his body to be laid to rest with Ruth in Beckenham, Jessie left no legal instructions.

Letters of Administration were duly prepared and Mama was informed as next of kin. She renounced this duty as she simply could not take on board that Jessie had gone and I took on the probating in June. I was just in the depths of this paperwork when we had notification from Henry's maid that he had taken a turn for the worse. When Jessie had been with him we had spent many days at Bexhill on Sea and I had noted with some concern my brother's pallor, his lack of appetite and the time he spent alone in his bedroom, but our focus had naturally been on Jessie, who by this point required round the clock care. Poor Henry, his decline from eligible bachelor, 'man about town' with his customary topper and ram-rod straight posture to frail, stooping, housebound old man was pitiful to watch. He had for the past year or so hardly ventured beyond the grey, venerable church at the bottom of his street, and rarely left the house at all when we were nursing Jessie. He died on

28th June, a blistering hot day – perfect seaside weather. Mama's face when she heard the news was one of total disbelief. The three funerals certainly made us all question our own mortality. My own health is not that good at present and I am fearful of what will become of Mother if I die before her.

My last entry. The final chapter in my tale is written today on the 17th April 1895 – the day I have reached my half century. We decided to have a joint celebration: my 50th birthday together with an opportunity to show off our new house. Or should I say flat. There were many reasons for this move – the main one being to distract Mother from her daily tortuous search for her invalid daughter, closely followed by a need to be located nearer to the office. I have been going into Griffins far less in recent years. You can tell that my involvement has diminished as I have focused on family events in these final few pages. Not that I have been pushed out at all, far from it, over the years I have to confess that I have felt myself equal, if not superior, to many of my male counterparts, but I am getting old and tired. Since it became a Limited company, and on Richard's death, Charles has been Company Secretary and we have also taken on a new Director. A young gentleman by the name of Francis Blight, who we poached from a rival publishing house. I have offered him a directorship as part of the package and he brings with him a solid managerial background and many contacts in the world of technical publishing. This is the direction I see the Firm continuing to develop. I know I've nurtured a strong line in Theology and Philosophy and we have remnants of Classics, English Literature, Law and History, but it is Science and Technology which remain our core subject categories. Our catalogue is growing with our reputation and I see nothing but a rosy future given the continuing trend for technological advances across all areas of science. We have been fortunate in recent years in employing a number of loyal and hard working staff. Men who have quietly accepted my involvement and bowed to my authority and simply got on with the job in hand. One employee stands out above the rest as he has been a faithful ally to me over the past ten years. Mr Brody first came to Griffins as part of the editing team, following many years at a rival House but has since taken on a number of different roles. A thin, silent man with a shuffling gait pervaded by an indescribable air of faded gentility – of having known better days – he has shown considerable patience and kindness to me over the years and has been a diligent worker. No task was too menial. Despite evidently having received the education of a gentleman, he never refused to perform menial office tasks such as signing receipts, going on errands or acting as copyist and he has provided an excellent role model for younger recruits. He too is due to retire in a couple of year's time, but I am hoping his legacy will live on. I fear some of the youngsters these days are not quite as willing to take on as many different tasks as their predecessors but in retrospect I am probably being unfair.

I must just tell you briefly about our flat at Ridgemount Gardens. It is near Gower Street and Number 30 is on the ground floor. We had to have a ground floor flat as Mother cannot manage stairs any more and this allows her to have a bedroom on the same level as the front room where she spends nearly all her time, sitting by the window staring at the tiny strip of garden that runs the length of the street. Caroline, her servant, is amazingly patient with her and the pair are quite attached to each other, Caroline having been with us for over ten years following the death of her own husband in 1882. The house is very smart I must say, thanks to Nellie's vision and her appointment of a top team of upholsterers and decorators. Although much smaller than our other houses, it perfectly suits our needs. The parlour is a sitting room and dining room combined and there is a small storeroom and a large cellar which has really helped to accommodate our possessions. My room is particularly over furnished as I have acquired most of Jessie's collection and love to sit at my desk and quietly observe their varied shapes, hearing again her voice full of delight and joy as the gifts were received.

Just as Queen Victoria is showing increasing signs of becoming more fragile and is appearing in public very infrequently these days (just two years short of her Diamond Jubilee year), so too has Mother barely socialised publically since the death of her children. My birthday was a time for celebrating a new beginning for us in London. We are not alone as, by now, one fifth of the entire population of England and Wales lives in Greater London. Mind you most of London's residents now live in the suburbs rather than in the city where we have chosen our flat and I like the fact that in the evening, when commercial life closes down for the night, we residents can reclaim our city. Nelly is less convinced and does not enjoy being so central. I agree with Eliza Lynn Linton (a female journalist who works for the *Morning Chronicle)* who feels *"in London you live; in the country you breathe"* as I have come to love city life and thrive on the energy of the capital. I do however agree with Nelly that London is a very dirty and smelly city with worsening pollution that is an inevitable by product of burning fossil fuels. The clouds of dust and smoke that hang like a shroud over most of our streets is also not good for Mama's chest and has prompted many a trip to the country or the seaside in pursuit of cleaner air. Without the need to be near the Firm both Nelly and Alice are left with fewer reasons to be in such a built up area, although both have done their fair share of shopping it has to be said. Liberty's on Regent Street is their favourite destination. I am far less interested in browsing the many departments but I confess to still enjoying the mechanical lift even at my ripe old age and it is this attraction that draws me occasionally to join my sisters on one of their many shopping jaunts.

And so I sit on the evening of my birthday with happy memories of a day spent in the bosom of my much depleted family. I am not afraid of entering my final chapter. I have been one of the lucky ones born into a life of privilege. Even though our foundations were shaken as I have described, we have survived the ordeal of losing Papa and spending years fighting for our livelihood without falling apart because we have known the safety of true love. Despite many a disagreement we have stood firm Mother and I, our principles intact and I think, no I know, that Papa would be proud that his legacy lives on. Now is a good time for an established publishing house specialising in technology, as scientific advancement seems to be gathering momentum with every passing year. Look at my beloved Germany – right at the forefront of such developments. It is a shining example of modern life. I just hope that Great Britain (so intent on concentrating on the colonies) does not get left behind. I am sensing that we are shifting to a time when our Empire is becoming over-stretched and under-defended but at the moment we continue to reap the benefits of our colonies. I know I have been lucky to live in this time; a period when Britain has been truly great and I'm proud to have witnessed such improvements in economic, political, intellectual and moral progress and yet I feel we are becoming complacent, arrogant even, as our Queen ages and our politicians argue. I can see other nations learning from our experiences and I fear we are in danger of being left behind. I don't mean in the production of consumer goods as we have a huge market to sell our products to – far greater than America and Germany for example – and we continue to lead the way in agriculture, finance and distribution. Thank goodness for the efficiency and dynamism of our Stock Exchange I say. Like Henry, I too welcome this newly mechanised world in which we now live, not least because it has reduced our household bills in recent years. Prices of food and industrial goods have declined sharply, steam power has mechanised many trades and British industry has been boosted by greater purchasing power, although we at Griffins have worked hard to keep a check on wage increases to keep our expenditure down. We have, however, been able to reward the loyalty of our longer-serving staff and as I have gradually reduced my working hours, the extra salary I was awarded last year has proved a bonus.

My work at Charles Griffin & Co Ltd has not come to an end. I still go to the Warehouse most days but I'm supported by Francis who is shaping up to be a top manager and of course Charles who is my first port of call if I have any new material or any issues with our authors. I also have high hopes for young Charles Rae who has recently moved to Tonbridge School in Kent and is already showing an interest in the business – not that his father would have given him any choice, it would be his duty as eldest son to enter the Firm.

As well as the business and my family, I have another focus these days: my work in the Church. Since our move I have found a new place to worship: St Peter's in Regent Street and there is plenty to occupy me there. Along with Alice and Nelly, I have volunteered as a helper at the Working Girls Club. An apt title really given I have been a working girl most of my adult life, although these young girls have none of my privileges, my choices and my lifestyle and deserve a chance in life. I love my Sunday classes with the girls. Many were denied a proper education and are learning to read and we spend valuable time together discussing the teachings of the Bible. And so I look back on my life with contentment. It may not have followed the path I had initially hoped for as a child, nor indeed the one expected of me as a young Victorian lady, but it has been fulfilling all the same. What the future holds for me is in God's hands but I feel at last that Papa's beloved Firm is safe.

I dedicate this book to the next generation of Griffins in the hope that they will read it and marvel at how different their lives would have been had their GrandMother not been so brave and strong and against all the odds managed to keep the Griffin's publishing house alive.

Epilogue

Whenever I read a novel, I am disappointed if I am not sufficiently informed of what the future holds for the main characters, even though I appreciate I am meant to use my imagination. None is required in this case as this is a book based on fact and I have all the evidence needed to document exactly what happened to the family and to the Firm from the time we left Elizabeth about to write her will. I have focussed on the Griffin line from which I descend, as it was this branch that stayed in the Firm and whose fortunes were bound up in the publishing world.

Elizabeth Eaves worked tirelessly for Griffins until her death on 6th February 1899, dying before her mother Jessie, who by this point was the grand old age of 76 years. At the time of Lizzie's death the family shareholders in Griffins had fallen from ten on foundation to just five: Jessie, Mary Ann, Charles James, Helen and Alice. There were no family members working as Directors but whilst Charles James was not on the Board, he assumed the Chairmanship and was voted as a director at the First General meeting after Elizabeth's death. Charles' son Charles Rae had by this time left school and spent time at William Heinemann and Simpkin Marshall Hamilton – a book publisher and wholesale bookseller respectively – learning the trade and was primed to support his father. Like previous and future generations of Griffin boys, he was destined to learn the ropes from the bottom up and started work at the Firm in January 1902 as a clerk before moving into the sales department.

Meanwhile his Grandmother Jessie had never recovered from Lizzie's death. Not surprisingly, the family chose to move again, but this time it was without Alice who back in February 1897 at the ripe old age of 34 years had surprised the family by marrying. This is likely to have been a high point for Helen, Lizzie and Jessie just three years after their *annus horribulus*, especially as her betrothed – Thomas Muckalt- was by all accounts quite a catch. Thomas was a lawyer based in Hest Bank, Lancashire, but he maintained London connections so we can assume that in his capacity as a provincial lawyer, he met Alice in London. Alice moved up North from this date and late in 1897 or early 1898, she bore her first child: Jessie Agnes Rae Muckalt – the child was later to be mentioned in Elizabeth's will, added in a codicil. Lizzie was Jessie's Godmother and bequeathed her watch and chain and gold necklet to the child. Alice went on to bear another child – Thomas – a couple of years later but by then Elizabeth was dead. Although Alice and her husband were both allocated shares on Lizzie's death, within a few months Thomas had transferred all his share to his wife and there was clearly a rift between the families but we are not sure why. When Alice died in September 1913 she naturally left her shares to her husband but when Thomas himself finally died some 20 years later, he stated in his will that he had no shares as he *"did not claim the interest given to him by his said wife in her will by deed registered with the Inland Revenue"*. Young Jessie followed her Godmother's path and remained a spinster, whilst Thomas married, but neither had any interest or dealings with the Firm (presumably due to their father's lack of contact).

Back to Helen and Jessie senior's move following Lizzie's death. The couple chose to relocate outside of London and never returned to the metropolis. Caroline Freeman, Jessie's faithful servant moved with them and they settled at 12 Sea Road, Bexhill – not far from Henry's old address and in a town that they clearly knew quite well. The final straw for Jessie was possibly the news of the death in Sweden of her eldest child Mary Ann Eliza Rae (or Polly as we knew her) on 22nd September 1902. We are not sure quite what happened to Jessie from that date until her own death on Wednesday 10th March 1909 at the age of 85 years. She was described on her death certificate as 'of The Vineyard, Ticehurst Sussex' - a building long since demolished but by all accounts this was part of Ticehurst House, described as one of the oldest mental hospitals in the UK. We can assume that Jessie's poor, tired mind, stricken by the loss of so many of her children had quietly given out. Her will was proved on 3rd May 1910 to Francis Blight as sole surviving Executor. It had been made out at 12 Sea Road, Bexhill on 15th June 1899 – not long after she had moved there with Helen. The will was witnessed by John D Vallance and one of his clerks. The executors were her son Charles James Griffin and Francis Blight, to each of whom she left £100 (or 10 each of any Charles Griffin and Co shares she might hold as they chose). To Helen she left all her furniture, plate etc. She left only one bequest: £200 to J Agnes Muckalt (Alice's daughter) for her to receive when she reached the age of 21.

And so ended the life of a remarkable woman.

So what happened to Helen? Apart from the 'near marriage' back in 1886, Nellie had devoted her life to care for her mother and to run their household. When her sisters and mother died she must have felt very lonely especially as Jessie was clearly senile in her final years. Ironically, her own involvement with the Firm increased at this point almost by default. When Lizzie died Helen not only had more shares transferred into her name, she was also elected onto the Board on 24th March 1899 – another family member to support Charles James. After Jessie's and Mary Ann's death she acquired yet more shares and by 10th March 1909 Helen was one of only two Directors of Charles Griffin and Co Ltd following the death of Charles in 1907 – an event I shall come back to.

Helen moved again after Jessie's death with Caroline who transferred her loyalty and affection to Nellie and on 24th October 1911 she was resident at The Dell, Buckhurst Road, Bexhill on Sea although this was not her final address as, on 1st March 1912, she acquired the freehold to 4 Rotherfield Avenue, Bexhill on Sea. Helen drew up her will on 9th March 1927 at the age of 67. In it she appoints Charles Rae and John Daniel Vallance as her Trustees and Executors and the second clause seems to be prophetic: *"I desire that my funeral be conducted in a plain and simple manner and that my remains be buried in or near to the place in which I may happen to die and be not transported to some distant place of interment"*. In light of how she died, this statement is interesting. Perhaps she was planning her own demise even then? Sadly, Helen Florence died sometime between the 14th and 29th June 1927, the uncertainty being because she committed suicide by drinking spirits of salts (an acid poison) in Warren Wood, Balcombe Sussex at some time unknown between these dates. We are not sure if anyone ever carried out the second clause of her will.

Back to 1907, the year that left Alice Emma Griffin (Daisy) a widow. Other than the tragedy of Leonard's death, Daisy and Charles James appeared to have enjoyed a happy marriage and Charles (although maybe not using his top mathematical brain) was, for many years, a successful traveller for the Firm. Looking at a commission statement for the period between 1889 and 1890 it would suggest that he drew a relatively modest salary in that period (£187 10s 0d) and on top of that he received commission of £179 2s 3d. Despite working in the Firm for many years and also holding the position of Company Secretary, it was not until after Lizzie's death that he was elected a director in March 1899. We know his exclusion from the Board was a sore point with him for years as, during this time he had attended Board meetings as Secretary and inserted several complaining notes into the margins of the minute books. There was a good reason for this however, and one that is referred to and documented in the Board Meetings on several occasions: his love of the bottle. Maybe without Daisy he too would have drunk himself into an early grave like his brother Alex? Who knows? What we can assume is that his drinking was a concern for the company directors and on one occasion Charles himself was forced to record several paragraphs in the minute books to the effect that his job as a traveller could only continue if he remained teetotal for the following months: he was clearly some way off being considered reliable enough to be taken onto the Board. We are not sure exactly what prompted this ultimatum. Presumably Charles had run into some kind of trouble, and his drinking had escalated, and he certainly suffered from gout in later years.

Francis Blight, the Managing Director, was criticised by younger members of the Griffin clan, largely because he was thought to have blocked Charles on several occasions. However under his managerial directorship, the Griffin catalogue achieved its largest technical coverage since Charles Griffin's tenure before 1860. Throughout all of Charles' troubles, Daisy was a faithful and loyal wife, and the couple celebrated their silver wedding anniversary on 18th November 1905. On 1st July 1907 Charles retired. It may be that he was unwell: he was suffering from appendicitis at the time. Within a few weeks he had died *"after a brief illness and an operation for appendices"*. The company recorded the death and a trade notice was produced by C G & Co printed with a modest black-edged mourning band. Charles was buried in the same grave in which Leonard had been laid rest in Chingford Mount Ceremony on 28th August 1907. The sum of £3 17s 0d was paid for digging the grave to 13 ft depth. A further fee of £2 s 6d was paid on 31st August to turf the grave.

Even before Charles' death, his son Charles Rae Griffin was placed in a quandary. His wedding had been planned and arrangements made for 7th September 1907 but the engaged couple expressed their concerns about going ahead with the celebration to Charles senior who by that time was dangerously ill. Before he died, Charles insisted that the wedding take place whatever happened and so the couple went ahead with the ceremony. Most of the congregation were in deep mourning, and we can assume it was rather a sombre affair.

We have a lot of details about Charles Rae and his wife Norah Margaret Lee, not only because we have been passed information down the line by their son - my Grandfather – but also because Charles Rae was a keen photographer and his life is well documented in his pictures. After his schooling in Tonbridge, Charles' inclination had been towards mechanical engineering and so he took on extra training in engineering and electronics. This knowledge stood him well in his years as Managing Director of Griffins as did the experience in two rival firms undertaken prior to his starting at the family firm. Unlike his father, Charles Rae showed a strong work ethic, a sharp business mind and more importantly, was not addicted to alcohol. More to the point, he was a Griffin, and these qualities resulted in a quick progression onto the Board of Directors and a long and successful career as Managing Director following spells as supervisor of the Reading Department (where the new manuscripts were sent) and head of the Firm's advertising. He met his wife-to-be through the Congregational church in Highbury, had a long and happy marriage, producing four children – the eldest being my Grandfather, Charles Falkner Rae Griffin in June 1908, a child who immediately became known as Rae to avoid confusion!

Meanwhile under Charles Rae's direction the Firm had been going from strength to strength during the war years. In November 1911, Charles Rae's mother Daisy transferred 51 shares to her son (these had been in a Trust and due to come to him on her death but she clearly wanted to give him more power in shareholding meetings). She also arranged that her remaining 44 shares be given to her son as a gift and these were transferred by Vallances in December. By 1916 the family were based in Mornington Crescent, Chingford. It was at this address that their third child was born – John Oswald

Griffin, a brother for Charles and Nancy Margaret (who had been born in 1911. Each year, from the start of the First World War, Charles was sent mobilisation papers. Each time the Firm submitted application for exemption from such service due to his vital job of working on technical books, which were used in all three military services. The applications for 1914, 1915 and 1916 were successful but that for 1917 was not, and on Friday 9th March 1917 Charles volunteered for service in the Royal Naval Air Service, signing on at Alexandra Palace as an AM1 (Air Mechanic First Class). We hold an anxious letter from his wife (whom he affectionately called 'Nano') written on the very day he enlisted. It is headed *"the darkest day I have every known"*. This may seem a little dramatic but the family will have already been touched by the horrific casualties of the First World War from friends, family and acquaintances, and Norah was herself to lose a brother during the conflict.

Oh the blank, my darling, my darling, I miss you with every bit of me,

it's been the longest afternoon & evening I have ever experienced, but

I'm glad to say I've cried myself dry & feel ever so much better this

evening & more so after I received your p.c. ...

> *The children have been very good; Nancy particularly was a darling all the morning alone... Rae cried when he got to bed. Misses you ever so much & prayed for all the people wanting their Daddie's! Miss Davis has been very sweet today, I'm profoundly grateful for her. You missed her out this morn. at prayers!!*
>
> *Saturday morn;*

Darling, your dear precious letters came & we gloated over them, so glad you have some congenial companions & have someone to look after, some mother's boy...

Today Mother writes begging me to bring Rae & Nancy over tomorrow to see Auntie Maggie, so I shall I think leave John it's too cold...

Write tomorrow.

Meanwhile by the time of the First World War, no other British publisher had a stronger technical list. From Mining to Manufacture, from the supply of Electric power to Waste disposal, Griffins had books describing trade practice. The distinctiveness of the Griffin books even extended to its red covers and right through into the 1970's, the Griffin list – by then with a different main specialisation – retained a few world renowned texts on how to develop and use dyestuffs; how to design and build docks and harbours; how to spray metal to create such things as non-stick utensils; and so on. Many of these had their roots in the books developed during Francis Blight's tenure. Francis' expectations were that Charles James' son Charles Rae and his own son Horace Blight would end up taking over management in due course. Horace, a qualified accountant had joined the Firm as Secretary quickly becoming a Director and for seven years the management team experienced a period of stability and the business thrived.

The First World War stimulated the sales of exactly the kind of books that Charles Griffin & Co Ltd published as the country strove to become more efficient. Such sales also boosted the country's (and the company's) export sales. There were also new wartime requirements, and the Firm produced more than one book on Aircraft manufacture and the development of special metals and other materials.

Like Charles Rae Griffin, Horace Blight also joined the war effort but sadly he was killed. Francis' dream of a natural progression of his family in management was no longer possible, but he arranged for his son in law, Arthur Downer, to join the Firm to take on the Accounts department. He joined the board as Secretary and held shares, as did his wife and her mother. The position of Company Secretary had first been offered to John Joseph Griffin (residing remember in South Africa until his death on 18th April 1922), but he politely declined the offer and this left Charles Rae and his son Rae as the only Griffin men actively working in the Firm. The rest of the family took an interest from afar and capitalised on its success as shareholders.

Griffins was as much affected by the depression of the 1920/30 period as any other company. It weathered that storm for two reasons: belts were severely tightened, and any recovery for the country would need to be led by manufacturing. Griffin's published books that people would need all the more urgently. It also benefited from incredibly loyal, hard working staff. *The Centenary Volume* of the Firm written of course in 1920, makes particular reference to the number of 'old timers' – staff who had stayed with the Firm for, in some cases, over twenty-five years. The staff, we are told, regularly 'begged' to be allowed to work late into the evenings and frequently sacrificed their Saturday afternoons to ensure they kept up to date with their work.

1927 was an important year for the family and the Firm. In all the time since Lizzie's death Francis Blight had been Managing Director and the Board consisted of Blight, Charles Rae and Helen Florence. Blight retired seven years later, 1927 and in October Charles Rae became Managing Director. With Helen's death a new set of Directors was elected. Charles Rae became Chairman and Managing Director with Arthur Downer (Blight's son in law) and Daisy (Charles James' wife) being appointed; and in 1928, Charles Rae's son Rae joined the board. Always interested in engineering (particularly Aeronautical and Mechanical) Rae's involvement in editing new books soon strengthened the list in these fields.

It was around this time that the future key specialism for Griffins came to the fore. Apart from one book on probability theory, published in the mid-1840s, the first book on this key subject was issued just before the First World War. Yule's *An Introduction to the Theory of Statistics* was the first and only textbook available at the time to teach a subject that was becoming a vital tool in academia and industry. (Other publishers quickly saw what was happening and built up lists, but until the 1960s, Griffins was still one of the largest and best publishers of Statistics). Yule's book acted as a recruiting sergeant for others. Many big names in the subject chose Griffins as their publisher for that reason. One of Yule's statistics students (studying Geography as it happened) was later brought in to revise the book, and he too produced a classic text, the seminal *Advanced Theory of Statistics* by Maurice Kendall. He was later knighted for his services to the subject.

During the Second World War, the Firm survived largely because of the tenacity of Charles Rae. Too old to serve this time, he kept the company going despite paper rationing and staff leaving to go into the forces. One of those who went was his son Rae, who was recruited into the editing and book production arm of the Ministry of Aircraft Production. Rae like his predecessors had an inventive mind and was very practical. Whilst many of the technical books the Firm published interested him, we know that given the choice he would not have entered publishing. His passion was flying and his ambition in life was to own an aircraft manufacturing business. Grandpa Rae had, as a young man, not only built a car from scratch – a Bentley no less – he had gone on to build a plane. He knew his duty however as eldest son, and he did not pursue a different career. Charles and Norah accepted that their second son John's ambition was not to become a publisher and supported him to further his chosen profession: as an architect. A very successful architect in fact, ending up with a large practice with his own sons involved and in due course inheriting and enlarging it still further.

After the war, things slowly returned to normal, but technical publishing was becoming difficult to keep profitable. Subjects like statistics, using a lot of mathematical symbolism, called for the most expensive typesetting and relatively small print numbers. It was increasingly difficult for small independent companies to keep going, and mergers and closures followed.

James Griffin, my father and Rae's eldest son, joined in 1956 (leaving for two years of National Service and returning afterwards). For a time, during the early 1960s, three generations of Griffins were on the board at the same time!

Late 1961, Charles Rae was persuaded to retire, but sixty years of travelling to London to work had become so routine that within a few months of stopping he had died, in April 1962. And so the company was led by James Griffin, my father, with his father Rae still working full time at this point, along with a much diminished staff.

The lease of the Drury Lane office, to which the Firm had moved in 1925, expired in 1974. London, like the rest of the European Economic Community that Britain had joined just one year previous, was struggling after the energy crisis and there was a period of political and social instability, with a three way struggle between the Conservative and Labour Governments and the unions. The Board recognised the need to cut costs, and it was decided to retreat to an out-of-town address, which was only possible by putting warehousing and order-processing into the hands of an agency (Book Centre of Neasden). James and Rae supervised the move and will have gone through a similar process to Lizzie and her team when they relocated from Stationer's Court. As ever in their working life both men were 'hands on' in their roles, James being young and strong spent many hours lifting boxes, loading vans and sweeping shelves and floors in the dusty warren of rooms that made the warehouse in Drury Lane. Little did he know how dearly this activity was to cost him later in life.

Meanwhile offices were found in High Wycombe, which the Firm was to use for the next ten years or so. Halfway through this period Rae followed his father into retirement, but sadly, he too was unable to enjoy this for long before he died in June 1983.

My father James was a book loving, hard working man who was happy enough to follow his predestined path to enter the Firm. However, his time as Managing Director was the hardest the Firm had ever had to face as the company was hit by the downturn in the economy and, unlike in previous depressions, the company's specialism in highly technical books was not its ticket to survival. In 1979 there occurred a milestone in British history with the election of the first female Prime Minister, but the Prime Minister's tenure was not a happy time for the Firm. The years 1979-1982 were particularly tough as Margaret Thatcher launched a monetarist revolution in Britain and cut public expenditure and the basic rate of tax, whilst interest rates were increased. This led to soaring unemployment and a shrinking economy. Griffin's customer base was severely diminished and whilst privatising state owned industries was the Conservative answer to re-flate the economy, it was the service sector rather than manufacturing that boomed (at least until Black Monday saw the stock market plunge and the pound devalued). Demand for specialist books on engineering, manufacturing and science was squeezed at the same time that public spending cuts reduced higher education establishment's budgets for technical books (advanced statistical books being largely bought by universities, polytechnics and specialist colleges).

The 1980's saw little respite. In Britain, it was the decade where people decided they wanted lower taxes, and they expected to be able to make money. A positive outcome of the decade (and one that would surely win the approval of Lizzie, even if it did come a full century after our brave ancestors had been working in a man's world) was that women were meant to be treated as having equal potential as men. Before Black Monday shook the City's foundations making hedonism a little more frowned upon, the decade was all about wealth generation, entrepreneurial opportunity and the acceptance that those who have it flaunt it, leading to the birth of the much hated 'yuppies'. This was not a time to run a hard-pressed publishing house.

Unemployment went from half a million to three million and Britain became a country even more divided on the grounds of wealth. Working with a skeletal staff, taking on several people's jobs and capping his own wage, James struggled on, the family honour at stake as well as a young family to support.

After much personal angst (it's not easy having the burden of an inherited business) but being able to draw very little from the Firm, with staff numbers now down to the bare minimum and spiralling rent, paper and printing costs, my father had no option. Having supported his eldest sons through Cambridge University and with myself just off to London to study Geography at University College London, he was forced to consider a new future for Griffins. Just as Charles had no option but to offer a partnership with Bohn when he knew his time was running out, when James was approached in 1986 by a pair of entrepreneurial publishers, the offer was too tempting for the Board to refuse.

Having sold the international London Book Fair for a considerable personal profit, the prospective Griffin buyers had decided to plough money into small independent publishers. Terms were agreed to acquire the company name, copyrights and stock in the more profitable titles, and the services of James as Editor. The company itself was not bought, and became 'Richard Griffin (1820) Limited'. It was shelved pending resuscitation if required. Sadly it was only two years before James was forced to look elsewhere for employment as it became apparent that it was the Griffin list rather than his many years of experience in the business that was of interest to his new employees.

Clearly publishing is in the Griffin blood – at least for some! Having left university in 1986 and after a spell in a book shop, James' eldest son Andrew joined a rival publishing house to learn the trade just like his forefathers. Then in 2004 Andrew, wishing to start a publishing business of his own, decided to take over the dormant company. His present activities are very different from those of the company put into mothballs; but his various current ventures all sit within and alongside the Richard Griffin (1820) Limited stable. The Griffin trade mark – the wide spreading oak tree – survives to fight another day, albeit in a different context and it will take all of Andrew's entrepreneurial skills and hard work to tempt Griffins to rise phoenix like out of the ashes. His involvement in publishing is a small consolation to my father, who continued a career as a freelance Editor working for a variety of organisations before retiring in 2003. This was much to the relief of my mother who, having supported her husband through the lean years, the traumatic sell out in the late 1980's and the uncertain life of the freelancer was keen to spend some leisure time as a couple.

It is with great sadness that my father's involvement in the Firm could well have cost him his life and not just due to over work. Having bravely fought cancer in 2005 he was struck down with a new unrelated disease in January 2010. A cancer – Mesethelioma – which is usually caused by exposure to asbestos many years earlier. The only likely cause: the dust released while clearing out Drury

Lane over thirty years ago, a time when the dangers of this commonly used fire resistant material was virtually unknown. As with everything in his life, my father accepted his diagnosis with calm resilience, bravely putting up with months of painful and fruitless treatment (much worse the second time around with no hope of recovery). As the rest of us raged at the unfairness of life, he quietly went on with the task of dying, spending his last days intent on lessening the pain of his family.

There have been no more female managers running Griffins since Elizabeth and even now, the majority of Publishing Houses (mostly large conglomerates as the independents have often been swallowed up along the way), are run by men. The history of many long running businesses are likely to be just as fascinating as Griffins and behind any family run Firm, powerful and intelligent women are likely to have provided a defining influence. However, back in the 19th century very few will have openly taken up the helm, as Elizabeth was forced to do, and even fewer will have survived purely because of the tenacity and determination of two women determined not to see the business fail. Even before Lizzie's open involvement in the firm, Jessie was the true pioneer, working at a time when women were still seen as decorative homemakers. Without either women the history, not just of the firm, but also the fortunes of all of Charles' descendants (myself included) would have been very different indeed.

Appendix1

JOSEPH GRIFFIN (1751/52 to 1838)

As with all families, Lizzie's life was shaped by her ancestors. Even back in the late 1770's almost a century before her tale, the foundations of her life were established, centuries of parenthood shaping family values and beliefs and providing a genetic pool that showed entrepreneurial tendencies, intellect and musical ability. The bedrock for these foundations was the family and we believe that the fortunes of young Joseph Griffin were transformed when he married his wife, Mary King in 1778.

They married in St Leonard's Church Shoreditch and both Joseph and his bride made their marks in the register. The fact they could not write was not uncommon at this time and showed they had not been educated, but we also know that the couple gradually accrued more wealth as they moved properties, taking on the rent of a larger house as their family grew in size and this would suggest that he was firmly entrenched in the merchant class, as an employer rather than an employee. There were six baptisms of children born to the couple spanning the period 1784 to 1802.

When the records show the birth of what we suppose to be the eldest child – William Samuel Griffin on 2nd March 1784 – the family were living in Holywell Lane in Shoreditch. William was born the same year as the City of London Police Force was established and between 1784 and 1786, when Elisabeth Griffin was born, the family moved a few hundred yards to Webb's Square. Joseph will have leased this property rather than owned it, as was typical of that time. Following the two elder children, Richard Thomas Griffin (Lizzie's Grandfather), Sarah Griffin and James Griffin were born (in

1790, 1792 and 1796 respectively). We know nothing more about Elisabeth, Sarah or James.

We have strong evidence to suggest that the couple took their family to worship in the church where they got married, and where they had their children christened – St Leonard's of Shoreditch. The church was a very powerful institution at this time and Joseph will have listened to the sermons with rapt attention, as it provided him with a link with the educated world.

Details about Joseph's early-married life may be patchy but we can assume that he was employed at this time, possibly setting up his own merchant business. We can surmise from the relative success of the children we know about, that he gave them a good start in life, and the link that William, Richard and John Joseph went on to have with the book trade in particular, probably had its roots in the experiences of their father in this line of business. In later years Joseph was described as a merchant trader, possibly with bookshops in Glasgow as well as London, and as a member of the merchant class and with money to spend he would be increasingly buying into the trappings and lifestyle traditionally associated with the upper classes.

It is worth spending the time to consider the context for Joseph's chosen profession. The book trade was very different to modern day industry. For a start, most people were not able to read or write because the education system for many would have been Sunday school and not much else. In addition, for many years books were sold on the following price system: selling a few at a higher price was better than selling thousands at a lower one. This meant that by the end of the 18th century, and early 19th century, books were gradually becoming more expensive and not less. To make matters worse, many new novels were written in two or more volumes, making their cost out of the reach of all bar the richer members of society. New books were generally introduced in Central London, before being shipped to shops outside the capital. It is not surprising therefore that book sales were small and for some in the upper class this was how they liked it, as they feared cheaper prices would open up books to the lower classes that would then be in danger of becoming infected with dangerous ideas. In the late 18th century most popular novels only had print runs of around 4,000 copies. There was another reason or this and that was that most people bought second hand books from pedlars who sold low production books, such as chapbooks (these were 24 page booklets with a page cover illustrated with a wood cut). Initially the most popular chapbooks were traditional or folk stories but by the 19th century, there were a range of more adult oriented books of songs, jokes, myths or legends or retelling of famous events and covers were generic and rarely linked to the story. These chapbooks were generally sold by street vendors. The other main place to buy books in the early 19th century was from a second hand dealer.

Our estimation is that Joseph started working as a bookseller in London, possibly owning a shop and also a stall or table in a market. Is it therefore conceivable that he had multiple outlets, employing tradesmen to sell his books at various market stalls or overseeing his bookshops. Having started by buying stock from auctions and from people who came to his stalls, as he expanded he would almost certainly have also bought second hand books from the bigger more established booksellers. Over time, it is fair to assume given Richard's fortunes, that he would have managed to save sufficient money to rent a space to store his books, but the money he will have made on books alone is not likely to have been substantial and when business was poor he will undoubtedly have looked to sell other items, such as stationery to boost his income. He will have competed for business not just with other booksellers, but with coffee houses, some of which stocked extensive libraries – such as Tom's in Devereux Court and George's in Temple Bar, or book clubs. One reliable source indicated that he also sold philosophical and scientific equipment as well as books.

It is worth remembering at this point that the library as we know it today was not a usual method of obtaining books. More common was a club where members paid an annual subscription which was used to buy books, then, after they had been read by members, they were sold off or divided amongst subscribers. Becoming a member was not always easy as newcomers had to be on good terms with an existing member to join in the first place. By the time that Joseph was operating as a bookseller, coffee houses were themselves lending out books, for a fee and in effect became libraries and it was seeing the financial advantage of this system that undoubtedly encouraged booksellers to offer a similar service. Certainly as we will find out later, Joseph's son Richard was keen to exploit this market. However Richard never aspired to becoming a seller of 'penny bloods' or 'blood and thunder's' (chap fiction staples of the late 1830's), small 8 page booklets with paper covers which usually revolved around violent crime and had a gory wood cut on the front cover. It is perhaps fair to assume that Joseph was also not in this particular market, but rather preferred more specialist books, especially as between 1830 and 1850 there were at least 90 publishers (known at this time as booksellers) of penny fiction and the market was becoming saturated.

By 30 March 1820, Richard Thomas Griffin had founded his own company in Glasgow. In due course, Joseph and his wife moved up to Glasgow and were apparently living in the suburb of Gorbals to the south of the river. The exact year in which Joseph and Mary Griffin moved to Glasgow is not known, but we might speculate at the early-to-mid 1820s. It was during this period that John Joseph Griffin moved north. Being the youngest of Joseph's family it might well be the case that he would stay closest to his parents, who were in any event quite elderly by this date – Mary would be about 65 and Joseph nearly 70.

Joseph could well have been a consultant to Richard when he was setting up the Firm, and could have introduced his son to his own contacts if he had a past or current bookselling business in the City. Meanwhile, Mary will have enjoyed a quieter and comfortable retirement, corresponding with her London based family by letter and enjoying occasional visits from their children and grandchildren, but on Wednesday 3rd June 1827, she died [Glasgow Herald], leaving the 75-year-old Joseph alone. She was buried five days later in St Andrew's by the Green church, where Richard was on the vestry. When Mary died, Richard paid £7 10s 0d to reserve a 'half layer' (i.e. a shared burial vault) in the burial ground of St Andrew's by the Green – the church where he worshipped with his family and where Joseph and Mary had also been devout members of the congregation.

Joseph went on to live for another 11 years after his wife's death and died of dropsy at the advanced age of 86. Sadly he outlived his son Richard, but he was left an annuity to help pay for his care when his son died in 1832. We must now turn to Joseph's second son, Lizzie's Grandfather, Richard Thomas Griffin, the founder of the Firm, whose untimely death shook the foundations of what had rapidly become a highly successful enterprise.

Appendix 2

RICHARD THOMAS GRIFFIN (1790 to 1832)

Richard is perhaps the most important family ancestor in our tale precisely because he was the founder of the company that Jessie and Lizzie fought so hard to preserve. Whilst we believe that his father helped to establish his sons in the publishing world and certainly paid for their education and apprenticeships, it was Richard's entrepreneurial ambitions together with what appears to have been a fruitful marriage that enabled him to realise his dream. Richard Griffin & Co (RG&Co) was founded after Richard had spent several years in the book trade. In 1815, he undertook a five-year agreement to work for Thomas Tegg at 111 Cheapside, London, and this document still survives. As Richard was 25 years old, this was not, therefore, a traditional apprenticeship, but rather a period of employment during which he was 'learning the ropes' in Tegg's trade.

Thomas Tegg was an important figure in the early life of the Firm. He was a bookseller/ publisher in London who became very successful during his lifetime, ending up a leading figure in the City, living in an ex-Lord Mayor's house and elected as a common councillor for Cheapside. One of his particular strengths was to select other publisher's books that were selling slowly, making a low-price offer for them and then selling lots of them on for a small profit. He also published many books in his own right and was in effect, the forerunner of the special offer 'book sale' which set up in shops with short leases or town halls for the day. It was to the 111 Cheapside shop he occupied just before the Lord Mayor's house that Richard came in 1815. Richard's older brother William Samuel witnessed the agreement for Richard to work with Tegg.

Very soon after he started working at 111 Cheapside, or even before, Richard must have met the girl who was to become his wife, Elizabeth Eaves. Perhaps she came into the shop and Richard charmed her with his attentive manner and thorough search for suitable reading material? Or maybe the Eaves family were friendly with Thomas Tegg – a man who was definitely a member of the 'nouveaux riches' – and Richard was introduced to the Eaves as a 'bright young thing'. The wedding took place after Banns had been called on New Year's Eve 1815, and both parties were unmarried and said to be living in 'this parish'. New Union Street (where Richard lived at the time) was within St Giles Cripplegate parish .

Over the next five years, Richard developed his bookselling and publishing skills, such that by the end of this period he was ready to go into partnership with Tegg. Before detailing this partnership, however, we should consider Richard's children, as we believe that he fathered at least one child before or just after his marriage - although not it would seem with his wife.

We know from our records that his first child was a daughter – Sarah Bond. Presumably the daughter of an unknown Miss Bond, Sarah's birth date remains in the shadows. Richard admits in his will that she is his 'natural daughter'. We know nothing of the details of where Richard met Miss Bond but it was not uncommon for men to have affairs outside of marriage. Illegitimacy was rife as respectable married bourgeoisies often seduced girls of lower social standing, having one or more children by them and then supporting those children alongside their legitimate offspring. Some were even brought up in the same household. This was not the case with Sarah but Richard did support her financially throughout his life and her presence was clearly accepted by the rest of the family who acknowledged her existence by expressing concern for her future after Richard's death.

Back to Richard's early married life. On 18 April 1819, Richard and Elizabeth had what was perhaps their second child together, Charles Griffin, Jessie's husband and father of Lizzie. The baby was baptised in their local parish church St Giles without Cripplegate in a ceremony that was to mark their last celebration in London.

Because he was born four years after their marriage, it seems unlikely that Charles was their firstborn. Yet the evidence for any other child born before this date is restricted to a handful of cashbook entries in the account books in which there are references to a 'R Griffin Junior', which we originally assumed was simply a formula for Richard's son, i.e. Charles, since he is described elsewhere as *'filius unicus'* (only son). It now seems much more likely that this first child died before 1831, the year that Richard himself made a will in which he describes Charles as his 'only child'. Presumably the young Richard was born in London between 1816 and 1818 and died in Glasgow in his teens. To love and nurture Richard for this number of years only to have him cruelly snatched away before he reached adulthood must have been devastating for the couple and will have had a profound effect on both parents. It also focused all of their attention on Charles, a far sturdier child, who took after his father in looks and temperament. Charles will have known the full force of his parents' expectations and will have been groomed from a very early age to take over the family firm. Of course at this stage, no one could have imagined quite how soon his services were to be needed.

Back now to Richard the bookseller/publisher. A 50:50 partnership document was drawn up between Tegg and Richard to set up a new company, Richard Griffin & Company to be based in Glasgow with Tegg handling the London trade. The document consists of four handwritten vellum sheets measuring approximately 20 x 18 inches (50 x 45 cm). Each page bears a revenue stamp for £3 0s 0d. The firm was set up to print, publish and sell books.

Tegg would have had no problem in parting with some of his stock to cover his half-share in the partnership (at its greatest period, his shop was said to have contained a million books!) Richard, however, must either have raised a large loan, possessed a lot of money himself, or had family connections that were prepared to make such an investment.

Richard and his family probably moved to Glasgow late in 1819 or very early the following year.

Let us consider for a moment why he chose to head north for his new business venture. Glasgow was an important city for book traders in the 19th century. It was a thriving, bustling city – the perfect location for an entrepreneurial businessman keen to establish his new publishing firm. Glasgow was a city of political influence, boosted by the enormous shipyards and ironworks that were springing up on the banks of the Clyde. The Clyde also provided means of an inland navigation of some importance. When Richard and Elizabeth made their home in Glasgow, the city was going through a period of great change. Glasgow had long since possessed wealthy merchants, largely trading in tobacco with the West Indies and American Colonies. Tobacco lords were still in residence, strutting up and down in their scarlet coats, curled wigs and cocked hats, arrogant in their riches from the European tobacco trade, from the slave trade and from their own estates in the American colonies.

Edinburgh had established itself as a printing and publishing centre for Scotland but in 1638 Glasgow's Magistrates invited George Anderson to leave Edinburgh and establish himself in Glasgow as the city printer. Printing continued to flourish and Glasgow became a publishing centre to such an extent that the Press of the city obtained a European reputation under Robert and Andrew Foulis from 1741 onwards. Glasgow had also become a centre of the Hand-Loom industry. However, Richard chose an interesting time to settle in Glasgow. Just a year previous, in 1819 the city was in the midst of a radical uprising. Hosts of unemployed workmen (who had previously been mainly self employed at Hand-Loom weaving and had lost their jobs with the advent of mass production at the spinning mills) took to the cobbled streets to draw attention to their plight. The authorities set up relief centres for the homeless and about 324 weavers were employed to level off the slopes around Glasgow Green (an area later chosen by Richard and Elizabeth to set up a fashionable home). However, the authorities failed to pacify the masses and calls for radical reform resulted in plans for a revolution.

On 4th April 1820, the British Government thwarted their plans to attack Glasgow from the South and the radicals were wounded, caught and tried – the ringleaders sentenced to death and many other prisoners transported to Australia.

Meanwhile, Glasgow was establishing itself at the forefront of technical knowledge. The pioneer of technical education was John Anderson, Professor of Natural Philosophy in the University of Glasgow. When he died he left his fortune for the foundation of 'Anderson's University' later to become The Royal Technical College - a place where Richard's younger brother John Joseph was to study and teach. It is in this context that Richard brought his business to Glasgow. No wonder then that he chose this location to specialise in the publication of technical and scientific books. However, the full force of industrialisation had yet to come, and Glasgow was still at this time a contained city, with market gardens and orchards in the Old Town, not a dim and distant memory. This was a time when salmon still survived in the Clyde and where salt was still sold to cure the fish in parts of Saltmarket.

The shop that Richard rented for his bookshop was number 75 Hutcheson Street and was situated at the corner of Hutcheson and Garth Streets. Although we have no official details of any opening ceremony, it is highly likely that the opening of the shop was widely publicised and Richard will have certainly wanted to draw as much attention to the new venture as possible. Setting up the bookshop must have taken an extraordinary amount of planning and organisation – some of which is likely to have taken place in London before Richard moved up North. The Public Library he founded, although not opened until the 1st January 1821, must have been on the plans early on and Richard is likely to have earmarked the floor space for this section, even perhaps choosing the corner frontage for that reason. During the initial set up of the bookshop, the library area is likely to have been sectioned off, or possibly Richard used it to display extra stock or as a storage area. Elizabeth will not have seen her husband for the weeks running up to the opening, giving her plenty of time to shop for the 'perfect dress' to be seen at the opening ceremony. In the meantime, Richard will have spent every waking hour in the shop overseeing the workmen as they built shelves, installed counter tops, signs, and cupboards, painted the walls and scrubbed the floor. Then there were the book deliveries to order, sign for, check, store or display, staff to employ and train, stationery to print, advertising to organise and windows to dress, whilst at the same time, keeping a firm eye on the company's finances. Richard clearly rose to the challenge and must have steadfastly worked through each day, happy to see his ambition finally being realised, likely encouraged by this father, who was also a regular sight at the Hutcheson Street address.

The location he chose was right in the heart of Glasgow a short walk from the Royal Infirmary founded in 1792 where Joseph Lister was later to begin antiseptic surgery using carbolic acid for the first time (in 1865) and not far from the Royal College of Science and Technology where Richard's younger brother John Joseph later studied. We have two contemporary wood engravings of Richard's shop at this time – one outside in 1821 (see page 222), the other is an inside depiction in 1825. The detailed engravings give us a wonderful insight into the layout of the shop, and how Richard presented his new venture to the city. The outside view seems to be the frontage of Garth Street and shows Griffin's Public Library – the frontage on Hutcheson Street being the main bookshop.

Glasgow directories show 'Richard Griffin & Co, booksellers and publishers' at this address from 1820 to 1825. When choosing his trademark/book plate, we think that Richard was inspired by The Arms of Glasgow – an oak tree with a bird, a fish and a bell the motto being *"let Glasgow flourish by the preaching of the word"*. The House of Griffin adopted the oak tree as its symbol with the motto

"Quis Separabit nos?"– which strictly speaking should have been written *"Quis nos Separabit?"* – meaning 'who shall separate us' and is part of a quote from the Bible, the rest of the phrase being *"who shall separate us from the love of God?"*

As to the stock, the first production record book survives, with costing details for books published by the company. The first activity, however, was presumably marketing the books supplied by Tegg, and acquiring stock from other publishers to sell on. Some of these ventures were formal 'agency' collaborations, with one or more other firms being listed as selling the books; while sometimes the consortium shared the cost of publication and were then listed as co-publishers.

On 1st January 1821, Richard launched his new venture: 'Griffin's Public Library'. Advertising prints for this service survive. The exact date of the advertisement is not known, but it describes a collection of titles, particularly in physics, metaphysics, theology and natural and moral philosophy, daily newspapers and caricatures offered to subscribers – selected for *"instruction and amusement"*. Griffin's Public Library was a forerunner of Glasgow's many great libraries, including the palatial Mitchell Library, which opened in 1877 in temporary premises on a site on Ingram Street with a stock of 14,000 volumes (it now boasts the title of the biggest reference library in Europe).

1823 saw the first involvement of Richard's younger brother John Joseph Griffin as an author. This was *Chemical Recreations*, the book that was to run to six editions by 1826. It was written for amateur 'natural philosophers' anxious to undertake experiments in chemistry.

To help his business, Richard joined various local trading groups. On 14 March 1823 he became a Burgess and Guild-Brother of the City of Glasgow, by purchase and as his company became established he broadened his portfolio and in time began lending money. In a world before banks offered mortgages or loans to 'ordinary' customers, Richard like all well off men of the age, would have made his money work by lending money and thus spreading his own investments.

In 1824, Richard joined a number of other Glasgow worthies in having his portrait painted. One of the other sitters was Dr George Birkbeck, the founder of the Mechanics' Institute with which Richard's brother John Joseph was deeply involved. The artist was William Bewick who, on 4th August 1824 produced a portrait of Richard – a watercolour with chalk tinting. The drawing has also been engraved (or perhaps a pen-and-ink sketch with tinting). Both of these survive, and the National Portrait Gallery holds photographic copies.

Richard Thomas Griffin. 1790-1832.
Married Mary Eaves

The publishing side of the business began with the production of works on religion and poetry and general literature for adults and children and education and gradually became more specialised on technical education. Influenced by Glasgow's growing reputation in the field and the forthcoming technological expansion, and fuelled by Richard, John Joseph and later Charles' personal interest in mechanical engineering, chemistry and scientific advances, the Griffin specialisation was a wise and logical choice. The specialisation also had roots we believe in Joseph senior's business and the combination of bookselling with the sale of the appliances of chemistry and natural philosophy gave direction to the bookselling branch and laid the foundation for the publishing branch of the Firm.

Richard was clearly a deeply religious man. He had been elected on to the vestry of St Andrew's by the Green on 22nd February 1827 just a few months before his mother Mary died and was buried in the churchyard. Having been baptized in St Leonard's church in Shoreditch and then worshipped at St Giles without Cripplegate where he subsequently married, he was clearly seeking a like-minded church when he moved up North – hence his choice of St Andrew's - built in 1751, the first to offer Scottish Episcopalian worship. Perhaps Richard simply followed his father's lead as Joseph may well have had links with the church during his own time in Glasgow and father and son certainly attended the church together on Sunday's, Joseph being taken by carriage from South of the river with John Joseph and his wife Mary. The Griffins quickly became established as one of the most devout families in the congregation, regularly attending meetings and offering financial support.

In 1828 Richard was appointed to the Musical Committee of the Episcopal Chapel vestry. This is the only evidence we have until the second half of the century of the musicality of any of the family. Several of his grandchildren (including Lizzie), were definitely musical, and it does seem logical to suppose that Richard was at least interested in music – he must surely have been thrilled to hear the organ in the church. Glasgow was fortunate to be the recipient of a number of classical performers, some not yet famous, others already well known and it is quite possible that Richard and Elizabeth enjoyed concerts at the Assembly Rooms in nearby Ingram Street.

Early in June 1827, Richard's mother Mary died, and was buried on 8th June in the Episcopal Chapel burying ground. Four days after this, Richard paid £7 10s 0d to reserve a 'half layer' in the burial ground. The site of the grave is given as 'No. 12 betwixt the postlethrails and the chapel'. It is clear that he purchased this, for himself and his family, on the occasion of this family death.

On 3 June 1829, he was issued with a passport [number 3517] by the French Ambassador to the English Court. This entitled him to make a passage from London to Calais or Boulogne, travelling alone, and it calls upon the authorities to make such a journey safe for him. The stamps on the passport reveal that he travelled to Calais on 5th June, reaching Paris on 9th June, after an epic journey by horse-drawn stage coach from Glasgow via London. He stayed there for only one day, leaving on 10th and returning via Boulogne on 12th June. It would appear that he travelled straight back to Glasgow, and was certainly back by July.

We do not know exactly why Richard went to France. There seem to be two possibilities. One may have been to cement an agency for French goods, the other in some way connected with his brother John Joseph Griffin. John did make a journey to Paris in 1829 and it could have been a follow up to Richard's trip.

Only a few days after he returned from France, Richard took Charles to a new school. We know that Richard and Elizabeth placed education very high on their list of priorities. It is likely that by that time, their elder son Richard had died and this will have focused all of their attention on their remaining son. Choosing the right school for Charles will have been just as important as it is today, and is likely to have been a key topic of debate in the Griffin household. Richard will have made the ultimate decision on his son's education. The Scottish system of schooling was pretty haphazard until the passing of the Education Act in 1872, which made primary education compulsory. Primary schools were under the jurisdiction of the Kirk Sessions and secondary education was only available in the larger towns where it was controlled by the Town Council. Given Richard's wealth, he chose to send Charles into the Private schools system and such schools provided not just an academic education – focusing on Reading, Writing and Arithmetic – but also offered a range of ex-curricular subjects such as music and cookery. Charles was lucky. Children were generally seen as useful to their parents and were enlisted even before the industrial revolution in a variety of work from a very young age. Lack of parental support to education was a key problem as many parents had a cavalier and careless attitude about securing their children's education as well as withdrawing them too early to put them to work, and very few could afford to educate privately. Apprentices started from well under ten years' old and were based on a very strict servitude towards their masters. This was not an easy time to be a child and Charles was fortunate his parents could afford to educate him both at primary and secondary level. Despite only being thirteen at the time of his father's death, his own apprenticeship into the family firm did not come until he was 19 years old.

At the end of 1829 (17 December), Richard made provision for his family by paying John Wilson 'Ground Annual secured to Elizabeth Eaves or Griffin in life rent and Charles Griffin in fee, the amount of the Ground Annual being £30, (totalling £600 in all)'. Clearly Richard felt the need even at this time to make provision for his wife and son in case anything happened to him. We know that he died a long, painful and unpleasant death, and this desire to provide for his family's welfare in the long term may indicate that his health was deteriorating, and his realisation that this was a fatal condition fuelled his need to put his affairs in order.

Fortunately, the business continued to thrive.

On 22nd July 1830, money was lent by Richard to the company of Bumpus & Griffin. John Joseph Griffin is the partner in this firm, and stated to be 'bookseller of London'. Richard was not only being kind to his younger brother in this case. Investing in the Bumpus partnership must have made perfect business sense given the success and stability of Bumpus' bookshop empire. John Bumpus operated from Newgate Street, London at this date, and this would appear to be the date when John Joseph went formally into partnership with him. In all, Richard made loans of £859 11s 3d to John Joseph and/or to Bumpus & Griffin. Clearly there was a very close connection between the families. Of the total paid out, £200 0s 0d is described as a personal loan to John Bumpus.

Around this time, the family must have moved into 13 Monteith Row, possibly requiring more bedrooms to house their servants (who they tucked away at the top of the house) and a desire for a less noisy location. Although until the directory of 1830/31 we have no definitive information about where the family lived, we know that for a time their home address was Hope Place, Woodside Street, a row of houses that no longer exists in modern Glasgow. It could well have been Hope Place where the family lived from the first day until they reached Glasgow and Monteith Row was certainly in a less urbanised area and was by all accounts a plum location, right overlooking Glasgow Green and within a short walking distance of the office in Hutcheson Street and their church at St Andrew's by the Green. Richard and Elizabeth could well have had their eye on the development in Monteith Row, whilst they were living in Hope Place, possibly when they took their children to play on the Green. The row of terraces of rather plain, but nevertheless, spacious three storey houses looking South onto the Green were built by Thomas Binnie in 1823 and 1830. The couple could have been one of the first occupants – possibly the very first – of the new houses and would have benefited from the feeling of space at a time of rapid city development just a few streets away.

Costs that we have already seen show a continuation of Charles' education (5th February 1831: 'Mr Walker Kilfs, £46 19s 11d) and the family's churchgoing ('Episcopal Chapel, £5 0s 0d'). On 5th April 1831, the ledgers show the purchase of '4 waggons coals from John Thomson, £2'. Clearly this was for Richard's new house. However, perhaps for the catastrophic health reasons we have already hinted at, this account was not paid for two years.

So far, Richard's life was ever on the up! His firm seems to be going strong; he had enough money to lend considerable sums against securities; he was established as a senior member of the Glasgow merchant fraternity, especially those in the book trade; and he had moved into a substantial house in a fashionable area. He clearly loved his job and had great ambitions for the firm. He also revelled in the rapid expansion of the city during his time at the heart of the old town.

When he died in October 1832, Richard is said to have 'lain upwards of a year on his death bed'. Moreover, he must have foreseen problems ahead, because he drew up a will on 8 July 1831. A considerable body of legal paperwork has survived, not only in the family archive but also recorded in Glasgow's legal records. The will is the earliest of this sequence.

Richard appointed four people as his executors – his wife Elizabeth; Peter Aitken, jeweller; John Carfs, bookbinder; and Robert Malcolm, printer. All these are 'of Glasgow'. The will instructs these executors to pay all his debts and funeral expenses; to 'obey and fulfil any instructions left by me either in my own hand writing or having my signature attached'; then to pay a lifetime 'alimentary' annuity of £30 to his father. It is to be in weekly instalments and 'subject to the inspection and approbation of my said wife'. All the rest of his estate is to be paid to his wife and son 'in the same proportions as by the law of Scotland' would be due to them. The document was duly signed before his lawyer and his clerk (John Kerr, Writer in

Glasgow, and Robert Walker). Our knowledge of Richard's estate stems from this will and from an inventory of his estate and other legal documents, all deposited in the 'Books of Council and Sefsion or other Judges' books'.

For a year after the will was first drawn up, it seems that Richard went on acquiring assets and his business affairs continued into 1832 – presumably from his sickbed. He clearly wanted to leave his affairs in order and must have experienced considerable angst at the future of the business he had created. Although reassured by his brother's involvement, Richard must have lain in his bed thinking about what he would leave behind trying to ensure he left the business in impeccable order. He even budgeted for a smartening of the Firm's premises shown clearly in this ledger - 11 February 1832 Graham, Carpenter, £7 16s 10d'; 15 May 1832 'Half year's rent for 64 Hutcheson St, £75 0s 0d'; 17 May 1832 'Johnston, for painting the shop inside and out, £67 17s 5½d'.

Family circumstances were changing. On 15 June 1832, Richard added his youngest brother John Joseph Griffin, described later as a 'bookseller of London', to his list of executors. This was 'seeing that my brother… has since [8 July 1831 when the original will was written] become a resident in Glasgow'. At this date also, he willed £300 0s 0d to Sarah Bond, to be spent on 'her maintenance clothing and education… exclusive of the sum I am already bound to pay for her board during the next eighteen months.' The executors were also appointed as 'curators to her until she attains the age of majority.'

In this same will codicil, Richard also left £10 0s 0d and any interest, to the 'Owners or Managers of the Episcopal chapel; of Glasgow'; (this was actually writing off the earlier £10 loan to them). Another clause in the 15 June 1832 codicil allowed his executors to use the services of a 'ffactor' [the ancient way of writing 'Factor']. This person was 'to act under them the more effectually to fulfil their instructions'. The name associated with this was Ambrose. It is a fact that 'Mr Ambrose' ran the Griffin family affairs in Glasgow in the 1850s and 1860s, after the family moved back to London. He continued to act until 1872.

One significant document is on file: most of the draft of a new copartnery document, showing how John Joseph was to become part owner of RG&Co. Clearly, Richard's health was giving him cause for concern. John Joseph was needed to carry on the day-to-day running of the firm.

The wording shows that John Joseph 'late bookseller in London and now in Glasgow' is part of the team. The capital invested (by Thomas Tegg and Richard) is said to have been £8,000 0s 0d. Thomas Tegg is to supply books at cost price; Richard and John Joseph were to give their time to the business, John Joseph in lieu of any capital input. The partners agree to continue as 'Booksellers and stationers' in Glasgow, although they were also to act as wholesalers in Scotland and Ireland (as well as retailers in Glasgow.) The new co partnership is to run for seven years from 30 June 1832 (the original foundation date of 30 March was altered to conform to their preferred working date). The profits are to be divided into 9/24 parts to Tegg, 9/24 parts to Richard, and 6/24 parts to John Joseph.

In the morning of Monday 29 October 1832, Richard died. As we have seen he had been bedridden for over a year, and the cause of this is stated in the burial register as 'ulcer bowels'.

Both the sphere of work and home life were naturally profoundly affected by Richard's death. Having written John Joseph into the partnership, RG&Co could continue under family guidance. From John Joseph's point of view the company was providing his own bread and butter. But it also represented the bread and butter of Richard's family. So for everyone's sake it was vital to keep the firm going.

So we can turn to the final aspect of Richard's short but eventful life: what he left for his family. First there were funeral expenses to be paid for, which began with a 30 October 1832 entry 'Printing funeral letters, 17s 0d'. Then there were the usual complicated mourning and funeral expenses to the paid for. It would appear that Elizabeth's love of shopping was not abated by her husband's death. As was entirely fitting at this time, it was important to show the world your suffering and Elizabeth was determined that her husband's departure was given the correct attention for a man of his social standing. Richard himself may have planned his own funeral but it was Elizabeth who spent many days sourcing the perfect mourning clothes not just for herself, but also for her son and her servants. Quite how much she spent is apparent from the household account books of 10th November 1832 – a few weeks after Richard's death:

Rent for Monteith Row	£22 10s 0d
Servants wages due	£3 10s 0s
Flemington, for mourning	6s 9d
Grimshaw, Undertaker	£4 14s 0d
Robson, for mourning	12s 0d
Stephens, for mourning	£1 5s 0d
Ingles, for mourning	£11 15s 8d
Mirrlees, Undertaker	£8 0s 0d

There were also various outstanding household bills to be paid (entered at the same date) as Richard's estate was wound up. A line would have had to be drawn under any credit accounts in his name (for traders and service providers) so that his estate could be finalised.

Meek, Perfumer	£1 5s 0d
Thomson, Grocer	£1 2s 6d
McArthur, Grocer	16s 6d
McCulloch, Grocer	£3 7s 4d
Gibbs, Wine merchants	£8 9s 0d
Laudeman, Wine merchant	£1 19s 0d
Ralston & Co, Hatters	£1 10s 0d
Willis, Carver	3s 6d
Lang, Ironmonger	17s 0d
Boyd, Cabinet maker	£1 5s 0d
Coals	£1 7s 0d
Coals	8s 0d
Aitken, Jeweller	£16 11s 3d
Dr Buchanan, Physician	£40 0s 0d
Monteith, Shoemaker	13s 0d
Penfold, Druggist	5s 0d
Dick, Taylor	£6 6s 0d
Dyer's account	7s 0d

In the above list, we assume that 'Dyer' is a person. Aitken was one of Richard's executors. Dr Buchanan is presumably the 'Dr Andrew Buchanan, surgeon, of 45 West Nile Street' [1832/33 directory]; who continued as the family doctor and adviser for some years. Death, like marriage, brought the family and community together.

The executors – actually John Joseph - of Richard's estate made an inventory of all his assets as at 1 November 1832, amounting to the following.

John Bumpus, London	£671 17s 8d
Scottish Union Insurance	£25 0s 0d
John Wilson	£600 0s 0d
Mrs and Mr Bruce	£800 0s 0d
James Walker	£200 0s 0d
Robert Golder	£250 0s 0d
Samuel A Oddy, London	£7 1s 10d
Richard Griffin & Co, Glasgow	£3,064 8s 4d
Peter Adam	£300 0s 0d
Furniture at Monteith Row	£284 6s 10d
TOTAL ESTATE	**£6,502 13s 10d**

The above total was divided as:

Sarah Bond	£300 0s 0d
Charles Griffin	£4,951 15s 10d
Mrs Griffin	£1,250 18s 0d

Since Richard had invested in a life rent for 13 Monteith Row, it seems logical to assume that his widow and son continued to live there after 1832. The Mitchell Library has indicated various addresses for 'Mrs Richard Griffin' between 1836 and 1846. After Monteith Row they record 'Provanside, Stirling Road' [which we know from other records was number 1 Provanside]. Later she moved to 20 Buccleuch Street. This last move was subsequent to Charles Griffin's marriage in 1843.

Richard was clearly respected by his peers and a very successful bookseller and publisher. Had he lived longer, his business would have matched any of the other big names operating in the city. William Collins, for example, had his office just to the east of the Andersonian Institute (now Strathclyde University). He began his publishing career only a year before Richard. The two men knew each other well and later Charles's children also asked the advice of Mr Collins and received it. Before we move to Charles, the next chapter is devoted to John Joseph, the man who took the helm of Richard Griffin & Co, driving the business forward until Charles was of an age to work in the firm. A man who was to become one of the most respected and well known scientists of his generation. Under John Joseph's direction, the firm continued to focus on technical publishing and book trading, building on the solid foundations laid down by Richard.

(*Original Wood Block.*)

GRIFFIN'S PUBLIC LIBRARY,
HUTCHESON STREET, GLASGOW,

1821.

Appendix 3

JOHN JOSEPH GRIFFIN (1802 TO 1877)

John Joseph Griffin, great uncle to Lizzie, brother in law to Jessie, was a highly influential character in her tale, and one who as an intelligent and respected scientist, author and businessman, really deserves a book in his own right. However, for now, we shall establish his place in our story, before concentrating on his time spent on Richard Griffin & Co following the death of his brother Richard. It is important that we understand John's involvement in the business as he was the person that Jessie first approached on her husband's death and it was to John that Lizzie was to turn too on numerous occasions when she needed advice. The reason for this will become apparent, as will the devastation they both felt when he refused to take on the post of Trustee when the situation became desperate.

John Joseph's involvement in the firm was perhaps rather thrust upon him by his older brother's death, but given his father's trade and his own interest in literature, it is not surprising he stepped into the breach. Despite harbouring ambitions of his own, he rose to the challenge of managing the bookselling and publishing arm of the business, whilst continuing his own studies. It was not until his nephew Charles was old enough to take over the reins that he could concentrate firmly on his work in the world of Chemistry and continue to build up what was to become an internationally renowned business of his own. Because of his relative fame in the world of Chemistry, we have more documentation about John's life, although this is mainly focused on his academic achievements.

We must remind ourselves where he fits into the family tree. He was born in London in 1802, the youngest child of Joseph Griffin. Richard's migration to Glasgow late in 1819 or early in 1820 presumably left only the 17-year-old John at home with his parents.

We can be confident that John did receive schooling, if for no other reason that he was a fluent French and German speaker (able to translate technical books from those languages). Having said which, in 1841 he reported that he had no German conversation and was unable to follow all of a theatre visit he attended. Furthermore, the two books he translated were re-translated a few years later. Perhaps his German was not quite as good as we at first thought. Indeed, for his 1841 continental tour, John packed a German dictionary (but not a French one). Moreover, the rest of his life proves that John showed an early aptitude for scientific subjects.

At some point, however, he moved up to Glasgow, because before 1823 he attended Chemistry classes there. Perhaps, after all, he did go north with Richard.

The course, which John had attended at the Andersonian Institute, was designed for working men who wished to develop their theoretical knowledge. John was probably highly excited about his move up north. If he did move then he would have been in his teens, and Glasgow would have been an attractive location given its reputation in the technical field.

John must have begun this work a good while before he completed the course himself in 1823, for the simple reason that Richard published this book on 23 September in that year. In fact, John still considered himself a student himself, since he dedicated the book to his 'fellow students'. The RG&Co production books show that John was paid £10 0s 0d to supply the copy, and was entitled to 12 free copies. The book was called *Chemical Recreations: A series of amusing and instructive experiments…* illustrated by… engraved figures which were to remain in print until the end of the nineteenth century, by which time it was in its 10th edition.

Chemical Recreations sold out immediately on publication and was reprinted nine times over the years. The evident success of the *Chemical Recreations,* and the Chemistry Course at the Mechanics' Institution, led to a trading opportunity for RG&Co. In the early editions of *Recreations* John sent his readers to shops where Wedgwood ware was sold to buy, for example, lipped beakers at 6d, 9d and 1/-. If RG&Co were to sell such apparatus as well, they could supply their readers' needs and make more profit in so doing. Thus, in 1826, they decided to open a new shop at number 64 Buchanan Street with John managing it. It was called 'Griffin's Chemical Museum'. We must remember that John was only 24 years old at this time, as yet unmarried, but he was clearly hooked on chemistry and its applications.

John past his twenties, by day working with his elder brother Richard selling books and chemical apparatus; by night he attended lectures, wrote books, and undertook experiments. He may well have started his Scottish life with his parents in the Laurieston district of Gorbals but in June 1827 his mother Mary died and we think his father moved out of Glasgow to Partick – then a separate village West of Glasgow. It was probably then that John chose to move nearer his work in the centre of the city.

In his true adventurous spirit John decided it was time to better his own education through travel. He spent a prolonged period in France before travelling on to Germany to study at the University of Heidelberg and it was March 1830 before he returned to Glasgow. Richard will have kept a close contact of his brother's progress in Europe, probably corresponding with him by letter, particularly if he had any specific query about the scientific equipment side of the business. He also invested in his brother's London venture with John's London business partner, John Bumpus, Richard lent money to Bumpus personally, to John and to the partnership they formed together.

John's return to Scotland must have coincided with Richard's final illness. (Maybe he actually returned because of it, knowing how much he owed his older brother and feeling a strong sense of duty to his elderly father and to his sister in law and young nephew). So, when John reached Glasgow he must have assumed more responsibility for the running of RG&Co, as well as forging ahead with his own chemical interests.

He moved to a new address [1832/33 directory], number 36 St Andrews Street, which is quite close to Monteith Row and Hutcheson Street. 1832 was a momentous year for several reasons. At the end of it Richard died. John was one of the executors of his brother's estate, handling all the paperwork associated with winding it up. Moreover, he had to assume total responsibility for RG&Co. To top it all, at some time during the year he married Mary Ann Holder.

During much of that year, John was involved with Richard's executorial work. It was he who acted for all the executors in drawing up an inventory of Richard's assets (30 April). It was he who arranged for and managed all the legal documentation required after a death (1 May). It was he who made sure that death duties and debtors were properly paid and recorded; and it was he who ensured that Richard's annuities (to his father and to Sarah Bond) were paid (11 October).

The situation as 1837 began, then, was that Richard was four years in his grave, Richard's son Charles was not yet 18 and still attending the University of Glasgow; RG&Co's original shop was still selling books in Hutcheson Street with Griffin's Chemical Museum in

Buchanan Street. John had taken over the reins at RG&Co, was married with three children, who were by that date just under four, just under two and six months old. It would appear that in 1837, the bookshop was removed from Hutcheson Street (by then renumbered as 75), and the whole operation came together again in 115 Buchanan Street.

And then disaster struck.

The baby was the least able to fight off disease and James died on 22 January 1837, the family making a mournful journey to St Andrew's by the Green a few days later. Then both the other two children succumbed in quick succession, Sarah on 8th February (*Glasgow Herald*), buried on 11 February; and Richard on 23 February, buried 25 February. Clearly they probably all died of the same infection, Sarah and Richard definitely dying of influenza. Interestingly, the *Glasgow Herald* of 13 February 1837 in which Sarah's death was announced, and that of 24 February saying that Richard had died, both state that they died 'at Buchanan Street'. Whether this was where the family had moved to, or signifies that the babies had been taken to the shop on those days, we do not know.

John and his wife must have been devastated. Yet the family's spirit won through, and within a few months of this triple tragedy, Mary Ann was pregnant again and we can only imagine the trepidation she must have felt during her pregnancy and the early years of all of her subsequent children's lives. Meanwhile John's work continued. During 1837 he exhibited chemical apparatus, which he had specially adapted for experiments on a small scale. This was at the British Association meeting in Liverpool.

RG&Co's Buchanan Street shop was entitled 'Griffin's Bazaar' on a poster which appears in the 1837 edition of the firm's *Book of Trades*. In 1838, according to the Mitchell Library [1987] Glasgow Post office directories, list John's nephew Charles working for RG&Co. Perhaps the catalyst was the death of Joseph senior who was buried on the 18th April that same year: as one generation dies another steps into line? John may have found himself in a slightly awkward situation. There was later no doubt in Charles' mind that he was to inherit RG&Co. Yet at the age of only 19 he was clearly too young to be able to take over. At the same time John had until then been in sole charge of the company, and no doubt was directing it in the way that suited his own interests. Charles spent these early years observing and working his way through the ranks in a crude form of apprenticeship, leaving his uncle at the helm.

Meanwhile John's own academic career continued to thrive. Not only did he give papers to the Glasgow Philosophical Society he was appointed as their Librarian, which was a position of even greater significance than it sounds. The libraries of the Glasgow Philosophical Society, the Andersonian Institution and Glasgow Museum were all brought together under John's supervision.

The publishing side of the business carried on as before. The Griffin's Scientific Miscellany series began in 1839, and apparatus was sold as well as books. The Scottish Book trade Index lists 24 Canon Street [not listed in the modern A-Z] as the firm's address from 1839 to 1842. They presumably moved premises from Buchanan Street because they needed more space? Certainly the stock of scientific instruments must have been quite bulky to store and display. During the next few years, John continued to write scientific books which were to further his reputation in the field. Then, John was one of five Glasgow chemists who were invited to be amongst the 75 men forming the Chemical Society (later the Royal Chemical Society), the oldest chemical society in the world. In 1849 John was elected to the Society's Council.

At some time on or soon after 17 July 1841, John set off from Glasgow on the Carlisle Mail on another lengthy tour of the continent. This was partly to meet German, Austrian and Bohemian chemists and equipment makers, but also to enjoy himself. He must have left his nephew Charles in charge of the firm, and was presumably happy to do so. The journey covered Berlin, Chemnitz, Wittenberg, Dresden and Prague. It took 2½ months and ended in mid-September. The whole trip cost £230 0s 0d, which sum can be checked back from his diary summary to the firm's books. His final port of call was Antwerp, from which he sailed to London, arriving on Thursday 16 September 1841.

His return appears to have been to a new house in Provan Place. This was presumably not far from Provanside, where his sister-in-law and her son Charles lived. Directories show John at Provan Place from 1841/42 through to 1844.

We assume that John returned from his continental tour with a pile of new contacts, chemical samples, and a lot of goodwill. 1842 was said (by one source) to be the year in which Charles Griffin officially joined the firm, although we have seen that it is likely to have been the year before. The relationship between John and Charles Griffin had apparently become strained, presumably as Charles matured. It was during this year that John decided to go down to London. He moved to 53 Baker Street, and set up his Chemical Museum as 'J J Griffin & Co.' (JJG&Co). The address is given both as '53 Baker Street' and 'Portman Square, Baker Street', which indicates that the building was at the southern end of Baker Street.

In 1848, a large sum was paid to the previous publishers to purchase *the Encyclopaedia Metropolitana*. Counsel's opinion was sought, on whether the text could be split up and published as separate books. This was delivered on 19 August 1848. This represented a considerable investment for the firm, which was not without financial risk. 1848 also saw the publication by JJG&Co of a reprint from *Encyclopaedia Metropolitana,* and the decision was made to break up the work into separate books, several of which appeared very quickly.

Although John had moved, he remained the London partner of RG&Co (the Tegg connection had ended some years before). John therefore wrote progress letters to Charles, several of which have survived. These mention that trade was very slack and that cholera was rife in London at the time. The cholera epidemic had yet to peak in Scotland.

John may well have relished the moved away from what he saw as his brother's business but he certainly maintained his interest in publishing as well as furthering his own scientific interests and building up his equipment sales. In 1849 there was a new edition of *Chemical Recreations,* the 9th. It was printed by Bell and Bain of Glasgow, and published by JJG&Co, of 53 Baker Street, London, Thomas Tegg., London, and RG&Co of Glasgow. It was in 1849 that John was elected to the Council of the Chemical Society. He was to hold this post until 1850. Meanwhile, John had also acquired an engraving machine that enabled him to produce equipment graduated in French and English. John's own business was going from strength to strength and on 1 March 1850, he took over the business of John Ward (which had been founded in 1811), thereby adding philosophical apparatus to his other categories.

JJG&Co were granted two medals for their exhibits at the Great Exhibition of 1851 and this offered the perfect marketing opportunity for the equipment side of the business. The categories were 'Graduated Glass Instruments', the description being 'Exceedingly accurate and good', and 'Economic and convenient chemical apparatus'. The graduated instruments came as a result of John's purchase of the engraving machine in 1849.

Until 1852, Charles and John had continued to operate over 300m miles apart; but in that year John relinquished his part of the business. This could well have been amicable as John would have been very busy dealing with his own expanding company.

Despite being 50 years old, John's energy showed no sign of abating and he continued to move his firm and his home over the next few years. He moved his company out of 53 Baker Street in 1852; it would seem to 119 & 120 Bunhill Row (described as his manufactory); while he himself moved to 10 Finsbury Square. So he removed from the west end to the city, which is interesting in that it bucks the trend of city retailers migrating to Oxford Street. For a couple of years John was busy writing and publishing a variety of books, (including one of his most prestigious titles – Robert Hunt's *A Manual of Photography*) and in 1854 he published the final (10th) edition of *Chemical Recreations*. However, by 1857 John's health had begun to suffer and he was ill for the whole of 1857, during which time he worked on a new book – *The Radical Theory in Chemistry*, at his home: Longton Lodge, Sydenham. The book was finally published in 1858. It must have been during the last couple of years of the 1850s that his sons Charles and William joined him in JJG&Co. It was also about this time that Charles Griffin removed the head office of RG&Co (and his own family) to London.

At the time that Lizzie took up her tale, on the death of her father in 1862, her Uncle John was approached to become a Trustee and given his previous role as manager of Griffins in Scotland he seemed the obvious choice to take over the reins until Jessie's eldest son came of age. Sadly he was unable to take up the challenge. We will not dwell on John's final years but suffice to say, that he was still busy writing and overseeing his own highly successful business. Like Jessie he moved house often over the years, and was living in a newly developed and highly desirable area of Islington by 1864. His address, 5 Douglas Road, appears in correspondence with members of his nephew Charles Griffin's family; they lived only a few hundred yards away from Douglas Road – a fact that must have been a comfort to Jessie.

Over the next two years, John's business continued to thrive, and it was in the mid-1860s that the squat-spouted glassware known as 'the Griffin beaker' was introduced. It was still being sold by Griffin & George in 1980. These beakers came in several sizes that nested together. Even in his advanced years (John was 64 years old in 1866) he continued to write, publishing *Chemical Handicraft* and several more scientific papers. After various house and office moves, John finally settled in 31 Park Road, Haverstock Hill, where he lived from 1870 until the end of his life. At the age of 75, on 9 June 1877, John died at his home.

We are now ready to turn to Lizzie's beloved Papa. The man whose death propelled his widow and subsequently his daughter into the strange and mysterious world of business.

Appendix 4

CHARLES SHARPE GRIFFIN (1819 to 1862)

Charles Griffin. 1820-1862.
Married Jessie Jane Rae.

So we reach Charles, beloved husband of Jessie, father to Elizabeth a man who fought so hard for the firm in his short life, and whose legacy shaped the future of generations of Griffins.

Having enjoyed what on all accounts appears to have been a happy childhood as the much adored only son of Richard and Elizabeth, an only child for much of his life, after the death of his older brother and the absence of his illegitimate sister Sarah. Born in London in 1819 but raised in Glasgow, Charles attended a boarding school in Kilpatrick from the age of 9 years old, but his privileged world must, like his own family, been jeopardised when his own father became ill so young in adulthood.

It was left to his uncle John Joseph to drive the business forward whilst Charles finished his education, right up to degree level as, in the latter part of the 1830's, he attended the University of Glasgow. He then spent time learning the trade and the exact date Charles entered Richard Griffin & Co is not known. The earliest directory to list him is dated 1840/41, (Charles Griffin of Richard Griffin & Co., home: 13 Monteith Row); data for this directory could have been collected in 1839. At this date Charles would have been aged 20.

At some date before 23 January 1843, Charles met the girl he was to marry, Jessie Jane, who is one of the women we are celebrating in this book. Jessie was the 15th and youngest child (and the youngest of two pairs of twins) of James Rae, Sheriff-Substitute of Linlithgowshire. There is no doubt that she came from a wealthy and influential Scottish family. Linlithgowshire was later part of the county of West Lothian, to the immediate West of Edinburgh, and is now part of the administrative region of Lothian. The capital of the county was Linlithgow, in which town was a royal palace. The courts where James Rae administered justice remain in the town. We know that following the death of her father, Jessie, her mother and other unmarried sister

Helen, moved to Glasgow and in 1843 (when the banns were called) she is described as residing in Barony Parish, Glasgow.

On 23 January 1843, banns were called for the third time in the parish church of Barony Parish (St Stephen's). Andrew King, the minister married the couple on Friday 27 January 1843 'at Glasgow'. Charles is described as a bookseller; Jessie Jane's father is stated to be 'the late James Rae'. This ceremony appears to have taken place according to the rites of the Church of Scotland presumably reflecting the denominational preferences of Jessie Jane and her family. Provan Side was within Barony Parish, so maybe Charles had switched his preferred church, in which case perhaps he may have met Jessie as a fellow member of that congregation.

The *Glasgow Herald* carries an announcement of the wedding, stating it to have been

> At Garnet Bank, Sauchiehall Street, Glasgow, on the 27th instant by the Rev Andrew King, Mr Charles Griffin, Glasgow, to Jessie Jane, youngest daughter of the late James Rae Esq., Sheriff-Substitute of Linlithgow.

Charles and Jessie's first child was Mary Anne Eliza Griffin (the little girl that was known to all the family as Polly). She was born on Saturday 11 November 1843 in Glasgow, the eldest of nine children to be born in Scotland. The *Glasgow Herald* said: 'At Provan Side, Stirling's Rd on the 11th inst, Mrs Charles Griffin: a daughter'.

Elizabeth Eaves Griffin (our Lizzie) was born on 17 April 1845 in Glasgow, Charles' second child. Her second forename was, of course, her grandmother's maiden name.

By September 1845, we can assume that Charles was managing the bookselling side of Richard Griffin & Co, with his Uncle John Joseph the chemical museum and apparatus side. Presumably publishing decisions were taken between them. On 31 August 1846, Charles purchased a 'half layer', being 3 square yards in the Fir Park Necropolis, sharing with Dr F R Lowe (Beta 57). Lowe was the husband of Mary Ann, nee Rae, a sister of Jessie's. Charles paid £9 9s 0d for this, at 63/- per yard. The monument was described as an 'Egyptian vault' Clearly Charles had at this stage, no intentions of moving away from Glasgow. Later his rights were sold to Mrs Ann Haig of Edinburgh.

On Friday 22 January 1847, Charles' mother Elizabeth died, and was buried in the vault that Charles had purchased. The burial register of the cemetery shows three committals to the Griffin vault, headed by Charles' mother Elizabeth. On 23 March 1847, Charles's household will have rejoiced when his first son had been born. He was given both of his grandfather's names: Richard Thomas.

Family tradition has it that tension grew between Charles and his uncle around this time. Presumably Charles wished for more autonomy, inevitably eroding the control that John had exercised for many years. Suffice to say that by 1848, John had moved south to London, leaving Charles in Glasgow.

A second son, Alexander Jamieson, was born on 31 July 1848. Charles seems to have approached his friends and business colleagues when it came to godparents. We have no direct evidence, but it seems quite possible that Alexander's second name reflected the surname of his godfather, and there was one eminent Richard Griffin & Co author of that surname.

It was at about this time that Richard Griffin & Co acquired the rights to one of its most successful books: the *Encyclopaedia Metropolitana*, although whether Charles, John Joseph or both men were instrumental in the negotiations we don't know. This *Encyclopaedia* with its strong focus on mechanics, engineering and the sciences to serve manufacture and marks another step in the direction the firm was making towards its specialisation in technical works.

In the autumn of 1850, Charles' third son and fifth child, Charles James Griffin, was born on 23 October and so the household at 1 Provan Side consisted of the following.

> Charles Griffin, Head, Married, 32, Publisher, born London
> Jessie Jane Do, Wife, Married, 26, Publisher's wife, born Linlithgow
> Charles J Do, Son, Not married, 5 months, Publisher's son, born Glasgow
> Jane M Kechnie, Nurse, Married, 21, Wife of a sailor, b Haddington, Coulston
> Marrion Snedden, Servant, Not married, 26, House servant, b Old Munkland
> Eliza Rennie, Servant, Not married, 25, House servant, b Stirlingshire, Alvie.

At this date, Charles and Jessie Jane's family consisted of Mary Anne (7½), Elizabeth Eaves (6), Richard Thomas (4) and Alexander Jamieson (2¾) as well as Charles James. Although both parents were at home for the time of this census, the children were staying with Helen Rae (one of Jessie's sisters) at 10 West Bay, Inverkip, and a village on the North West Renfrewshire coast; presumably they were packed off at this point to give their mother a rest after the birth of baby Charles. This census was the first to ask for the identity and relationships to the head of household; the exact ages, and the parish of birth. The number of servants is also worth noting, Charles and Jessie were clearly firmly entrenched in the upper middle classes and Jessie will have had considerable help running her expanding household.

Two years later, on 8 February 1852, the next child, Jessie Jane Griffin (clearly named after her mother) was born; sadly, she was disabled although she lived a full life. We are not sure of the extent of her disabilities – it could have been a form of cerebral palsy or complications during the birth, but we know that her mind was unaffected. Even more tragically, almost a year later, another daughter – Helena Griffin – was born on 8 March 1853. She may have been born with a medical condition or she could have simply had a raging temperature that led to the convulsions that killed her. She only lived for eight weeks, dying on the 8 May. Helena's was the second burial in Charles Griffin's vault, being buried there on Thursday 12 May 1853.

On 30 April 1853, the Senate of the University of Glasgow granted Charles the right to call himself 'Publisher to the University of Glasgow'. Charles was notified of this appointment in a letter dated

2 May. This title was held until his death. Clearly Charles had become extremely important in the publishing and educational establishments in Glasgow. The association with the university was also reflected in the use of the University arms by Richard Griffin & Co. The illustration of the Glasgow city arms (the tree, the bell and the fish with a ring) in a stained glass window over the door of the company's premises (presumably at 39/41 West Nile Street) was published in the firm's Centenary Volume.

Charles' fourth son (eighth child) was born on 24th May 1854 and was named John Joseph Griffin. That this son was named after his uncle may possibly have been something of a peace offering from Charles to his uncle at a time when we believe that business dealings were a little strained. Jessie must have only just got out of her mourning clothes after burying Helena before she was pregnant again.

For several years after John Joseph's removal to London, publications, exhibitions, advertisements, etc were presented as co-published by Richard Griffin & Co and John Joseph Griffin & Co. In 1853, the first such indication of Richard Griffin & Co's move to London is that this is the last year in which a catalogue is issued with only '40 Buchanan Street, Glasgow' on it. By 1855, entries read '4, 5 & 6 Warwick Square, London, and 40 Buchanan Street, Glasgow'. The London office was, it would seem, in place by 1855 (note that John's company was operating in London at the same time but at completely different addresses). It is therefore very likely that Charles himself had removed to London to develop these new premises, leaving Jessie alone with her family in Glasgow.

One more child was to be born in Glasgow, and his connections show how far Charles had progressed in his dealings and friendships with eminent men. Henry Brougham Griffin was born (so his birth certificate confirms) at 7.30pm on 15 December 1856. [It is normal practice to put the time of birth on twins' certificates, but unusual on solus births. We have no reason to suppose that Henry had a twin.] His godfather is known to have been Henry, Lord Brougham, a prominent member of the government of the day. In 1830 he had been made Lord Chancellor and did much to facilitate the Reform Bill, although his political career ended in 1834. However, he remained a strong advocator of technical education (being one of the founders of the University of London in 1825). His association with the firm and his personal friendship with Charles developed over the years and Charles published all of Brougham's writing.

The family's formal exit from Glasgow was made with a flourish. A dinner in Charles' honour was given – tickets priced at 12s 6d each – by the Glasgow Incorporation of Stationers. It took place at Carrick's Royal Hotel in George Square on Thursday 3 November 1859. Two toast lists survive, including four loyal toasts, one to Charles Griffin and one to his fireside [i.e. offering domestic good wishes to him], plus 15 other toasts ranging from 'The Literature of Scotland', to 'The ladies'. Mr Park sang a song. The names of those who proposed or replied to the toasts included:

- Professor John Eadie (a Richard Griffin & Co author), associated with the toast 'The Evangelical Clergy of all Denominations'.

- Dr Fletcher Reid Lowe (Charles' brother-in-law), associated with the toast 'The Educational Institutions of Glasgow' [Lowe was a teacher at the High School of Glasgow].

- Mr Duncan, associated with 'The Papermakers of Scotland'.

The *Glasgow Herald* of Friday 4 November 1859 reported that a large number of Charles' personal friends were present, and that Charles was moving his 'extensive publishing house' to London. The chairman congratulated Charles on his 'enterprise and business sagacity'. Charles, replying, mentioned 'some of the philanthropic objects which had engaged his leisure hours, with a view to the elevation of the working classes.' In another speech 'many regrets were expressed that Glasgow was to lose the benefit of [Charles'] zealous and faithful endeavours to promote innocent and healthful recreations amongst the working classes.'

It seems that Charles must have made a special journey back to Glasgow to attend his dinner. Charles will have watched the relocation of his uncle's business with interest and when the firm finally closed down its Glasgow operations, like John Joseph Griffin Ltd it did not sever its connections with that city. The family must have travelled between the two cities for personal reasons – to catch up with family and friends left behind and Charles was after all, still the Appointed Publisher to the University in Glasgow. Clearly the move to London was the right one as there was continuous development of the business and numerous volumes were issued. Although Glasgow was expanding industrially, there was a huge manufacturing centre in London. Entrepreneurs came to the capital to develop their products and many factories and workshops sprang up all over the City. London was very different to the place Charles left as a baby. The population had expanded rapidly (from 1801 it went up by 20% every decade and by 1845 it was recognised as the largest City in the world). This was the place to base a growing international business and Charles was determined to exploit the trading benefits, improving transport links and political and commercial importance of the city.

Quite how Jessie coped with the move is pure speculation. She was after all Scottish by birth and had left her family, friends and support network to start a new life in an unknown city. With a husband working long hours (and as we have learnt, still travelling back and forwards to Glasgow to tie up loose ends) she will have been left alone to cope with setting up her household and settling in her Scottish born children. The fact that Charles was a small baby when he moved up North meant that he too must have felt a big wrench leaving Glasgow. The older children may well have been excited by the move but we can imagine tears and trepidation in the weeks leading up to this monumental event.

Meanwhile, the firm survived its biggest relocation to date and continued to thrive. The publication of individual works that had started life as part of the *Encyclopaedia Metropolitana* continued. A strong series of books written by the eminent engineer William John McQuorn Rankine was published from 1859. These were extremely influential teaching texts on the theory of engineering and of physics. Rankine was Professor of Engineering at the University of Glasgow from 1855 to his death in 1872.

Charles' fifth daughter, Helen Florence Griffin was born in Sydenham. The family must therefore have travelled south well before 17 October 1860, possibly the year before her birth and Dr Aitken (one of Charles' authors) agreed to be her godfather. Sydenham was a very desirable location at the time. A little later in the century, Mrs J E Panton in her book *From Kitchen to Garret* (1888) recommended the higher parts of Sydenham as a good location due to fresher air, lower rents and roomier houses. Privacy, comfort, convenience and spaciousness were all key considerations in choosing a suburban residence and the house the couple chose appeared to tick many of the right boxes. The house, called 'The Lindens, Laurie Park' (sometimes described as 'Laurie's Park', and also 'Lawrie Park'), was close to the site to which the 1851 Great Exhibition 'Crystal Palace' had been moved in 1854. Pairs of four-storey semi-detached villas were built on this estate, and many seem to have born the name of trees. The houses demonstrate the desire not only for privacy but also for individualism in terms of design and the semi-detached house gave more scope for both than the previous fashion for terraced housing. There was quite possibly another reason for this choice of location. Charles' uncle John Joseph was living very close to Laurie Park in the late 1850's and Charles could well have stayed here before his family moved down from Scotland and at the very least will have been a frequent visitor.

In terms of the firm's business location, book imprints in 1860 and 1861 bore the address 10 Stationers' Hall Court. This area (and Warwick Square close by) was the traditional publishing centre in London at the time. It continued to be so until blitzed during the Second World War. The 1860s proved to be significant in the history of the firm and family in one other way; it was in 1861 that Charles bought out his uncle John Joseph Griffin's interest in Richard Griffin & Co. The formal date for winding up the Scottish end of Richard Griffin & Co was 30 June 1862.

At this point, the family tradition goes, Charles Griffin like his father before him became conscious that his health was deteriorating. We are not sure exactly what affliction Charles had but have evidence it was a long and drawn out illness – very like (or perhaps even the same as) his father. Medical advances were significant during the late nineteenth century but Charles lived and died at a time when provision was very basic. At least by 1858 the Medical Act had ensured that all doctors were properly qualified, but Charles will have had to leave his physician Dr Buchanan in Scotland and find a new doctor and without X ray (discovered in 1895) or ultra sound scans, his diagnosis is likely to have been as vague as his treatment. Because of his ill health, it is assumed, Charles decided to take a business partner, and to develop a new company on a 50:50 basis.

It may be that family tradition is wrong, and that this move was merely one step in Charles' drive to develop his company. Had Charles only realised, however, that this plan was to misfire on his family, he might have pulled back. On the other hand, the wording in some of the letters of sympathy received when he died make it quite clear that Charles had a very serious illness, and had been suffering from it for some time. The partner chosen was Henry Bohn a well-known publisher of many kinds of book, including the remarkable 'Bohn's Library'. So influential was this Library, that it has given rise to a colloquial phrase in the English language. The expression 'to bone up' on something, meaning to revise it before an exam, etc, should actually be 'Bohn up', because it refers to revising using Henry Bohn's collection of knowledge.

The date of the new partnership was agreed as 1 January 1861, after which the company became 'Griffin, Bohn and Company'. The firm traded from the same address as before. By March 1861, Henry Bohn had to take over the day-to-day running of the partnership more or less completely. He wrote, on 1, 4 and 5 March 'Mr Griffin is still unwell and away', and in April 'At the present time, Mr Griffin is labouring under a serious illness'.

The census of 1861 provides another fixed point of reference for us to consult and was held on 7 April. Household number 103 – The Lindens, Lawrie Park – was in the parish of Beckenham (within the subdivision of Bromley). Charles' household is recorded as follows.

Charles Griffin, Head, M, 41, Publisher employing 35 clerks, etc. London
Jeſsie Jane Do, Wife, M, 36, Scotland
Mary Ann Do, Daur, U, 17, Scotland
Elizabeth Do, Daur, U, 15, Scotland
Jeſsie Jane Do, Daur, U, 9, Scholar, Do
John Joseph Do, Son, 6, Scholar, Do
Henry Brougham Do, Son, 4, Scholar, Do
Hellen Do, Daur, 5 mo, Kent, Beckenham
Susan Hockley, Serv, U, 23, Nurse, Somerset, South Cadbury
Catherine Anderson, Serv, U, 27, Cook, London
Diana Bligh, Serv, U, 20, House maid, Herts, Hatfield
Mary Woods, Serv, U, 18, Nurse maid, Surry, Woking

That Charles employs 35 clerks is a measure of the importance of his company. The size of the staff at work and at home announced the economic position of the employer. Charles and Jessie were employing four servants at this time and the villa must have been spacious in order to accommodate them all. Whether Susan Hockley was in place as a maternity or a sickbed nurse is not clear. If she was the nursemaid, she will have been employed to look after the children – a full time job in the Griffin household with four under the age of ten and three extra teenagers in the holidays.

The household was not yet complete. Jessie was pregnant again (quite how Charles managed any activity in the bedroom is a mystery – perhaps he saw it as a welcome distraction?) The youngest child was a girl called Alice who was born on 15 February 1862, in Norfolk Street, but her birth was not registered until some six months later [which was technically illegal]. Then Jessie came to the London registry office from her home 'Coombe Lodge, Swanscombe, Kent'. Undoubtedly, the delay in the registration must have been caused by Charles' health.

Whenever they moved to Coombe Lodge, it does not feature by name in the 1851 or 1861 censuses. Swanscombe, lying four miles east of Dartford, of which it is now a part (at the southern end of the M25's 'Dartford Crossing') was, in 1861 a small village of 414 houses and a population of 2,323.

Although we know that Charles was not able to attend his office every day, he continued to play an important role in managing the business until his death. During this partnership, GB&Co acquired the rights to what is probably the best-known book that Griffins ever published. This was Henry Mayhew's *London Labour and the London Poor*. The rights were acquired from the previous publisher, whose two-volume edition never enjoyed the same success as did the GB&Co three- and later four-volumed versions.

Amongst other prestigious publications was the *Dictionary of Contemporary Biography*. Charles wrote to everyone of importance, asking for biographical pieces for inclusion in the dictionary. This must have been issued at least twice, (perhaps GB&Co acquired the rights to another publisher's earlier issue, we are not sure), because they often sent out pasted up versions of existing text and asked for updates. The resulting replies were carefully kept, and in later years sold to the British (Museum) Library, where they can still be consulted in several volumes in the Additional Manuscripts collection.

Sadly, on 5 August 1862, Charles died at his home aged 41 years. The family were left devastated by their loss. Of the ten children, The three elder girls at this time were Mary Anne Eliza (19), Elizabeth Eaves (17) and Jessie Jane (10). The three elder boys were Richard Thomas (15), Alexander Jamieson (14) and Charles James (12). The four little ones were John Joseph (8), Henry Brougham (6), Helen Florence (2) and Alice Edith (6 months).
On 5 November 1862, Henry Bohn wrote to a Mr Sanderson:

> You will be sorry to hear that poor Griffin is no more, and has left a widow and 10 children to deplore her loss. She is, however, I am glad to say, a very sensible woman & a good mother, which is everything to the young ones.

The business presented a problem. With Charles dead, there was no breadwinner in the family Firm (or in any other employment).

Agents were pressed into service to manage Jessie's interests, and one Glasgow letter-writer stresses:

> I am truly thankful for the exertions of Mr Collins and Mr Ambrose [the proprietor of William Collins the publisher, and the family's Glasgow lawyer respectively] I would not have believed that either of them would have undertaken such responsibilities for another, and although some things may not meet your entire approbation I would say have patience, and you will find that they are doing their utmost for you.

In a few years, the writer hoped, they would 'bring the business to such a state that it can be carried on with its own capital.'

Jessie was the only family member to take on the role of Executor, after John Joseph refused, and she had of course the most at stake if the company foundered. We have evidence that suggests that, whilst she was clearly a bright and ambitious individual, her vision for the business was not unrealistic and it was unfortunate that the managers the family was forced to employ until Richard was old enough to take over, were often not up to the challenge. We have absolutely no doubt in our minds that the Griffin Publishing house would not have survived without her dogged determination to fulfil her husband's dying wish. Generations of future Griffins, myself included as my father was the last Managing Director of Griffins, owe their livelihood to the bravery of Jessie and her daughter Elizabeth. Their story – told by Lizzie – is one I hope you enjoyed.

www.ingramcontent.com/pod-product-compliance
Lightning Source LLC
Chambersburg PA
CBHW052027020726
47501CB00004B/1286